Morgan G. Watkins

In the Country

Essays

Morgan G. Watkins

In the Country
Essays

ISBN/EAN: 9783337227265

Printed in Europe, USA, Canada, Australia, Japan

Cover: Foto ©Andreas Hilbeck / pixelio.de

More available books at **www.hansebooks.com**

Essays

BY

THE REV. M. G. WATKINS, M.A.,

RECTOR OF BARNOLDBY-LE-BECK.

———

" Divini gloria ruris."

———

LONDON:

W. SATCHELL & CO.,

19 TAVISTOCK STREET, COVENT GARDEN, W.C.

1883.

CONTENTS.

———

PREFACE.

By the courtesy of Messrs. CHATTO & WINDUS, Messrs. SMITH & ELDER, and Messrs. LONGMANS, GREEN, & CO., these Essays are reprinted with very slight alterations from the *Gentleman's, Cornhill, & Fraser's Magazines.*

COUNTRY ESSAYS.

Devon Lanes and their Associations.

THE great Italian poet, at the commencement of his song, finds himself lost in a wood, dark, rugged, and solitary. We shall begin by placing our readers in a labyrinth, bright, smiling, and picturesque. Nothing is easier than to find this maze in the outskirts of most Devonshire villages. The West is proverbially the land of green lanes, and though you must not go too far west, or the stone walls of the Cornish hills will disenchant you, no one can find it hard to lose himself in the network of lanes that surround any village in Devon. Let us transport our reader, then, to the lanes that skirt the myrtles and fuchsias of Budleigh-Salterton. Much like the "hollow lanes" of Hampshire, about which Gilbert White discourses so lovingly, they far surpass them in prodigality of floral wealth, and abrupt change of scenery. Curious legends and old-world characters are to be found in them ; railroads have for the most part avoided them, and there are no more pleasant associations than those which crowd upon the mind in threading these lanes at any season of the year.

Labyrinthine, indeed, are the lanes of South Devon to the stranger who wanders in them, hopelessly enclosed by lofty banks crowned with tall hedges, that twist in and out, and are

A

interlaced by others, and circle round again under the blue
spring sky, like the fabled stream that never blent its waters
with the ocean.   Passing beautiful, too, are they, filled with a
changeful loveliness of bright-coloured flowers and pendent
ferns and darting dragon-flies ; while creeping bindweeds knot
themselves round gnarled oak-stems, with leaves more artisti-
cally cut than those of the acanthus, and berries, green, black,
and red, like the wampum on an Indian warrior.   Here the
hedges almost meet overhead, and graceful festoons of flowers
depend like *lianas* in a tropical forest, as you will see them nowhere else in England.   There the bank on one side falls gently,
and what a prospect opens on the view !   Fair meadows bathed
in sunshine, with the Otter river winding through them, lie
below; yonder are the red Devon steers, grazing up to their dew-
laps in buttercups ; beyond them dusky moors melt into purple
haze, and every here and there you catch a glimpse of the far-
off Tors on Dartmoor simmering in the mid-day glare.   Then
again, the other side of our lane sinks abruptly, and the sea
spreads out far below, with a white sail specking it here and
there to take away from its impressive infinity.   And birds sing
and bees hum amongst the bright-yellow furze-flowers, and a
stream that, like yourself, has lost its way, tinkles merrily adown
the bank from the coppice.   The lazy hawk hovering on your
right does not even deem it needful to wheel off in alarm.   So
irresistible is Devon in her beauty that you fall in love at first
sight, and may be quite sure that like every loveable maiden,
the more you see of her the more will her unobtrusive gentle-
ness endear her to you.

A glance at the physical features of the country shows how
these picturesque lanes were formed.   The aboriginal track-way
over hill and dale, rudely marked out by stones laid at intervals,
just as the Devon coastguardsmen still guide themselves over
the cliffs at night by lines of stones so deposited, sank gradually
into the soil.   Mud from the path was flung on either side.

Violent rains cut deep furrows in the road; during winter the path became a water-course where it was not a bog, and this continued for centuries. Then came an age of improvement; the adjoining moor was divided from the road, after the native fashion, by banks of earth, trees and bushes took possession of them; and while every season washes the road away, every time the farmer mends his fences the banks above gain height. Thus each year deepens the lane. Frost often brings down one of these banks, which are topped by hedges, in some cases thirty feet above the traveller's head; and this "rougement," as they call it in Devon, must be replaced before the lane is passable, so that their depth seldom diminishes, and perpetually increases.

Many of these lanes are extremely ancient. Round Dartmoor especially they go back to Celtic times, or beyond them to that dim pre-historic antiquity, where even archæology loses itself. Their natural formation, as we have described it above, overthrows a theory which has before now found favour with ethnologists, and which would contrast the generous, open-hearted Roman with the skulking Celt. The Roman shows his character according to this fancy by his wide, elevated streets, driven for the most part in a straight line through the length and breadth of the land; while the other's nature was to hide in circuitous hollow lanes, fighting in trenches, as it were, while the legions manœuvred in the open. What little the ancients have told us of the Celts negatives this view. Though superior force and a higher civilization drove the ancient Briton to the fastnesses of Wales and Cornwall, the Celt was brave to rashness, ready, as Aristotle says, "to dare even the waves with his sword."

Returning to the lanes, another feature which strikes the stranger, besides their twistings up and down the hill-sides and their depth, is their narrowness. It is very difficult, and in many cases impossible, for one vehicle to pass another in them.

Sometimes a gate has to be opened, and one or other must drive into the field ; sometimes by waiting in a more open space it is just possible for the coming vehicle to graze by. When the great man of the country drives in them he has outriders to clear the way for him. This narrow roadway gives the history of locomotion in Devon. Originally these lanes would only be traversed by foot-passengers and beasts of burden, the predecessors of the pack-horses, laden with " crooks " of faggots or furze, so often met in them at the present day. Then came the broadest view on the subject of transport our forefathers could hold. The curious narrow wain, without wheels, consisting of a rough body, drawn on two thick shafts which rest on the ground behind, came into vogue. Specimens of it may still be seen in use on the hill farms.

Amongst the minor embarrassments of these old lanes is meeting an infuriated ox running a-muck. If you are not prepared to scale the steep banks at a moment's notice, you should be ready-witted enough to provide yourself beforehand with a straw. It is a west-country superstition that even if you meet his satanic majesty you can cut him in half with a straw. We hesitate about giving another receipt, as we never came to such close quarters as to give us the opportunity of trying its efficacy. It is of little use to ladies, who are most likely to be caught in the plight we have fancied, still here it is. You have only to spit over his horns, whether it be ox or devil, and he will instantly disappear !

There is another bit of Devon folk-lore we may as well mention, for a traveller in these intricate lanes will often have the chance of putting it into practice. If you lose your way, take off your coat, and having turned it inside out, put it on again. You will immediately find the right track. It may easily be conjectured that the proverb, " It is a long lane which has no turning," could never have been coined in Devonshire, although that other equally true one, of marriage being like a lane, from which, when once you are in, there is no getting out, is manifestly indigenous.

Autumn brings a beauty of its own to these quiet lanes. Heather and golden gorse stray from the moorland down their banks—the last bright flowers of the year—just as two or three purple and pink cloud-flakes often linger in the West long after a glorious sunset. The tall hedges are a tangle of convolvulus and honeysuckle, filling the calm evening hours with fragrance. Mid-day, which, sooth to say, is during July somewhat oppressive in these still retreats, has now its own clear, sharp breeze. Deeper shades of red and yellow are passing over the leaves. You may often meet here two or three bare-armed children from the cottage on the hill-side, staring at you with round blue eyes as they gather blackberries, which have left numerous specimens of nature-printing on their cheeks. The biggest boy maybe stands on a donkey's back under the nut-trees, clutching at their treasures, with no fear of the patient animal beneath him moving on. Mother is far away on the moors gathering " worts " (whortleberries), to sell to visitors at the neighbouring seaside village. Home life is very uneventful to these cottagers. The children tell you, "Vather be to the zyder-press," and this answer will apply equally well to him, good, honest man, any day from August to November.

The stranger rambling in these Devon lanes is frequently surprised at a turn of the road to find before him in its sheltered "combe" an old mansion now converted into a farmhouse. Very picturesque does the transformation render it, with its thatched gables, deeply sunk dormer windows, and large lower casements, lighting what was the common hall, but is now the goodwife's kitchen. Merry beards once wagged there, and the best families of Devon—the Mohuns, Carews, Champernounes —may have flourished in the massive walls, whose heavy mullioned windows you see blinking in the sunshine. Gilbert and Drake may have circumnavigated the world there to an admiring audience over oceans of cider. All these worthies have long since passed away, but nature is still unchangeable. The heavily-laden horsechestnut-trees bow before the gentle breeze sweeping round the garden, and the Virginian creeper over the windows reddens, as they may have done one summer when shouts told far and wide that the Armada was in our seas.

Just such a house may be seen in a lane near Budleigh-Salterton. Sir Walter Raleigh was born in it. Its projecting porch and heavily-thatched gables have an old-world look about them ; but on the whole it takes its fame as a matter of course, and makes no great pretensions to be anything more than an Elizabethan country house. The hills rise above it at the back, stacks close in round it, you hear the cows lowing from the "linneys," the garden is full of old-fashioned flowers, and a genial atmosphere of peace hangs over it. The general features of the place must have changed very little since Sir Walter rambled about the quiet woodland ways which hem it in. Here he cherished boundless dreams of El Dorado, galleons and in- gots. Hayeswood in front and the hills behind must often have seen him, like another Alexander, chafing at the narrow horizon of his world. The first pipe smoked in England may have been puffed on the mossy bank where you sit at present. It is impossible to refrain from associating this calm spot with the courtier's after-life. How often must he have turned in fancy to this little homestead when fainting under a tropical sun, or chafing as a prisoner in the Tower ! The mind, they say, often revisits early scenes in the moments of death. Ra- leigh may have seemed to hear the sheep bleat, and called up in fancy the well-remembered outline of Hayes Farm against yonder green hill-side, as he closed his eyes and laid his head on the block.

Expeditions to such famous spots should be undertaken if possible during summer. Candour compels us to state that no

one would care to walk lightly shod in winter through the Devon
lanes. The road which, in more civilized counties, November
converts into "feather-bed lane," becomes here, in the native
term, "mucksy lane." You long, as you flounder in the mire,
for the ten-foot stride of the giant Ordulph, who lies buried at
Tavistock. As the hedges lose their bravery, the red sandstone
stares in all its nakedness from the banks. No storm or wet
daunts the pretty blue periwinkle from flowering here during
the winter months, and there is sure to be a plentiful supply of
wormwood at every corner, "good to prevent weariness in
travellers," according to Pliny's old-world wisdom. As the
long evenings close in, you may hear "eldritch skirls" in the
coppices around. That silent spectre passing overhead so
silently as hardly to disturb the streams of moonlight is only
the owl on his way, as in Shakespeare's days, "to woo the baker's
daughter." You need not mistake it for something uncanny.
The last of the Devonshire witches — Temperance Lloyd,
Mary Trembles, and Susannah Edwards—were executed at
Exeter Castle in 1682, though many a poor old woman in
out-of-the-way districts is still suspected of being "a white
witch."

It is still thought dangerous, though, to disturb "the little
people" at their revels on the sward by the lane-side which
falls back to the oak wood. You will do this if you whistle as
you pass by. Let them be in peace, unless you wish to be
"pixey-led," and left "stogged" in a deep swamp. It is ticklish
work meddling with Elbricht and his fairy folk. Be forbearing,
even you, my irate British farmer, if they will gallop your
horses over the moor at night, and Dobbin, your faithful
market steed, be discovered all over foam in his stall on two or
three mornings during winter. Why should the pixies be
debarred from a night with "the wish hounds" occasionally?
Open your window the next frosty midnight, and you will hear
the rout sweeping merrily away towards Dartmoor. Do not

even let your better half exasperate you by complaints of her dairy being rifled by them. It is true she has never ceased twitting you for that unlucky night's work, when you went down to the cellar, after she had retired to the upper regions, and unfortunately dropping the candle and the cork of the cider-barrel, had to stand all night with your finger in the bung-hole, to prevent the precious liquor running out. But bid her wink at fairy misdemeanours, and remind her she may then be invited to fairyland herself, and come back wonderfully enriched. Perhaps she may even stay there altogether. Such cases are not unknown in the West. In 1696, it is upon record that a certain Ann Jefferies, in Cornwall, "was fed for six months by a small sort of airy people called fairies," and performed many strange and wonderful cures on her return home with salves and medicines she received from them, for which she never took a penny from her patients.

The Devon peasantry are very superstitious, and the long, moonlit nights of Christmas, which are so fascinating to most people, bring their special terrors to the lone farmhouse, or the cottage half hidden by the pines at the side of these lanes. Their fancies do not for the most part take the fatalistic hue of the Welsh countryman or the still more gloomy complexion of the superstitions of the Channel Islander. The Devon yeoman has no fear of meeting a coffin obstructing his path when benighted in the narrow lanes, which is sure to betoken his own if he knocks it roughly over, or is otherwise than scrupulously polite in taking off the lid and replacing it the wrong way, when it instantly disappears. It is rather an un-defined dread that something *might* come which oppresses him as he looks over the glimmering waste of snow. Something did assuredly come, at dead of night, some thirty years ago, to the very neighbourhood wherein we have fancied our traveller rambling, the angle formed about Salterton by the left bank of the Exe and the sea. In the outskirts of Topsham to the lanes which ramify from there into the country, were noticed on several wintry mornings mysterious footsteps over the virgin snow, having great affinity (so the natives affirmed) to the cloven hoofs popularly assigned to a certain nameless personage. These tracks advanced steadily without any apparent divarication, walking over roofs, walls, and other obstacles that might reasonably be supposed capable of baffling a hoaxer. The story quickly spread to the London papers, and all kinds of guesses were made respecting the footprints. Some ascribed them to natural causes, such as the visit of a large wild-fowl, &c., but found small favour with the country-side for their trouble. The mystery was never satisfactorily cleared up. Long after most people, however, had forgotten the whole occurrence, the neighbouring peasants did not dare to stir from their hearths after nightfall.

Often as we have threaded Devon lanes after sunset, we cannot testify to having seen anything more fearsome than bats or owls. They are full of beauty (as well as mud) even in winter. Here a delicate snow-wreath glitters in the moonlight, waiting for sunrise to lend its pink and amber flushes, the death-tints of the graceful folds. There a deep recess in the bank bristles with icicle spears, as if determined that summer shall never more hang fondly over the ferny treasures within. The old trees sigh overhead as their last leaf flutters to the ground ; and now a deeper plunge than usual into the quagmire recalls us to the sterner realities of life. We were fast nearing some enchanted land of fancy, and lo ! we find ourselves ankle-deep in mud !

Pluck up courage, and press on through the wintry lanes a little further. The faint chimes of St. Mary's at distant Ottery are flinging their Christmas greeting over many a mile of moorland. We are passing the old " cob " walls and grey-headed barns of a substantial farmstead. The cocks will crow here all

night before Christmas day, according to the beautiful legend of
the county, to bid

"Each fettered ghost slip to his several grave,"

and the very oxen at midnight will fall down on their knees
before the manger.   The next turn brings us to the Otter,
rushing along some forty feet below with angry stream, very
different to the pleasant murmur with which it glides through
the land in summer.   Notice how abrupt are the transitions of
the lanes.   We can now catch the distant roar which tells of
the sea chafing awfully amidst the rocks of the Salterton reef.
How changed, too, are its waves from those which in August
ripple gently over the many-coloured pebbles on the beach,
much as some gigantic Viking might have dallied with the
yellow curls of his princess.   Now they form a black, seething
torrent, flashing here and there into huge foam-crested rollers,
that chase each other wildly on, and leap, and strike, and roar
again with rage as the sturdy rocks stand firm, and they can
only swirl round and break against their next neighbours in
the mighty charge.   Fully to appreciate the Devon sea, it
should be visited from one of the quiet lanes :!. ' ˉᵖen on to
the beach, when a good southerly breeze brings it in, and all
the green expanse is flecked with many a white "sea-horse"
riding gallantly on, as though after some imaginary hero
of Ivry.

   One more Christmas association, and then we will pass to a
brighter scene.   Curiously enough, the blue-scented violet
which lends such a charm to the lanes of other counties, is
very rare in Devon, and the mistletoe is never found there.
Glastonbury seems its headquarters in England, and whole
truck-loads of it are imported every Christmas for the festivities
of the West.   Its absence in Devon and Cornwall calls up an
awful picture of the womankind of other days, when such
amatory trifles as violets and mistletoe were not encouraged in

the land.   In some such mood do the Latin poets look back
with reverence on the austere virtues of the Sabine dames, who
dismissed their husbands to work in the fields while they ruled
the house and spun quietly at home.   Doubtless the Devon
swains are duly grateful as they see the pearly berries littering
the stations on the Great Western, that their lines have fallen
upon more osculatory days.

   If the Devon lanes are fair in summer, fairer in autumn, and
not without a certain loveliness in winter, in spring they are
simply radiant with beauty.   Let us breast yonder hill with
April's sunshine fleeting in vast sheets of splendour over the
heather.   The lanes are rather intricate, and if a damp place
here and there speaks of spring-showers, you will often recover
your equanimity by finding some rare plant, such as the pretty
little *pinguicola Lusitanica*.   On these spangled banks, all the
wild-flowers of the West seem following the example of the hares,
and running riot over mossy cushions and ivy-clad stumps.
But we are out of the lanes now, and with just one look from
the hill-side, plunge into the glades on the other side, and soon
reach my favourite grange.

   Can anything be more spring-like than those whitewashed
cob-walls covered with roses?   Through the "barton," past
the Alderneys, looking so well pleased with their lot, we will
approach the house.   The entrance is very massive and low.
Follow me through the flagged passage to the parlour.   Here is
our hostess, with the heartiest of welcome to sit down and rest
after our ramble.   And now Lucy comes in, with the fair hair
and blue eyes of the West, like her mother, "on hospitable
cares intent."   What will we have?   New milk? cider?
cream?   Take my advice, and choose the latter.   Here it is
in a lordly dish, mantled with gold and redolent (as good
Devonshire cream should be) of wood ashes.   Lucy will pile
you up a platter of it, with plenty of preserved "mazzards"
(wild cherries), and if you have not enjoyed your ramble

through the lanes, I am sure I shall earn your gratitude by introducing you to such a repast. Now that we have seated you in the low window-sill, by the large beaupot of roses, we bid you heartily farewell, and will tell you in conclusion, that whoever you be, and wherever you may ramble through the Devon lanes, you will find their beauty much heightened by the courtesy, hospitality, and kindness you will invariably experience from those who live amongst them. One of the greatest pleasures of after-life will be to look back, from toil and care and anxieties, to the sunny hours you have loitered away in the lanes of Devonshire.

At the Seaside.

LIKE the modern love of the picturesque and the enthusiastic devotion to the minutest sights and sounds of natural history, our longing for seaside pleasures is a direct growth of the peaceful times which followed the Great War. Late in the last century a few bathing-machines made their appearance on the southern coasts. George III. showed the fashionable world that life was endurable at Weymouth. But residence at the sea and dalliance by its summer waves was a luxury which no prudent families could enjoy during war-prices, or when Napoleon and his flotilla waited on the opposite shore to swoop down upon England upon any dark night. After the general pacification, artistic and imaginative pleasures gradually succeeded to the all-absorbing interest of the Peninsular War. Of late years the general diffusion of wealth has combined with these to send people to the seaside. Quickened modes of crossing the Atlantic and the Channel showed men that the sea was no longer the *oceanus dissociabilis* of Horace. The increase of railways, too, facilitated the conveyance of children to the sea, so that family life suffers no interruption by the prevailing habit. Wordsworth's advocacy of mountain and sea scenery, in which he has since been followed by all the poets of the reflective school, was aided by Scott's objective painting of nature, and has greatly contributed towards a love of the sea. Like most social phenomena, therefore, this enjoyment of seaside pleasures is the result of many different causes.

Just as the children, however, round their sand-fort, or the
lovers on the cliff-seat, do not trouble themselves about the
reasons which brought them there, but gratefully accept the
cool air and lovely view, we are well content to leave such
speculations to the statist and future historian.   The white
sea-birds call shrilly, and the incoming tide is ruffled into
silver foam on the long, yellow sands.   It is the time for enjoyment and not for social science.

The most miserable kind of happiness at the seaside is to be
found by visiting Scarborough or Brighton solely for the purpose
of mingling in their fashionable gaities.   The frivolities of life
may well be reserved for Mayfair and the season.   To fly
thence to a fifth-rate imitation of them at crowded hotels by
the sea is to contemn the influence of its fresh, vast solitude,
and deliberately to put out of sight its opportunities for quiet
recreation.   Yet at a certain period in most men's lives, as in
the existence of States, the pride of wealth and luxury thus
degrades the sea to minister to its pleasures, and the delights
of the Bay of Baiæ in the time of Augustus, or of Biarritz under
the French Empire, irresistibly claim their votaries.   Fortunately, human beings recover from this temporary aberration by
milder remedies than those which visit an empire; and the
maiden whose sole delight lay in dancing away the blessed
hours of moonlight on quiet waters in a fool's paradise at
Scarborough, lives to rejoice in watching her children wetting
their feet in the pools of a dull Cornish fishing village.   Those
old days retire into dreamland ; save for their amusing contrasts
with the present, we gladly bestow them as alms for oblivion.

On the other hand, the happiest mode of enjoying the sea is
to put on an old coat and thick boots, and then,

> " Procul negotiis
> Ut prisca gens mortalium,"

to give oneself up to thorough indolence and receptivity of

seaside influences. Telegrams should be strictly interdicted, and only the most unimportant letters forwarded. The holiday should be set apart for some intellectual treat—reading the Laureate's last poem or George Eliot's latest story. Some study, however, out of the ordinary line of a man's business ought to be professed—say geology, or investigations into the marine zoophytes—to redeem idleness from the charge of being idle; or a big book may be taken to the sea, a history or a stiff theological treatise, to be able to put the amiable sophism upon ourselves that we intend to work, to give, in short, a back-bone to a molluscous purpose. We lately met a clergyman on a six weeks' tour in Scotland who had thus taken with him Butler's *Analogy* and the judicious Hooker, for much the same reason, we suppose, as the ancient Egyptians were wont to introduce a skeleton at their feasts. Solitude at the seaside is a great mistake. Dürer very suitably introduced the sea as the background of his *Melancholia*. The immensity of the sea overwhelms the personality ; but let a man have wife, sister, or friend with him, and then the presence of a kindred soul, and the ordinary everyday remarks upon the sea, vanquish the un-vanquished. Above all, no one should seek the sea for enjoy-ment who is compelled to economise and strictly scan the day's expenses. Butchers have a trick at the seaside of not supply-ing the finest joints and of charging unconscionable prices, while landladies proverbially must make hay while the sun shines. Unless a man can wholly fling base domestic cares to the winds when he visits the sea, let him spend, say three weeks there entirely free from anxiety, instead of the month he at first purposed, which would demand nice calculations and unsleeping thrift. Nothing so soon mars a holiday as care. It is the bunch of hyssop in our autumnal cup of joy.

Though it is easy when inland to fancy the sea's delights, to lavish poetic phrases on it, and to persuade oneself, when dis-inclined to travel, that imagination can satisfy as well as sight,

a subtle, ineffable charm does indeed overhang it, which no
creative insight, no wealth of language, can catch. From
Homer to Tennyson the poets have been at work upon it and
cannot express this magic charm. Stansfield's pencil has per-
petuated its rougher moods, and Turner its sunlit glories; we
hang enraptured over Mr. Brett's realistic limnings of its summer
purples and Mr. Hook's green swells from which the salt spray,
torn off by the rising breeze, almost strikes fresh upon our
senses, yet is there a further secret which their artistic touch
cannot grasp. The seaside dweller sees it on the dancing
waves when the joyful light of dawn comes rippling over them
from the gateways of the East, and in the clear sparkles of a
noontide sea. He woos it, too, in the tender aërial blues which
float around its face just before the moon seeks her throne in
the cloudless azure above. This nameless charm is compoun-
ded of glitter, profundity, and extension. No painter has
seized it so vividly as Claude, and Wordsworth happily suggests
its manifold mystery in the lines—

> " Stealthy withdrawings, interminglings mild
>   Of light with shade, in beauty reconciled."

This indefinable sea-charm can only be realised when actually face to face with it. The sea itself can alone satisfy its
votary. It is this nameless spell which year by year summons
so many susceptible natures within its influence. Like a coy
beauty, we cannot win her, and yet we cannot content ourselves away from her presence. Every one recognises the
power and grandeur of the sea in a storm, but only the finest
souls are stirred with its marvels when a summer calm holds it
in submission, and it is mostly in summer only that people
know the sea.

How many have wished to recollect their thoughts on first
seeing the ocean ! Memory cannot recall them. This is a
penalty men pay for travelling at so much earlier an age than

did their fathers. Other generations saw the sea for the first time when the mind was formed. Then they could register their feelings as they called Thalatta! Thalatta! Thus in Keble's case it was not until he was twenty, and had taken his degree, that he first caught sight of the sea. Yet this mature vision had its drawbacks. Childhood, and especially boyhood, lost that sense of vastness and power which the sea confers, and the most critical periods for budding genius missed in consequence the mental stimulus which thus accrues. A certain feebleness of language, a falling short of that grandeur of sentiment which marks the greatest poets, may be noticed in Keble's verses, and these defects may probably be attributed in great measure to this want of sea influences. Contrast (of course, in style only) the flights of Byron's poetry, that

> " Eagle with both grappling feet still hot
> From Zeus's thunder,"

with the polish and glow of *The Christian Year*. The difference is at once apparent. The one is a rush of imaginative vigour which will not be denied vent, and bursts through all barriers ; the other rolls obediently between well-ordered banks. The same feature is discernible in the Laureate's poetry, the outcome of early Lincolnshire impressions, where the sea is what the ancients would have called a sea that is no sea, a far-off power shrouded half the year in fogs and gloom. The only influence to be named together with the sea is the neighbourhood of mountains. The glow of aërial colour which is constantly flitting over them reproduces in great measure to a keen perception the perpetual motion and change of the sea. The world's greatest poets have fed their imagination on both.

Yet the first sight of the sea in childhood is none the less an epoch in existence if its stirrings of the soul cannot be recalled. The rapid locomotion that took us to it, the emancipation from lessons and the irksome regularities of home life, the sense

B

of an enlarging horizon of experience, these did but pleasantly
lead up to the mystery of mysteries on which hearts had so
long been set, and of which for months tongues had loved to
prattle. The child's wings were rapidly being fledged. To lie
down upon a strange bed amidst sea-sounds and unusual
bustle was another delight not unreproduced, we may be sure,
in dreams. But morn brought crowning bliss, to dash down
before breakfast without a hat and regardless of all nursery
proprieties, over the scanty turf of the " links," past the black
windmill where wooden bowls and spoons were turned, across
the deep-rutted sandy land never mended but by wind and
weather, with a scramble on the opposite side over the rough
stone wall, and then—one look, and there lay Fairyland !
Long yellow sands, fringed with fantastically-hung boulders,
led down to a vast grey water, heaving and sparkling into infinity, with here and there a golden ripple, and far away one
white sail which was carrying modern Robinson Crusoes to
islands of the blest, decked with all the wealth of tropic vegetation which a child's imagination could conceive. Yes, there
at last was the SEA !—

> " It is the sea, it is the sea,
> In all its vague immensity,
> Fading and darkening in the distance ! "

And then came a rush over the blown sandhills amongst dry
bladder-wrack and sea-waifs, where the shoes were filled with
sand ; the glance at the pink sea-stocks and globe campions
(all that at that time could be spared them) ; then the somewhat toilsome drag over wet sands dotted with savages' footprints to the edge, where (wonder of wonders !) a thin rope of
water came rolling up to break into a little sheet of foam, and
then another, which went over the ankles, till at length their
meaning flashed upon the mind. These were waves ! Then
ensued the return with large wistful eyes, and the old domestic's
reproachful shout, " Master Philip ! how could you go a-wetting

your feet before breakfast?" How well it all comes back upon the memory. Yet what a sea rolls between that point of time and the present! Ay de mi! ay de mi!

But the earliest recollection of the sea is not always so benign. As there are boys whose whole inner life opens out under its influence, so there are others whose first remembrance of it is like a frightful dream. They keenly recall the bathing to which they were injudiciously condemned before their nerves had acquired strength, and any familiarity with the waves had been established. The horrors of those first bathes haunt them like a bugbear, and they were conducted in a manner, we would fain hope, which is now everywhere obsolete. No greater refinement of cruelty could be fancied than to take a timid child into a bathing-machine on a rough day, undress him, and thrust him out to an old harridan waiting in the waves to give him the three orthodox dips. The more he screamed the longer did his amphibious persecutor keep him under, always waiting till his mouth was wide open before she immersed him. Add to these horrors the secret fear that she would lose hold of him in what terror magnified into waves mountains high, and the exhaustion consequent upon these mental agonies, and the wonder is that any child of that bygone generation ever again voluntarily entered water. Dreadful as the whole operation undoubtedly was, imagination has probably intensified its troubles, as years kindly erased from the memory its actual details; but a sufficient residuum of horrors is left to warn every parent that he cannot too gently accustom his children, especially if they are at all nervous, to sea-bathing. It is incalculable how mischievously the opposite course may act upon both their bodily and mental faculties.

Indeed, the influences of the seaside upon a child's mental faculties, especially his imagination, can hardly be overstated. If he be a genius, an embryo artist, poet, or novelist, the whole of his inner being expands, like the anemones which lie, gravel-covered lumps of jelly, till the grateful tide washes them into beauty, or the *delesseria* seaweed, which opens into a glow of rosy crimson as the flowing wave ruffles its quiet rock-pool. The ebbing and flowing of the tide is in itself a perpetual wonder, the first intimation to his budding intellect of the vast forces at work around and within our planet. The affluence of the sea in fish and the grotesque forms of some of them, the white-winged birds that circle and call over its waves, may hereafter lead his mind to these branches of natural history. The wide circle of heaven which arches over the sea, and the mode in which its tints are reflected upon the watery expanse, bestow endless lessons on the harmonies of colour, even if these instructions are unconsciously assimilated. But the ships are perhaps the most entrancing of all these influences, with their mysterious departures for strange shores, their white clouds of sun-kissed canvas, the sudden manner in which, after arriving, it may be during his nightly dreams, the child finds them safely anchored in the morning. Their presence intensifies his longing for seeing the world, and feeds that passion for adventure, inherent in all English hearts, which led his forefathers to range the deep and claim the supremacy of the seas, and which laid the foundations of our great colonial empire. For this reason those parts of the English coast whence few or no sails can be described are always inferior in interest, at least with masculine minds, to strictly maritime ports and shores. The vastness of the sea, without the counter-balancing spectacle of man's mastery over it, is apt to oppress rather than expand the mind. And if shipping forms a great element in the child's wondering love of the sea, how much more marvellous to him, from being just as full of wonder and yet touching him more familiarly, are boats ! In them he can himself tug at an oar and accompany the fishermen to their crab-pots, looking over the gunwale at the waving forest of seaweed, Undine's realm, beneath the lustrous swells, and then upwards at the rocks, grim and forbidding in a calm, and which but frown the blacker when the north wind hurls its breakers on to them, only to be repulsed in clouds of spray. Far out from them, too, runs into the sea a long reef of sharp-edged outliers, where the waves swirl as the fishermen row carefully past, while the child listens with eyes full of awe to their stories of the winter storms and the gallant vessels which have ere now gone to pieces on those cruel teeth. Terror added to beauty has a special fascination for childhood, though in a lesser way it affects us at every stage of life. It will be many a summer before the child can enjoy Mr. Ruskin's masterly analysis of the sea-charm that hangs around an old, wave-beaten, tarred boat, but he can feel something of the boat's influences from his earliest years. " In that bow of the boat is the gift of another world. Without it what prison would be so strong as that white and wailing fringe of sea ? What maimed creatures were we all, chained to our rocks, Andro-meda-like, or wandering by the endless shores, wasting our in-communicable strength, and pining in hopeless watch of un-conquerable waves ! The nails that fasten together the planks of the boat's bow are the rivets of the fellowship of the world. Their iron does more than draw lightning out of heaven, it leads love round the earth." *

A curious instance of the transcendent love of the sea in a thoughtful nature, and of the poor substitutes which trees or other natural features furnish for its overpowering charm, occurs to us as we write. In Dorothy Wordsworth's *Recollections of a Tour in Scotland* with her brother the poet, they met Mr. (afterwards Sir Walter) Scott, and Miss Wordsworth says : † " The wind was tossing the branches, and sunshine dancing among the leaves, and I happened to exclaim ' What a life there is in trees ! ' On which Mr. Scott observed that the words reminded him of a young lady who had been born and educated on an island of the Orcades, and came to spend a

* Ruskin's *Harbours of England.*   † 2nd ed., 1874, p. 265.

summer at Kelso and in the neighbourhood of Edinburgh. She used to say that in the new world into which she was come nothing had disappointed her as much as trees and woods ; she complained that they were lifeless, silent, and, compared with the grandeur of the ever-changing ocean, even insipid. At first I was surprised, but the next moment I felt that the impression was natural. Mr. Scott said that she was a very sensible young woman, and had read much. She talked with endless rapture and feeling of the power and greatness of the ocean ; and with the same passionate attachment returned to her own native island without any probability of quitting it again."

In boyhood the inner life, with all its emotions, bright fancies, and happy imaginations, retires for a time in the presence of the sea, while the bodily sinews and thews hail it as an ally which will brace them up for the battle of life. The sea is welcomed as a friend when the boy, with Byron's love of swimming, suffers the waves to bear him downwards on their bosom into the dark trough, then with one stroke rises up the green wall of the next swell, and as it curls into creamy spray which would overwhelm him and bear him backwards like a cork, head over heels, by one dexterous plunge dives under its rage, and, again emerging, slides calmly down into the next abyss, ready for another dive at the critical moment. What better discipline could boyhood have for the ups and downs of life than this wrestling with Father Ocean ? The delights of pulling a boat backwards and forwards in the harbour soon led to the first timid venture over the swells at its mouth to the open sea beyond, and form another early memory with most boys. And then ensued the entrancing joy of rocking on the waves outside, which was always accompanied by an unspoken dread that it might not be possible to row back again. Some-times a sailor really had to put out his boat and help the baffled wanderers home. Such minor dangers, too, as dropping an oar, being nearly swamped by a passing steamer, running down a choleric fisherman's boat and being pursued by him with an abundance of bad language and imprecations—these and the like adventures bring out in boys presence of mind and courage, a sense of power, and the habit of self-reliance, which prove invaluable in after-life. On every account he is a wise parent who annually takes his boys to the sea. Let him suffer their sisters to roam with them, tom-boys for the nonce, by sandy cove and rocky pool, gathering flowers, wetting their feet, and drinking in health at every pore, and he may laugh at doctors and fear not consumption, the Moloch to whom so many English youths and maidens are annually sacrificed. The *Fräulein* need not accompany the girls ; duets and marches may very well be left behind, for they are obtaining an education in outdoor life and gymnastic (as the Greeks called the arts which aim at ensuring bodily perfection) ; these, during our brief summer, should be permittted altogether to banish the intellectual claims which that people knew as music. For the same reason late hours and excitement ought to be rigidly interdicted at the seaside.

As for the golden days of youth by the sea, who shall venture to paint their pleasures ? What noble hopes are then cherished ; what high ambitions, what grand purposes entertained ! Life and the world and renown, with all their specious power and promise, lie before the young man. He has never known defeat hitherto, when he has once set his heart on anything, never been baffled in his plans. More potent than Archimedes, he feels that he holds in his hand the lever which will move the universe. Happy they who have a father at this dangerous period to check them in their extravagant longings, to teach them that power and genius must be directed to one point, not dissipated on manifold ends. Multitudes make shipwreck of the fairest prospects for want of sustained effort in one field of thought. So many foes are leagued against this

cardinal virtue, inseparable from success, that resolution is
sorely tried. And to falter herein is fatal. Especially may
one's own heart cause him to stumble. Unless youth betimes
stops its ears, like Ulysses, some siren, who as in his age yet
haunts the seaside, may lure him to idleness and so to destruction of many a bright dream; for the generous emotions
are strong, and the fire of love blazes forth at a glance or a
word. Most people possess a romance whose ghost is laid by
the sea, enclosed in a summer month and cast into the ocean
of the past. And most people, we may add, are fond at certain times of imitating the fishermen of the *Arabian Nights*,
opening the case and suffering the imprisoned spirit to spread
himself over the face of heaven and earth. " No man ever
forgot," says Emerson,* " the visitations of that power to his
heart and brain which created all things new; which was the
dawn in him of music, poetry, and art; which made the face
of nature radiant with purple light, the morning and the night
varied enchantments; when a single tone of one voice could
make the heart beat, and the most trivial circumstance associated with one form is preserved in the amber of memory;
when we became all eye when one was present, and all memory
when one was gone; when the youth becomes a watcher of
windows, and studious of a glove, a veil, a ribbon, or the wheels
of a carriage; when no place is too solitary, and none too
silent for him who has richer company and sweeter conversation in his new thoughts than any old friends, though best and
purest, can give him; for the figures, the motions, the words,
of the beloved object, are not, like other images, written in
water, but, as Plutarch said, enamelled in fire." But all these
attachments, which, like morning breezes, merely ruffle the
placid waters, as the years pass on culminate with many at the
seaside in that true and lasting devotion whose flower is marriage. Thenceforth the sea is sacred in the husband's eyes.

* Essays : No. V.—*Love.*

Its influences have largely coloured two lives, and those glories never wholly fade. It again becomes the all-sentient, sympathising friend, dowered with all the gifts of imagination and fancy, invested with the air of mystery it wore in childhood, which familiarity and absorbing activities in after-life had greatly obliterated.

In mature years men deal with the sea as with this old and tried friend. It invites them for the nonce to indolent repose. Instead of agitating with far-reaching hopes, it soothes with tender memories, soft reminiscences which charm the mind as a waft of its own fragrance delights the senses. The past, with all its joys and fears, attainments and griefs, opens before the man who seeks sea-solace when tired with life's toil. The future does not rise beyond the glittering horizon outspread before him. It is in manhood that we most enjoy the restful influences of the sea. The pensive sport of fishing chimes in well with this mood. Anchored so far out that the cliffs have lost their vivid colours, we idly draw up pollock and rock-codlings, while the boatmen spin their endless yarns of the good times for fish fifty years ago, "afore the French comed into our seas;" or accompany the flotilla of boats to the midnight herring-fishing, and watch the miles of nets drawn in with their many captives sparkling in the pale autumnal moonbeams. If inclined for more active sports, the fisher can cast his sand-eel from some outlying rock to the bass which come in with the rising tide, and rival salmon in their weight and vigour when hooked. Or, should he be an early riser, let him embark before grey dawn, hoist his sail, and let out lines for mackerel, the while he watches the rippling gold of sunrise dance to him over the eastern waves, and then call out the winged inhabitants of the rocks to their noisy morning evolutions. Sea-fishing is rapidly assuming the dignity of a recognised branch of angling, and in the excessive competition for trout-fishing and extensive system of preserving waters which at present prevail, there is every probability that each summer to come it will increase in popularity.

More frequently the familiar walks of the seaside, the long yellow stretch of sand, the white lighthouse, or the upland down, will induce a pleasing melancholy as manhood recalls the old loves and friendships of which they alone remain mute yet eloquent mementoes. Sundered from fair faces and winning smiles, it may be by death or circumstances strong as death, the whispers of old days, the aspirations long since crushed out of the heart, again wake to life. Sweet and bitter memories succeed one another as light and shade chequer the ocean spread out in front, while we lean on the stone wall by the ripening barley—

> " Oh, sad it is, in sight of foreign shores,
> Daily to think on old familiar doors,
> Hearths loved in childhood, and ancestral floors ;
> Or, tossed about along a waste of foam,
> To ruminate on that delightful home
> Which with the dear betrothed was to come ;
> Or came, and was, and is, yet meets the eye
> Never but in the world of memory,
> Or in a dream recalled." *

Even a window in Myrtle Cottage may in fancy frame a face unseen for thirty years, yet never forgotten ; and spite of the old boat on the little beach across the river by the wych-elms looking so commonplace, words were once spoken in it which for two people at least have changed the face of the world.

A merry peal of laughter and the pattering of many feet recall us to the present. We have wandered to the Children's Corner, where the sand-castles and mimic forts, each sapped one by one as the relentless waves sweep on, will not unaptly type the future fortunes and aspirations of many amongst these busy little ones. While blessing kind nature for their unconscious minds, who can avoid moralising over his own past at

* Wordsworth, *Poetical Works*, vol. iv., p. 136.

the sight ? And thus the benign offices of the sea to manhood are once more apparent. Retrospection with a view to contentment and thankfulness is chief amongst them. Present work, present duties, present opportunities, is the burden of the everlasting sea-melody to mature life. The music which those monotonous chords call forth from the past is the swan-song of a dead self. The father lives his youth over again at the seaside in his children, has his slower pulses quickened with their glee, and is taught thoughtfulness for others by their wants. Thus age is regenerated by childhood, childhood invigorated by maturity, and the influences of the seaside enable these periods of life to bear reciprocally upon each other. Paterfamilias may therefore find some compensations in the hard fate which annually drives him to the sea.

If a man have the least eye for colour, supposing other resources to fail him, residence at the sea may become tolerable by noticing the artistic effects of light on rock-scenery. A splendid effect is produced on a bare Highland scene in autumn when it is clothed in purple sheets of heather; an inland pasture is not easily surpassed in vivid colouring when a sunny June evening brightens out over it after an hour or two of rain. But the intensity of these hues is far exceeded by sea scenery. In addition to the geological structure of the rocks, which forms, as it were, the groundwork of the picture, the play of light from above and the strong reflected lights of the sea below bring out in enchanted lustre what before was sufficiently vivid, and leave the nooks and crannies in the deepest of shade. Canon Kingsley dwells with special fondness in his *Prose Idylls* upon the brilliant hues of his Devon rocks, and the changes which successively pass over their tints at sunset. But these variations of strongly-chequered light and shade are by no means peculiar to the West of England; they constitute a special charm of any rocky coast. Our painters cunningly seize upon them to give the tone to a sea-piece; and during a prolonged sojourn at the seaside, if a visitor analyses his impressions he will find that much of his affection for the place arises from the familiar yet half-unconscious manner in which his eye is daily soothed by the harmonies of colour it sees on the rock-walls. A seaside place without rocks, in the same manner, is insufferable after a few days; as well be set down in the desert or prisoned within four whitewashed walls. The sea, of course, can never lose its interest; its charm is always there; but landwards, to be met with nothing but sand and bents is depressing in the extreme. A novelist might well send a troublesome character, who is to be carried off the scene by insanity, to Skegness for a fortnight, which is described as consisting of "a streak of sea, a streak of sand, and a streak of land." Perhaps Cleethorpes might answer the same purpose in a week.

Let us take the sea-bird's wing to the frowning trap headlands of Cornwall, or rock in the fisherman's boat off the majestic sandstone cliffs north of Berwick, while the sun brightens out from the slanting grey curtain of rain-clouds on the horizon. The dark-grey rocks, through their crown of mist, one moment watch sullenly the silver showers that stream over their feet, and listen unmoved to the dull roar of the breakers; next minute the sunlight falls on their wrinkled faces, and, hey presto! what a change! A thousand unexpected points twinkle into prominence, and behind them a thousand cavities retire into deeper gloom, as the wave of light sweeps over the ˚craggy barrier to touch its grimness with a myriad delicate tints, and soften its savagery into beauty. But a poet's eye could alone do justice to the glorious spectacle—

> " Till now you dreamed not what could be done
> With a bit of rock and a ray of sun;
>   But, look! how fade the lights and shades
> Of keen bare edge and crevice deep!
>   How doubtfully it fades and fades,
> And glows again, yon craggy steep,

> O'er which,, through colour's dreamiest grades,
> The yellow sunbeams pause and creep !
>   Now pink it blooms, now glimmers grey,
>   Now shadows to a filmy blue,
>   Tries one, tries all, and will not stay,
>   But flits from opal hue to hue,
>   And runs through every tenderest range
>   Of change that seems not to be change,
>   So rare the sweep, so nice the art
>   That lays no stress on any part."

After the fairy vision, with all its positive tints, has passed on and charmed the spectator, there yet remain dim suggestions and half-fancied effects which no words can fix, so changeful, subtle, and evanescent are nature's kaleidoscopic variations; she fastens on each peak and cornice, each flaw where frost has chipped the rock-wall, each lichen spot which has softened its harshness, and then

> " Indifferent of worst or best,
>   Enchants the cliffs with wraiths and hints
>   And gracious preludings of tints,
>   Where all seems fixed, yet all evades
>   And indefinably pervades
>   Perpetual movement with perpetual rest ! " *

If we prosaically ask science by what magic spells these changes are wrought, Professor Tyndall will explain that they are due to the dichroitic action of light. The sky-particles or molecules of light are strewn everywhere through the atmosphere, and while the reflected light is blue, the light transmitted is orange or red.

There are persons who are satisfied with tamer scenery at the sea-side, who can enjoy Withernsea equally with Ilfracombe. The sea itself is all in all to minds so happily framed; accessories of sand or rocks or inland beauty seem to such people almost impertinent intrusions upon the one great feature. Fortunately for those who must have rocks, as well as for those

* Lowell, *Pictures from Appledore*, Poems, ed. 1873, p. 391.

contented with the sea itself, to say nothing of the varied range
of likings between these extremes, the United Kingdom offers
an endless choice of sea-towns, each with its distinctive features.
That isolation which pleases Germans at Heligoland may be
obtained by Englishmen at Rothesay, Colonsay, and many
other places in the West of Scotland, or in Inishmurray and
the numerous other islands sprinkled round the West of Ireland.   Other shores are renowned for sands or for fine sea, for
rock scenery, for fishing, for fashion, for boating, for every possible form of pleasure connected with the sea.   If one English
place were to be named where all the varied charms of seaside
life could be enjoyed in the greatest perfection, Whitby must
take precedence of all others.   To the attractions of breezy
heights, a fine river, and inland walks of rare beauty, it adds
temptations to the bather, artist, antiquarian, and geologist,
pleasant society owning little allegiance to the tyranny of fashion,
the finest of sea and waves, an old town which carries the visitor
back to the Middle Ages, a new one of which every stone tells
of Hudson, the railway king, a churchyard set on so high a cliff
that *Sic itur ad astra* might be inscribed on the steps leading
up to it, an abbey of which the graceful ruins areredolent of the
piety of Elfleda and St. Hilda, of St. John of Beverley and St.
Wilfrid of York.   Here, too, the great Council of Streaneshalch
was held, a cardinal event in English ecclesiastical history, and
the curious service of the three barons alluded to in *Marmion*
was rendered.   Altogether it is unique amongst English watering-places.   If the archæologist desire still earlier memories, let
him visit quaint little Boscastle, the "silent tower" of Bottreaux,
and, above all,

> " Tintagil, half in sea and high on land,
>   A crown of towers,"

or Milton's "great vision of the guarded mount."   In short, if
a pilgrimage to the English cathedrals is to read the history of
the land carved in stone, it may safely be asserted that the

archæology and associations of our sea-shores give in their most pleasant form, not merely the history, but the legends, poetry, and romance of the kingdom as well.

Old age finds no keener outdoor pleasure than to revisit the sea-shores familiar to it from childhood. Then memory and reflection summon the past to their silent sessions, as the man, cheered, it may be hoped, with all of love and deference which should accompany old age, watches at evening the fishing-boats hoist their sails to pass the harbour-bar ere the tide falls, and so, with their large brown spread of canvas, sweep majestically into the night. The grandchildren, it may be, play around ; their father walks up and down, unfolding to his approving wife, in the intervals of his cigar, the plan of his great work *On Di-morphism*, which is to waft him on to fame. All things around him, the aged man ponders, are full of hope and innocent enjoyment, each looking on to some higher stage, some blessing to blossom in the future. Has not this reflection a comfortable bearing on his own years, which are fast nearing their earthly term ? And if the inestimable boon be further granted him of knowing that his life has not altogether been spent uselessly and selfishly, if he be conscious of a good fight not unfairly fought, if not a few memories of kindly deeds beset him, of efforts made not wholly in vain to carry out the law of love in his dealings with others, if peaceable thoughts and pure fancies and righteous deeds and helping words have been the diet on which he has fed his soul, who would not envy him this retrospect of life, mellowed by the sea's freshness, and with each hard outline softened by its gracious influences? Then, turning from the past to the present, the sea spread out before him, with its sails mysteriously sinking below the horizon to seek another world, must needs remind him of the numberless philosophers and poets who have loved to view in it "that immortal sea which brought us hither," as well as the sea which rounds our little life, the unknown waters on which, when our anchors are once weighed, we must darkling make our voyage. The sea is thus the latest, as it was our earliest, instructor. Its vastness, its brightness, its union of perpetual agitation with central peace—all these qualities are now but symbols' of the future state, as they served in youth for the work of fancy, or of encouragement and solace in manhood. From this world's sea old age thus insensibly passes to the "sea of glass like unto crystal" before the throne of God. Finally, in order that it may strengthen the man about to suffer this "sea change" in a higher sense than Shakespeare ever dreamt, the notion of trustfully waiting is also inherent in the sea. Lowell seldom wrote grander words than when he thus dwells on this aspect of the sea and the home beyond:—*

> " The drooping sea-weed hears, in night abyssed,
>   Far and more far the wave's receding shocks,
> Nor doubts, for all the darkness and the mist,
> That the pale shepherdess will keep her tryst,
>   And shoreward lead again her foam-fleeced flocks.
> And, though Thy healing waters far withdraw,
>   I, too, can wait and feed on hope of Thee,
> And of the dear recurrence of Thy law;
> Sure that the parting grace that morning saw
>   Abides its time to come in search of me. "

* *Poems*, p. 381.

Amongst the Heather.

NOT the least breath of wind stirs the heavy masses of yellow calceolarias on the lawn, or finds its way through the open study window. A glance at the topmost twigs of the acacia, sensitive as they ordinarily are to the slightest curl of air, shows each pinnate leaf sharply brought out against a lowering sky. A thunderstorm is clearly impending, and we fall to thinking which book Elia, in his mild wisdom, would have recommended as the fitting one for such an afternoon. "Milton almost requires a solemn service of music to be played before you enter upon him;" ere long Nature's grandest diapason will be rolling overhead, while the lightning plays in and out from the canopy of cloud over the distant Welsh hills. All at once, as we open the book, a page of *Paradise Lost* discloses a sprig of heather. It is well preserved, owing to the plant's coriaceous nature, though the deep native purples are fled, being replaced by pale lilac. Satirical poets may smile at the speedy forgetfulness of the donor's name which ensues when such a sprig is given as a *gage d'amour*. Personal recollections soon fade from a dried flower, but local associations almost always assert themselves. The smell of a flower or tree in its living state is the principal spell which recalls distant places to the memory, as any one may prove experimentally for himself. The fragrance of yew-trees or furze bushes is thus particularly potent. The musty odour of death, however, confounds all these delicate scents, and it is the sight of withered

C

petal or dried leaf-stalk which now plays the magician to the mind. In this case remembrance flies back to Wallace's Hill in Selkirkshire, which overlooks the fair windings of the Tweed until the mighty russet shoulders of Minch Moor close the view. It brings back an autumnal Sunday morning and an idle ramble with a friend over the heathery slopes, until, sitting down by a Pictish fort, and gazing into the misty glens under Dollar Law and Broad Law, and then up at the brotherhood of envious hills which shut out the prospect from the Yarrow Valley, the home of love and poetry, in an absent mood this sprig of heather was plucked and carried so far homeward that it seemed but kindly to preserve it between these leaves, just as men grant a comfortable old age to a favourite horse. And now this little dry twig marvellously reproduces that morning's sights and sounds—the stagshorn moss winding amongst the heather-tufts with its delicate, amber-coloured spikes of fructi-fication; the whirr of the blackcock crossing a glen; the rush of a startled blue hare; the red mutch of the old woman walk-ing on the hill-path to Traquair Kirk; the distant peep at the massive walls of Traquair House, the last refuge of loyalty to the Stuarts, where Charles Edward's cradle is reverentially pre-served, and the front gates of the mansion may yet be seen overgrown with several inches of turf, never having been opened since its gallant owners rode through them to join the White Rose in 1745. Nay, the subjects, even the very tones, of the conversation once more awake to life, like the frozen notes in the fairy tale; and all this, thanks to the suggestiveness of a little dried sprig of heather.

It is matter of wonder why the thistle, with its defiant motto, has been adopted as the emblem of Scotland rather than the heather, which so regally mantles its hills. The rigid angularities of the national character live, indeed, in one; but the tender grace, the breadth of colour, the fragility, and yet the endurance of the heather, point to the higher and finer aspects of the Scotch nature, and the deep affection and strength of will which underlie it. The fact seems to be that, until the Union, the aggressive, prickly nature of the thistle only too aptly symbolized the rough and warlike disposition of Scotland. Few sentiments save patriotism found favour with its people before the middle of the eighteenth century. They took no thought of poetry or the refinements of life when the sword was at their throats and their ears rang with denunciations of Stuart or Hanoverian. When this question was definitely settled, and commerce took her place in peace upon her throne, border feud and national animosity alike faded into the emotional love of country and home, which finds its' expression in so many beautiful ballads and songs, the slogan being exchanged for those pathetic love-songs which are the glory of Scotch literature. Then heather was twisted in many a chaplet of song. Thus Thomas the Rhymer speaks of

"Flodden's high and heathery side."

And the ballad of "King Henrie" runs—

"Oh, pu'd has he the green heather,
And made to her a bed ; "

while it serves to heighten the pathos of "Faithless Donald"—

"When first ye climbed the heath'ry steep,
Wi' me to keep my father's sheep,
The vows ye made ye said ye'd keep ! "

The "brown heath" was Scott's favourite plant, and naturally occurs again and again in the Ettrick Shepherd's songs, perhaps never more beautifully than in his exquisite poem to the Skylark—

"Then when the gloaming comes,
Low in the heather brooms,
Sweet will thy welcome and bed of love be ! "

In prose no one has emphasised its cheerful appearance and

fitness to the localities it chooses better than Mr. Ruskin, and certainly no one ever drew it with exacter delineation of every curve and grace. When roaming over a Highland corrie, however, or marking the sunlight fall on the granite blocks of Dartmoor, all but swallowed, as they are in summer, by the purple ocean of heather that surges in upon their desolation, the traveller is apt to forget that there are more than one species of heather in the kingdom. There are seven (or, omitting *Calluna*, six) even in England, while the whole family boasts some 400 species, to say nothing of the innumerable hybrids and varieties which our gardens produce. Every one ·knows the common ling or heather (*Calluna*), which is the most widely distributed of the family, ranging as it does, from Labrador to the Azores, and spreading all along the western coast of Europe from the Atlantic-washed side of Africa, which is the original home of the race. The Scotch heather proper (*Erica cinerea*) is somewhat thicker and taller than this last, with reddish-purple flowers which delight bees, while its tender shoots are dear to the grouse and blackcock. The crossleaved heath (*E. tetralix*) once seen is never forgotten. Fairies might have modelled it in wax, as, rising four or five inches from the ground, it hangs its delicately-tinted, rose-flushed flowers over some boggy spot where the cotton-grass flutters in the wind and the plover whistles against the bleeting snipe, hence known in Scotland as the "heather-bleat." Whoever has penetrated to the angry coast of the Lizzard, either to see its curious churches or to gather its characteristic plants, must have recognized the Cornish heath (*E. vagans*) as soon as he set foot upon the magnesian limestone, while the ciliated heath occurs in isolated spots in the Cornish peninsula, and Mackay's and the Mediterranean heath are only to be found in the south-western districts of Ireland, being in truth outliers from the flora of the Spanish peninsula on the Continent. All these heaths are fond of lonely, wind-smitten localities, tenderly flinging their red and purple jewels over Nature's desolations, and as the long summer days die out, rustling their sere and withered flowers (which remain on the plant even when dead, and form the chief characteristic of the family in a botanist's eyes) among snow and wet, determined to do their best to cheer the waste places of the earth. The autumnal holiday-maker never fails to greet the heath as the symbol of all that is free and pleasurable in outdoor life, while to the inmates of the Scotch shieling heather stands in much the same relation for its economic uses as does the bamboo to the Gond or Malay. Even the gipsy and the tramp have reason to bless heather, as it helps them to a livelihood by making brooms, if only they can obtain or take right of common where it grows. And to many a mountain child the purple hillside is the only flower garden he knows ; but what a garden ! Reaching from horizon to horizon, itself the best of bedding-plants, requiring no care or expenditure, the greener after the worst of storms, when August's sun blazes most fiercely only more purple and luxuriant, the home of all that is elevated and purifying in heart and taste. For " it is not the written poetry which affects us most, but the unwritten poetry of our own youth, and mine is all bound up with heather, and fern, and streams flowing under the shade of alders." *

Not only are there many different species of heather, but despite the apparent uniformity of the common kinds when covering a moorland, the keen eye may discover differences in the texture and colour of the flowery carpet, which the dull wight, his vision unpurged by euphrasy and rue, thoughtlessly misses. Mark this grey scaur falling eighty feet from the pure blue skies overhead into the blackest pool of the Tummel, but fringed above with the deepest of purple heather, which lovingly runs as far down its face as the longest spray can find foothold. No wonder that an artist is painting the scene from his umbrella-

* P. G. Hamerton, *Round my House*, p. 54.

tent behind us, and no wonder that time after time he halts disgusted, no cunning of eye and hand sufficing to catch those living, glowing tints suffused with sunlight over the birch-trees, and dropping like a flower-fall (to coin a word for the nonce) into breezy space. Who has ever yet seen heather adequately painted? Miss Mutrie at present, Van Huysum in old days, would exactly limn a sprig of it ; but it is a very different thing to cope with a whole surface of glowing heather, with all its reflected lights, manifold depths, and fainter shadows, and trembling twinklings of rose-red passing into the grand sunlit fulness of purple perfection. From this living sheet of amethyst turn we the mental kaleidoscope to South Devon, where the heather-clad hills rise, say from the Otter Valley towards the west. The prospect has lost the prevailing charm of purple monotone, but it has gained in richness as compensation. Yellow bog-asphodel spikes and creamy white bedstraw, pink, white and blue milkwort, foxgloves and mullein with woolly leaves and yellow flowers, and many more contrasts of colour, like Proserpine's stores hurriedly emptied upon Enna, crowd every square yard of the stony moorland, while dwarf furze, ablaze with living gold, throws into prominence the red breadths of heather. Flora's richest gifts in July cover these bare hill-sides, topped here and there with dark pines, while blinding gleams of blue sea to the left and in front enhance the effect. It is very beautiful in its own way, but the soberness of Northern heather is lost in the general glow. This might be a lotuseater's paradise ; here there is room for imagination, for peaceful rest from work, and golden dreams. In Scotland, with foot on the heather, red as with the life-blood of its sturdy rocks, and running up their shoulders till stopped by the snow-wreaths which, even in summer, linger on the highest corries, the heart beats quicker and gathers strength for deeds. So Devon has her worthies who, as old Prince tells us, have sung and painted, and roved the seas in quest of adventures. Scotland's sons have left their bones in every clime, and everywhere stamped the impress of their stern patriotism and unbending perseverance. Devon has been the nursery of knights-errant—Scotland the stern mother of heroes.

Hants's heather, again, as seen on the North Downs, is uniformerly of a soberer tint than that of either Devon or Scotland. There is little admixture of other flowers, nothing to serve as foil to its amethystine glow. We look up to the man who is inflexibly virtuous, and respect him who is unswervingly accurate in his disposition of time ; but love seldom gathers round them, because kindly inconsistencies and the amiable failings so dear to ordinary human natures are unknown to them. So the heart finds it difficult to attach itself to the unalloyed heather of Hants. It is different with Lincolnshire, where scanty patches of the plant occasionally linger, pleasing oases to the artistic eye amongst the vast desert of skilled farming, the formal acres of turnips and mangolds threatening ere long to swallow up these purple outliers, which indeed are at present only permitted to exist on sufferance. The very rarity of these scattered banks of heather renders them precious. The beholder blesses them (if he be not a farmer), on account of their associations with Northern sport and beauty, freedom from cares, and a thousand other sentiments which break in acceptably on the anxieties felt all round him upon short-horns, labourers' unions, and foot-and-mouth disease. In Yorkshire the moors, with their heathery covering, are the next best thing to Scotland—are Scotland, in short, without its glamour and romance. When the brown streamlet under the hills on which we walk is seized at the end of the valley, five miles off, and turned into a vast tank, built by some company, to supply Manchester or Leeds with water, and the whitewashed walls of some hideous factory catch the sight on the acclivity beyond, sensitive natures feel that they have not yet got far enough North. The heather is the same, but its associations are in-

finitely poorer ; and, after all, association is a more powerful
agent than mere beauty :—

> " Oh, the wafts o' heather-honey, and the music o' the brae,
> As I watch the great harts feeding nearer, nearer a' the day ;
> Oh, to hark the eagle screaming, sweeping, ringing round the sky,
> That's a bonnier life—"

the outlaw may well say, than listening to the rattle of a thousand spindles, and living in a mile-long village, where every
house is the counterpart of its neighbour.

The growth of this modern passion for Scotch scenery has
been analysed by Lord Macaulay in a well-known passage. It
is little more than a century since Johnson penetrated to the
Hebrides, and came back to Fleet Street with as much fame as
a man now obtains after visiting the sources of the Nile. Gray,
the poet, seems to have been amongst the first to discover the
romantic beauties of Scotland.   In the Lake district, too, he
forestalled the encomiums of Wordsworth and his school.
Moderns, who leave their club one day and tread the heather
of Culloden on the next, little think what a business such a
jaunt was considered even at the beginning of this century.
Sportsmen who then took the journey carried multifarious supplies with them, and made arrangements for their stay resembling those which are made at present for a shooting trip to
Arkansas and the Rocky Mountains.   An amusing instance
may be found in Colonel Thornton's Scotch expedition, which
probably took place in 1784 or 1785; though, curiously enough,
in his stately quarto, published in 1804, he nowhere states the
exact year in which it was made.   The mere recital of his pre-
parations fills pages. Besides horses, dogs, guns, and fishing-
rods, with all manner of tackle and ammunition, he took a gig
and two baggage-waggons, complete camp equipage, two boats
(for the lakes), and even an artist !   All were packed on board
a sloop engaged for the purpose, and very racy are his exploits
by river-side and on the heather.   With the memory of Mr.

Milbank's famous bag of 728 grouse on Wemmergill Moors, August 20, 1872, in our minds, the following passage, concerning the gallant Colonel's achievements amongst the heather, is sufficiently amusing to the present generation :—

" I had had some suspicions that my famous treble battle-powder had received damage from a leak in the *Falcon* sloop, and this day's shooting fully convinced me of it. I never knew powder hang so much, and always firing dull; but there was no remedy. With good powder, I verily believe I could have killed thirty brace presently;" and then he takes the trouble to add, " Pero, Ponto, Dargo, Shandy, Carlo, and Romp, all whelps, behaved incomparably." *

Most enthusiastic of all sportsmen, however, when clad in his shooting-jacket and his feet on his native heather, is Christopher North. Who does not know his athletic frame, as he appears in Duncan's picture, leaning on his gun, his hat flung on the bank at his side, and his grand massive head and neck, such as Ajax might have envied, thrown back, as he sniffs the fresh moorland breeze, and, with kindling eye, breaks out into those eloquent rhapsodies wherewith he was wont to charm the last generation? What proud exultation for every gallant deed done of old on Scotch ground, and for all the rugged ballads that tell of them, now fires his heart ! Again, what keen delight in all the sports to which those heather-clads hills invite impels him to burst into ecstasies of excited yet wonderful description ! We pant after him in vain, as he breasts the corrie, intent on reaching the deer, unsuspiciously feeding behind the mountain's shoulder; now he leaves us far behind, as he stalks up the brae, " like a king rejoicing in his strength," while we, weakly mortals, painfully clamber below him, to shoot the ptarmigan on its summit; and again he reclines on the heather, mingling philosophic disquisition with recitations from Homer and Burns ; next moment to be rushing downwards to join a cours-

* Thornton's *Sporting Tour*, p. 151. London, 1804.

ing party, with which he hallooes the dogs on to some luckless
" maukin," and keeps pace with the fleetest of her pursuers,
till she " carries away her cocked fud unscathed for the third
time; nor can there any longer be the smallest doubt in the
world in the minds of the most sceptical, that she is—what all
the country-side have long known her to be—a witch." But
the activities of this true son of the heather are not half
exhausted. See him bird-nesting, salmon-fishing, "bickering"
with snowballs, fighting Jack the Tinker, shooting wild ducks
in the moonlight, when December's frost holds earth and water
in the hardest fetters, dog-fighting with gipsies after Falkirk
Tryst—had ever any one more intense delight in thews and
sinews, and the mere animal joys of living? Sit down now on
this heather cushion, with the graceful birches waving above,
and look down on beautiful Loch Tummel, while the enchanter
tells of village love and the sanctities of cottage life in the Highlands, and draws out the severe yet simple sentiments of piety
which bring together the minister's scattered flock every Sabbath
from distant shielings and shepherds' huts, seldom visited save
by the autumnal sportsman, and you recognise the tender, almost feminine undercurrent of feeling in the Professor's heart,
and own that he can skilfully touch the deepest chords of the
music of humanity. Now that political hatreds and insensate
party spirit have so greatly moderated their intensity, the man
emerges all the brighter from the clouds of partizanship. Long
may Scotland be proud of one of her warmest-hearted sons !

Besides poetry and eloquence, the sister art of painting has
caught marvellous inspiration in these later days of nature-study
from the heather which past generations looked on with contempt, as signifying the nakedness of the land, and shutting
them out from the acquisition of gold. Turning to Shakespeare
as a guide to men's thoughts in the Elizabethan age, Gonzales
can only think of heath as the last straw a drowning man would
catch at. It is something more worthless than even Virgil's

sea-weed—*vilior projecta alga* : "Now would I give a thousand furlongs of sea for an acre of barren ground, long heath, brown furze—anything ! The wills above be done, but I would fain die a dry death !" To heighten the horrors which spring from their prophetic announcement, it is on the "blasted heath" near Forres that the Witches meet Macbeth and Banquo, while the Clown in *All's Well that Ends Well* (iii., 2) infinitely prefers even old heather anywhere save in the country ; "our old ling and our Isbel's o' the country are nothing like your old ling and your Isbels o' the court." How different is popular sentiment at present, when crowds rush to the Academy in the height of the season to see a few square feet of Scotch landscape and red heather painted by Millais or Graham ! Landseer with his Highland views, and Ansdell with his homely shepherds, their flocks and dogs, have long been guiding the public taste to these objects. Year by year a larger proportion of our most able artists devote themselves to Scotch scenery, in which heather is seldom forgotten. Under the dull northern clouds, no other feature gives such a breadth of colour, such effective masses of purple to bestow the requisite tone on moorland or tempest. Even the barest crags, when spread with this rich mantle, testify to Nature's universal liking for the beautiful, and form a link by which to connect their rugged horror with human associations of love and tender protection. Turner and the great landscape painters of the Middle Ages looked to bright skies and flowers and laughing streams of water in great measure to supply this void, and, of course, they were powerfully aided by the clearness of their horizons, the vast expanse of aërial perspective which they could command. But a painter would frequently be in evil straits in Scotland, especially when debarred from a sea or loch, were he also cut off from the use of heather. With it he can flood his foreground with as warm a glow as Giorgione diffused over his canvas. Allow him a few dark strips of pine forest, and distant heather-clad mountains

touched with the setting sun's last rays, and, if he has sufficient
skill in handiwork, he may rival the savage witchery of
Ruysdael and Claude. The fulness, depth, and colour of
heather admirably adapt it to landscape composition, apart
from the sentiment obtained by its use. And what dignity
does it not acquire in the eyes of the lover of poetry as
he remembers that it was of heather, according to Æschylus,
that the telegraphic beacon fires were composed which flashed
from afar to Clytemnestra at Argos the news of the taking of
Troy!

But a Highland landscape is of itself sufficiently beautiful.
It merely requires heather to give it the predominant tone, and
interest a beholder by means of the many associations sure to
suggest themselves when he sees the purpled braes. Take, for
instance, the valley of the Garry in mid July. It possesses a
charm of its own; and yet Scotland owns a thousand more
valleys which, to casual observers, appear very similar when they
are flooded with heather-bloom, such is the magic of this humble
shrub. The prevailing colours in the open country on either
side of the Garry are reds and purples, derived mainly from
heather, but largely reinforced by clover and vetches. These
tints are set off by the flaunting blossoms of the broom on every
neglected corner, while the tender waxen *Erica tetralix* gathers
round the head of each mimic burn that cleaves the moorland.
Every here and there are patches of turnips, rejoicing the
farmer's eye with their healthy green leaves, as yet free from the
fly's ravages, while above them on the crags, and below towards
the waste spots, an ocean of heather surges in, like the flood-
tide, swallowing up, as it were, one by one the numberless grey
and black trap boulders which are piled up in confusion, the
gravestones of a long-buried world, and among which tower
foxgloves of great size and beauty. On one side is a barley-
field, in which the "blueys" are perceptibly colouring its ripening tints; the delicate pink of the corn-cockles, intermingled,

helps the effect. Above tower many huge spruce firs, like giants, with drooping robes of green that love to sweep the earth. Some of them have lost their lead, but another soon takes its place, and the disfigurement is speedily unnoticed in the clouds of foliage high up, its light-green tips all drenched in sunshine. Behind them the mountains break away into the skies, their shoulders covered with spires of young larch, while graceful birches come down the foreground intermixed with the heavy-hanging sprays of beech, like mountain nymphs which have left their stern seclusion to draw near to men. In the valley the bracken catches the sun's rays, and amidst its glitter the Garry may be discerned of the colour of strong tea, with boulders shining through its stream, like masses of cairngorm, when seen in the shade. Rain has fallen amongst the mountains during the night, and now the trees shake their leaves over the stream as it roars underneath, and the foxgloves near it dance in the echoes, and a thousand little burns, running into it, trickle everywhere through the lichen-spotted boulders! Indeed, seeing that all this country is the land of Burns, it is absurd for Glasgow and the neighbourhood to claim the designation in honour of the great national poet. What more typical view could be selected for a wild prospect of Highland heather? Only man is wanting, and at the next bend he is discovered in the shape of a salmon-fisher, trying the big pool under the Cradle-stone. But he is rather late, as this river does not fish well in July, and the chances are that, if he does hook a salmon in the pool, it will rush on the wings of this little spate over the sharp rocks at the bottom, and infallibly cut the line in half. And now the angler finds he has caught his " silver doctor " on the beach behind, and snapped off the barb. With the patience of his fraternity, however, he proceeds to put on another, only too thankful meanwhile to find a cushion of heather close at hand on which to sit. The roar of the water floats to the ear, softened by distance, the bee hums in the wild thyme, and the visitor to Scotland begins now to understand why its air and scenery are so invigorating.

To enter into the sentiment of loneliness which heather can bestow on a landscape, the traveller need only strike some ten miles to the east of the Garry, over the hills, at the back of the little village of Moulins. Here he will find himself surrounded with melancholy treeless hills and mountains, running down from Benygloe, with the little Brerechen burn winding through them, now half lost amongst a chaos of stones, now emerging into a crystal stream, and actually here forming a miniature pool under a three-inch cascade. But it is full of little bright-coloured trout, and ministers to the wants of many mountain sheep and countless birds, like a thread of joy running through their innocent lives. Here a blackcock gallantly defends the retreat of his three cheepers by feigning excessive lameness, fluttering up and settling immediately with loud out-cries. The sympathetic visitor follows him while the little ones escape amongst the heather, and soon he leaps up and speeds over the hill exulting that any one should fall into his trap. There lapwings flap about in an aimless manner, as if they, too, would imitate the tactics of the blackcock. Wheatears flit from mound to mound; corbies utter their forbidding croak from the hill-side, where a dead lamb is probably lying; little parties of curlew, with their scimitar-like beaks, dash over the dreary moorland; jackdaws, and occasionally a gull or two, scream in the distance; and a marsh-harrier beats the furze on the acclivities with as much regularity as would a pointer range for his master. This moor is a paradise for ornithologists. Birds are everywhere, and birds seen in their most confiding moods, for man's feet seldom penetrate this wilderness. As we approach the burn, what is all this screaming and fluttering? A couple of ring-ousels fly out of a cairn of stones where their nest is, and hover round, now resting on a rail with expanded feathers and much insulted dignity at their privacy being invaded, now screaming and rushing by in terror lest the traveller should pursue his investigations among the stones. Having escaped from these furies, a sandpiper proceeds to follow their example with still more emphatic flying and screaming. She must be deeply outraged, as she flies backwards and forwards, almost brushing against the heartless intruder amongst her domestic sanctities. If he possesses any kindliness of nature, he retires quickly from the angry matron, and devotes himself to the flowers which edge the little burn. They form the only cheerful gleams in the landscape; eyebright, milk-worts, white and blue; butterworts, like tall violets, with curious, greasy leaves; foxgloves, marsh bedstraw, sundew, and, once more queen of every mound, the *Erica tetralix*. The mere enumeration of them transports us to the brook-side and its sighing, fluttering cotton-grasses, always the symbols of desolation. No sign of man can be seen. The mists float together, and merge their soft outlines in grey cloud; the air grows damp and damper; and now a drizzle sets in, and the swelling moorland is swathed in folds of storm-clouds. Then the drizzle gives way to steady rain that soon passes into drifted sheets, as the wind eddies down the southern valleys.

Wrapped in our macintosh, it is high time to struggle back towards Pitlochrie. Luckily we possess a flask filled with dews even more potent than those the skies are distilling over our devoted heads (for Pitlochrie boasts an admirable whisky), and at length a huge figure descending the brae at our side, like the Spectre of the Brocken, joins us, and turns out to be a shepherd, contentedly smoking his pipe, itself made out of the *bruyère* or heather of Southern France, though commerce contracts it into "briar" wood. If heather ministers to dreariness and solitude, it also affords its own solace to some enviable dispositions.

"Saft the day!" he says, in answer to our greeting. "Ou

aye; it's a bit saft perhaps; but it'll no jist harm the hay much."

Yet half this deluge would drive a Southron squire or parson wild as he thought of his home-meadow. The virtue of resignation is strongly developed in Scottish peasants. Ere now we have seen them carting away barley sheaves in early winter, which had lain so long in the harvest fields, amongst the downpour of a wet autumn, that they had sprouted afresh and developed into a mass of living mouldiness, with a calm cheerfulness that spoke volumes for the solace of Calvinistic teaching. Much of it was useless for man, they told us, but it would do nicely for "the fools and the pigs." After all, fatalism, tempered with religion, is not an unsuitable philosophy for people who live in dreary, desolate heather-wastes, overhung with murky skies, and ever liable to be drenched with persistent rain. The sunny epicureanism of the Bay of Naples would be greatly out of place at Strath Brora.

Turn we again the heathery kaleidoscope to Dartmoor in summer. A sense of breezy vastness is borne in upon the soul, as on the slope of some granite-crowned tor, sinking into the heather which so naturally invites to rest, the eye scans the leagues of the ruddy plain, melting into blue hills and still bluer sky. From Hamilton Down, say, we are looking over "spacious Dertmoor," as Drayton calls it, over her swells and granite "clatters" to the beautifully proportioned tower of Widdicombe, so well known in the records of Demonology. Further north lies Manaton, Becky's Falls, and Lustleigh—ground dear to tourists. Far beyond these in the airy blue, the eye discerns Bovey Tracey, with its curious lignite formation, and a faint streak of white steam tells of the girdle which civilization is gradually drawing round this "ancient moor." There are not many localities in England, possessing features of their own, where so extensive a view, such perfect solitude, can be obtained. Three lovers of Dartmoor, well known in the West of

England, are more perfectly acquainted than any other men with every nook and corner of this waste of 130,000 acres, and one of them writes :—" Dartmoor is throughout a district of heather ; and it is only over a very small portion of the Lake country that either the ling or the common heath is to be found, and then only in patches. The many lichens that attach themselves to the granite, staining and marking it, and often hanging from it in long, grey beards ; the stretches of rush, fern, and bent grass; the beds of white, fluttering cotton reed (the ' cana grass' of the Highlands); these, with the broken rocks and the tors themselves, supply the neutral tints of the wild landscape, lighted and set off in due season by the glow of heather, the golden blaze of furze, and along the stream and towards the border country, by regiments, and squadrons of tall foxgloves. Many plants common in Wales and the North do not occur here. This alone is sufficient to give a special character to the colouring."

From these artistic pleasures we descend the other side of the high-land, and lo ! from the opposite shoulder of thinly-covered granite the world breaks in upon the dreamer in the shape of a coach and four, crammed inside and out with tourists, crossing the moor by the great central track from Tavistock to Moreton Hampstead, and Exeter. When the unwelcome dust subsides we pass the Vitifer Tin Mine, where the hills are seamed with the excavations of the ancient "streamers" (as the primitive Keltic miners are here called), and breast the hill amidst the whistling of numerous ring-ousels to Grimspound. A chimney of the mine, seen on the opposite side of the valley, links the men of to-day with the primitive tin-smelters who probably inhabited this British village. Or the mind may pierce still further the mist of ages, and view the men of the Bronze or even the Stone period within this fort, for no iron weapons have as yet been found near the ancient monuments of Dartmoor. What a retrospect to call up as we stand within

D

the rude granite enclosure of 500 feet in diameter, encircled by
a wall of granite blocks some ten feet in thickness, but nowhere
more than six feet high ! Could any other natural feature so
powerfully evoke the ghost of a long-buried Past as this
heathery moorland? Twenty-five hut-circles, also composed
of rough granite blocks, are far more easily traced than are the
remains of the Yorkshire pit-villages, and the spring of water
from which their ancient inhabitants drank yet runs within the
enclosure, so changeless is Nature when left to herself. Overgrown with ferns and heath, the place is much as it must have
appeared a year after the Romans or invading Saxons drove
out its natives. Archæology asks in vain whether the name
Grimspound is connected with a " boundary " (as in the many
Grim's dykes of other parts of England), or, in view of the
many dark superstitions of Dartmoor, whether it has aught to
do with Grima, said to be a Saxon name for the Evil One; or,
lastly, whether Grym, the fisherman and eponymus of Grimsby,
left here also traces of his presence. It must belong to Keltic
times, however, if it may be regarded as part of the group of
river and place names of this district ; Dart, Teign, Taw, and
the many compounds of Tor, itself connected with the Hebrew
for "rock " and " passing with an early migration westward "
from Tyre to these Dartmoor Tors.* Every stone before us,
therefore, may well carry thought backwards to these Phœni-
cian traders who, while buying the Cornish tin, left the San-
skrit name for it—Kastira—on the Cassiterides or Tin Islands,
and perhaps on Cassiter Street, Bodmin. To find another
link with that remote past, the very faith which now gives
England its national pre-eminence may have been handed
down to us by the men who once trampled this heather, and
have long turned to dust under it. Amid these deeper meditations on the stone monuments of the moor, the wayfarer re-
gains the ancient trackway below and makes for Two Bridges

* Earle, *Philology of the English Tongue*, p. 3.

on the West Dart before darkness falls, mindful of the moor-
men's rhyme—

> " River of Dart, river of dart,
> Every year thou claimest a heart."

Plenty of granite ribs broken from the moor's backbone strew
his path on both sides, and their grey glimmer will long be un-
subdued by night, as Browning has noted, with the subtle
observation of a true poet—

> " Piled stones that gleam unground away
> By twilight's hungry jaws, which champs fine all beside
> I' the solitary waste we grope through."—(*Fifine*).

And still heather is everywhere around, and runs down the
peninsula in front till it fitly enough dips down between the
Land's End and the Scilly Isles into that legendary imaginative fairy-land, the long-lost Lyonnesse,

> " A land of old, upheaven from the abyss,
> By fire to sink into the abyss again."

We must end with one more sketch from the " land of brown
heath and shaggy wood." It is an afternoon late in September,
giving another aspect of heather, and one well known to many
an Englishman. A few hours of fine weather are delusively
succeeding several days of persistent rain. The birches are
dropping masses of gold, the fir woods impenetrable depths of
gloom, whence come and go aërial whispers, preludes of
approaching storm, but, like Cassandra's forebodings, utterly
distrusted by two sanguine sportsmen who are striding over the
blanched heather-blooms on the open moor. Grouse have
already packed, and the gillie and couple of dogs which have
descended the slope before them have been worse than useless
on the upper corries. It is in no contented mood, therefore,
that they come down the hill-track by the shieling to the loch.
Its sullen surface, streaked with one flying sunbeam, and opening in the distance upon a grey sea ruffled into white, around

vast crags where the sea-fowl are wheeling and clanging in countless flocks, prescient of the tempest, deepens their sombre thoughts by the contrast it presents to its recent beauty. But who shall dare to describe seas which have lately been so well painted by Mr. Black? Where the moor dies out, and cultivation begins to snatch stinted crops of oats from its wide expanse, rises the Kirk, surrounded by grey lichen-tinted walls. As they pass through the burial-ground, the tombstones attract the strangers' notice. Wonderful figures of Death are carved on some, like a boy in buttons holding a scythe, and the artist has devoted extreme pains to the waistcoat buttons. Near these, in letters yet deeply cut into a granite slab, they read—

"HEIR LYES ANE VERTEOOS MAN IAMES SHIOCH SOM TYME BAYLIE OF HIS BROUGHE OF GLASGOW 1686."

Spite of the sombre afternoon, with that instinctive habit of playing Old Mortality so natural to man, they linger amongst the graves. The mists descend from the hills they have left, and draw nearer the dark enclosure, the deep, hoarse roar of the river resounds from below, and where the mist-wreaths occasionally lift, it seems to rush down from the skies in a turbid cataract, while the wrinkled gneiss of the Ben behind looms like the Matterhorn against its dark cloud-curtain, and the little burn that ordinarily sparkles happily down its face to-day flings itself down in masses of foam. Much heather mingles with the coarse grass in the sacred enclosure, as if man had made many attempts to extirpate it, but was now compelled to acquiesce in its usurpation. Outside it is much blackened in places where it has been burnt, while on the hill-tops it is soft and carpet-like, grateful to blackcock and grouse, and ankle-deep; whereas on the border land are tufts and bushes knee-deep, running into bogs where, like the Isle of Arran heather, it is nearly waist-high. A few pink flowers yet linger, but most of the shoots bear blanching blossom, and at every dozen yards a bluebell full of dew appears. Stagshorn moss crawls between the tufts over large grey stones, which sometimes occur in heaps, and these again intensify themselves into cairns on the top of each mound. Vegetation is brighter in the marsh below, where grass of Parnassus, red rattles, and the like, yet survive to mourn Summer. No small birds are in sight, but blackcocks are heard crowing on the hill-side to the left, and the sound harmonises well with the dreary landscape.

As the sportsmen emerge they meet a funeral entering : the shepherd has been brought down from the hill-side shieling to his last quiet resting-place. Reflecting how the same lot awaits monarch and slave—*omnes eodem cogimur*—the young men reverently take off their hats, and watch the minister with the ltttle train of mourners silently enter the yard. The shepherd, wont to rest in the shieling, its roof heaped up with peat and heather, will now sleep "until the day break and the shadows flee away," under the same familiar covering. The Englishmen miss the consolatory sentences of their own Burial Service, but the hard-featured Scotch faces before them are composed to a stern resignation. The minister has told them ere they started that they too have their life-work to perform faithfully, and the sense of being unprofitable servants is now being borne into their souls, as it only is on such occasions. Women as a rule do not accompany funerals in Scotland, and the widow sits by the turf fire in the shieling, rocking herself to and fro and "crooning" the while. The body is lowered, and the rich black earth heaped over it, and all turn to go : Donald, "puir beastie," his master's collie, lingers with downcast tail and ears, but is sternly whistled off. The men shake their heads and set their lips tighter as they retire, while one of the Englishmen, who is probably a poet in his small way, and

> "Hath among least things
> An under-sense of greatest"—

plucks a twig of heather from the neighbouring hillock, and

thinks how fitly heath should grow over a man whose life was
never dissociated from its present spell—whose greatest delight
it was to tread the heather braes, and hear the wild bee
murmur in its purple masses. And then the clouds break in
a soft deluge that overwhelms day, and, with another lover of
Scotland, the gathered sprig of heather, hastily thrust into the
pocket, may become a memorial of sober thoughts with which
Nature in her present mood appears to sympathise. The pale,
shrivelled blossoms, seen after many days, may haply blossom
afresh in high aspirations, the parents of noble deeds, linked to
them by some mysterious connection with the solemn spectacle
and accompanying reflections during which they were gathered.
For association, as we have striven to show, has wondrous
power; and sentiment is very far from being a weak incentive
to goodness, and heather suggests many pleasant reminiscences
to those who mentally connect it with a long series of autumnal
rambles. If the ancients (as its scientific name *Erica* shows)
regarded heather as a natural substitute for lithotrity, much
more wisely do we deem it a symbol of happy rest and
recreation.

Up Glen Roy.

HAVING lived long on the chalk of East Anglia, looking down upon marsh land and post-tertiary deposits, when a thirst at length seized me to see glacial action, and judge for myself of its power and extent, the geologist will understand that it behoved me to go far afield. Not that all evidences of the reign of ice had perished in the neighbourhood. In many fields where the sheep were quietly eating turnips, and by many gate-posts of the country where the careful farmers had placed them to stave off waggon wheels, large boulders of trap and granite told that wondrous tale of the Drift, which never fails to captivate imagination even in the most commonplace scenery. Every here and there, too, were beds of boulder clay in the neighbourhood, filled with that curious assortment of heterogeneous pebbles characteristic of the formation. But a still handier geological museum lay open to understanding eyes in every stone-heap by the roadside. Landowners in this district employ village urchins, when not "tenting" birds, to gather up the loose boulders and stones scattered over their fields during the drift period. These stones are of all sizes between a marble and a man's head, and, being of hard com-position, are greatly valued in a country of "cork" (as the natives term chalk) for mending roads. Hence it is that the practical geologist finds problems in every stone-heap; and, as he ponders on the only causes which offer a probable explana-tion of the difficulties connected with the transport of these northern strangers to the chalk formation, eager longings beset him to visit the North, from which these intruders came. The line of the Caledonian Canal, the Lochaber Glens, and the Monadhliah Mountains form a district where glacial action can, perhaps, be observed better than in any other part of the British Isles, save the remote Western Hebrides. So it came to pass that last autumn found me undertaking a pilgrimage northwards, and despite a strong gravitation to visit the leaf-beds of Ardtun, discovered in 1857 by the Duke of Argyll, and the Cuchullins, with their hypersthenic rocks belonging to the Laurentian series—the very oldest in that enormous succession of rock-chronology known to modern geology—contenting myself with the glacial scenery of Glen Roy and the vicinity. Others may, perhaps, like to accompany my footsteps.

How two pedestrians, drenched and travel-stained, reached Bannavie, at the western entrance of the Caledonian Canal, in mid October, it boots not to inquire. Suffice it to say, that for some six weeks the natives affirmed it had rained daily, save on Sunday afternoons, and on some days that it rained the whole day. The appearance of the country may easily be conceived : the moors resembled a gigantic sponge, while torrents flung themselves down the sides of every mountain, now plunging into deep, dripping recesses, whence continually floated curling masses of white vapour ; now leaping in full view, from rock-shelf to rock-shelf, while the air seemed to shake with their vibration and roar. No one has seen the full mountain beauty of Scotland until he has viewed it when suffering from such an autumnal deluge ; roads submerged, lakes brim full, and rivers roaring in full spate over their rocky beds ; while the bare brown mountains dimly loom through enveloping mists, their size enhanced by imagination, as it is impossible to trace their outlines in the cloud-rack that gathers round their shoulders. Coming up Glen Falloch the river had presented a splended sight. It came down rearing and leaping in terrific masses of white foam through its narrow channel, till it irresistibly reminded us of a charge of the Scots Greys, or of the

gallant band which followed the snow-white plume of the hero
of Ivry. The individuality of different rivers in Scotland is
strikingly brought out during a spate. In fine weather they
are simply broad or narrow, rocky or shingly, curved or direct.
But in times of flood the Tweed becomes awful, and, given the
chance, would signally falsify the bloodthirsty observation of its
tributary Till—

> " Though ye rin wi' speed,
> And I rin slaw,
> Yet where ye droun ae man
> I droun twa ! "

The Tay waxes stately, as befits the river that washes Scone
Palace, the North Inch, and other historical glories of St.
Johnston ; Spey is murderous, Findhorn treacherous, Ettrick
sullen, Spean magnificent, Garry brawls, Tummel rages, and
so on through half a hundred more, while Yarrow's murmurs
never pass into anger ; they rise, indeed, to mournful wails,
and intensify the sadness of its love-lorn, ballad-haunted banks ;
but its imaginative pensive beauty is only better brought out
when the silvery currents have fled for the nonce, and all the
horror of a blind thunderous torrent has seized upon it. In
the worst of weather its kelpies never lose their siren sweetness
of song. When trudging along, with knapsack on shoulders,
through the worst of these Scotch downpours, the pedestrian's
happy disposition enabled me to find numberless compensations of this kind for the lack of distant prospects, until I had
at length reasoned myself into the belief that under many
aspects Scotland never looked so well as on a rainy day. After
attaining this serene frame of mind, all discomforts caused by
wind or weather were transformed into factors which enhanced
the pleasures of freedom and exploration conferred by a rainy
walking tour. What a beneficent goddess is Adversity, if one
meekly bows before her scourge !

My companion had fondly imagined he could walk, though

fresh from Indian luxury, and had early paid the penalty of his rashness. At Tyndrum we had been driven ignominiously to the coach, and thence made our way to Oban, where, instead of reading its historical or antiquarian history from the guide-books, we found ourselves smiling at the Princess of Thule's amazement when she landed at so fine a town, and at so great a distance from "Sty-ornoway." Such glamour has Mr. Black flung over these grey western seas."

If I trust myself to speak of Glencoe, and Macaulay's ex-aggerations of its scenery, my readers will never reach Glen Roy, so they must be contented to ascend the Caledonian Canal in the very last passenger boat of the season. The hotel at Bannavie must have closed as we left; at any rate we ate for breakfast the very last rasher of bacon which it contained (very rusty it was), and brought away the waiter on board; while at one little station where the steamer stopped all the furniture of the waiting-room (one deal form) was put on board to go into winter quarters at Inverness.

Leaving the steamer at Laggan, and driving to Invergarry to obtain letters, a piteous disappointment ensued. They had all gone north to the Isle of Skye. A melancholy lunch in a dark room hung with the portraits of Methodist divines and prints of the Battle of the Nile, was not improved by the view from the window, where torrents of rain were falling through half-stripped lime-trees, showing the Garry tearing along in full spate behind them, and over all the mist-wrapped cone of Ben Tigh. But a walk of sixteen miles lay before me, and that in heavy marching order, for like Balbus, that friend of ingenuous youth, I carried *omnia mea mecum*. Half-an-hour after noon saw me trudging to the shores of Loch Oich, and thence along the south side of Loch Lochy, which recalled pleasant memories of the friends on board the distant *Gondolier*, in which we have travelled down the lake earlier in the day. Hills rose on the left; but, with the exception of sheep and an occasional

shepherd, no signs of life appeared. It was a keen pleasure in
that grey, wet afternoon to meet at length a shepherd driving
his black-faced flock. Artistic fancies at once crowded on the
mind. The sheep might have stepped out of one of Ansdell's
canvases; while, as no one but Apelles was suffered to paint
Alexander the Great, so none but Landseer could have done
justice to the colley. As for the tall, handsome shepherd, bearing on his shoulders a wearied sheep, whose legs he held under
his chin, the early Christian drawings in the catacombs have
immortalised this grouping, and art has ever since loved to reproduce it, while an endless association of endearing images
has crystallized around it. Their witchery in due time brought
me to the wild moor on which the mighty porphyry prism of
Ben Nevis is set. I had passed in front of its northern face in
the morning, and had seen a patch of last winter's snow yet
lingering high up on the dark precipices. Now two great
cataracts were flinging themselves wildly over its face—one in
a series of sinuous leaps, the other in two huge bounds, while
the air was vocal with their distant roar. Still it was with a
sense of relief that I reached Spean Bridge, with its neat little
hostelry, some time after darkness had fallen.

Much of this walk had taken me through that wonderful
fissure known as the Great Glen, the line of the Caledonian
Canal which cuts Scotland in twain. Geologists still contend
over the causes which produce this singular depression. It
may mark a dislocation of strata, and the chain of lakes which
form great part of its bed may be owing to successive subsid-
ences or fractures; while the rocks on either hand are but the
upturned edges of the mighty crack, with their faces weathered
and denuded by the storms of centuries. Or, which seems the
truer view, after the great fissure had been caused by dislocation, the deeply-scored sides, and especially the valleys (which
are now lake-beds, Loch Oich, Loch Ness, and Loch Lochy),
were the work of vast ice-action. " The Great Glen receives

the drainage of a wide mountainous region on either side, and
in old times a larger amount of ice probably flowed into it than
into any other valley in Scotland.   It received from the west
the large glaciers of Loch Eil, Loch Arkaig, Glen Morriston
and Glen Urquhart ; from the east those of the glens of Lochaber, and those which came down from the north-western
flanks of the Monadhliah Mountains.   Its sides show everywhere the flowing rounded outlines that mark the seaward
march of the ice ; and its rocky bottom, where visible, bears
the same impress."*   The geologist wanders through this district as through an enchanted land, to which he alone holds
the key, and on which, as a theatre for posterity's wonder,
marvellous scenes were once represented in days too remote
to admit even of a guess.   It forms a worthy introduction to
the glacial phenomena of its small neighbours, Glen Spean and
Glen Roy.

It was on the afternoon of a beautiful autumnal Sunday that
I ascended the Roy valley.   It had rained all night and most
of the morning.   Judge, therefore, of my delight when outside
the little inn I turned to see Ben Nevis, and found it covered
with snow, and that no longer the last of the previous season,
but the first of the present winter.   The early part of the walk
lies up the Spean valley ; and here it was impossible for the
merest tyro in geological science not to be struck with the
many evidences of glacial action.   Moraines, both lateral and
medial, may be traced in the numerous beds of *débris* and *détritus* with which much of it is choked.   Fine examples of
raised beaches, too, occur on either hand ; while Spean plunges
along its rocky bed below, cutting through the hard schist, and
suffering rains, frosts, and other natural agents to split it along
its numerous joints.   More strange than all, however, are the
long level terraces, sometimes crowned with a farm-house and
clumps of trees, visible on the right.   These contrast favour-

* Geikie's *Scenery and Geology of Scotland*, p. 180 : Macmillan.   1865.

ably, from their green appearance, with the desolate and rugged ground in their neighbourhood. The moor on the left side of Spean has clearly been once a lake-bottom, and these level terraces are due to the course of ages covering with vegetation the rough, unsightly edges of the accumulated rubbish from extinct glaciers. On the same side occur many hillocks of sand, some of which are denuded by wind and weather, and exhibit the characteristic marks of water-worn rubbish. Exactly opposite these, a huge boulder may be noticed, stranded, as it were, in a potato-field, which doubtless once upon a time fell there on the bottom of a sea or lacustrine bed from a floating iceberg. Many of the cottages, too (if not all of them), are built of these large ice-borne boulders—comfortable habitations enough, though their irregular walls suggest abundant rheumatism. Loosely fitted together, these remnants of ice-action are invaluable to the natives as a quarry. At the debouchure of Roy into Spean, where our path turns to the left, a couple of these long, natural earthworks remain, while the mountains of Glen Treig rise behind, Ben Chlinaig and his brethren, forming the boundaries of a typical Highland landscape. Here and there on the rising hill-sides shepherds are dimly visible collecting their flocks : near at hand, one is lying on a patch of heather, with his dog beside him ; while the young people of the valley—the girls mostly bare-headed, with twisted wealth of brown hair—stroll up and down, enjoying the unusually serene afternoon.

Most of the inhabitants of this district are Roman Catholics, under the care of a priest who visits them from a neighbouring glen, so that the Calvinistic rigour of a Scotch Sabbath is here softened into the peacefulness of an English Sunday. Soon a fresh geological feature meets the eye. On the right from the hill-sides, which continuously rise from the Roy River, banks of rubbish project at right angles, falling away abruptly into the water. These " lateral moraines," which strike even the most ignorant observer, are too well described by Mr. A. Geikie* to admit of abbreviation :—" In many a Highland glen it is easy to trace the suuccessive backward steps of the ice, as it continued to shrink up into the higher recesses of the mountains. Each moraine shows, of course, a point at which the lower end of the glacier continued for a while stationary, melting there, and throwing down its accumulated piles of rubbish. These moraines may be followed up the valley, mound within mound, each of which represents a pause in the retreat of the glacier, until at last we gain the upper end, where the stream of ice finally shrank up into the snow-fields, and where these, as the climate grew warmer, at last melted away."

Indeed, all this district is a paradise to the geological student, but we must hasten onwards to its most celebrated features, the Parallel Roads.

Shortly after leaving Bridge of Roy inn on the mail-coach road to Loch Laggan, rounded masses of rock may be noticed —the *roches moutonneés* of glacialists. Agassiz was reminded by the scenery here of the numerous moraines in the neighbourhood of Tines in the valley of Chamounix. To the right, ascending Glen Treig, its sides are scored, smoothed, and rounded by ice-action, while a lake is enclosed by these rockwalls in a depression probably scooped out by a primeval glacier. Far onwards, on the road to Kingussie, the traveller may note evidences of water and ice-action, and the long, level moraines previously described. Nature here tells her own story in characters which it is marvellous should so long have remained unknown to science. A day or two well spent in this district will teach a beginner more of geology than would multitudes of theories and whole libraries of books perused without practically seeing the mighty forces which have shaped the face of the country in their effects upon rock and mountain

* *Scenery of Scotland*, p. 193.

scenery. Sir W. Scott had some such landscape in his mind when he wrote—

> "Crags, knolls, and mounds confusedly hurled,
> The fragments of an earlier world."

Through woods of birch and oak sloping downwards to the Roy river, the road wound, with the pallid sunshine of autumn sleeping above it on the russet leaves, while every here and there Highland cattle browsed in the open glades, some of that peculiar grey colour which lights up like velvet of the finest pile. This shade of warm grey is seldom or never seen in England, and not even Rosa Bonheur's brush could do justice to its lustre when flooded with sunlight. A few wild flowers yet lingered on the banks; ferns drooped from the rocks; not a breath of wind stirred the foliage. It was the year's twilight before winter and darkness fell, and even now they were hurrying on apace. Three miles up the valley a lateral moraine is cut through to admit the road, and a huge block of water-worn grey granite lay on one side. To the left, high up in the rock-face, appeared a long straight shelf running upwards, evidently the first sign of the wonderful Roads; while opposite, over the little river, which here brawls in a deep cutting it has made for itself, are slight indications of no less than five parallel tracks. Passing onwards through some straggling farm-buildings—where the colleys, after the fashion of their kind, lay in wait behind a wall to spring out and startle the wayfarer with their outcries, and next moment to retreat with their tails between their legs, as if ashamed of their momentary valour—a lad directed me to walk a little further on, and then, "Ou ay, ye'll jist see the Roads."

At length, on reaching the head of the Glen, where it winds round to the right, the three celebrated Roads came in sight, level as if drawn by some giant engineer, with a monstrous parallel ruler, following its sweep to the north-east. There was no mistaking them. Grim, gaunt, and dark, they scored the

barren hill-side; while above them the rounded tops of the
rocks broke down into several openings gilded with the afternoon sun, and leading into the next valley on the north.
Fainter reflections of them, as it were, lined the opposite hill;
while below were heaps of détritus, moraines, *blocs perchés*,
smoothed circular hillocks, and every evidence of ice and
water-action. Sitting down on a boulder which could tell a
wondrous history in connection with its presence here, I
endeavoured first to impress the scene, with all its barrenness,
and yet its stern beauty, upon my memory, and next to account
for the three so-called Roads which lined the sides of the
valley. No distraction intervened. Bird-life is wonderfully
scarce in many of these desolate glens. Beyond a robin at the
farmstead, no bird was in sight to break the savage monotony
of the landscape. A silence that might almost be felt brooded
over it this afternoon.

Imagination easily peoples this Glen with the wild natives of
former days; nor is it difficult to reproduce the many skirmishes
of mountain warfare, the many deer-hunts of more peaceful
times, which it must have seen. Tradition, ever fond of the
marvellous, takes us back to Fingal's days, when the parallel
roads before the traveller are said to have been constructed as
tracks for the hero and his friends to pursue when hunting, or
as race-courses. Other stories suppose that they were levelled
to serve as defences for a camp or as actual roads to lead out
of the Glen. With what complacency does Science point the
finger of scorn at these explanations! How wonderfully does
her glamour transcend the wildest dreams of Ossianic romance!
" Instead of tracing back the origin of these mysterious parallel
roads of Lochaber to the days of Fingal, they stand before us
as the memorials of an infinitely vaster antiquity—the shores,
as it were, of a phantom lake, that came into being with the
growth of the glaciers, and vanished as these melted away." *

* Geikie, *ubi supra*, p. 201.

And yet this explanation does not remove them from the realm
of imagination. It only summons us to a still more fascinating
fairy-land than was ever traversed by the heroes of Morven.
No prosaic element is present in Mr. Geikie's theory. The
great level line which may be noticed on the south of the
Spean river, running along the hillsides, before the traveller
turns up Glen Roy, is only an introductory symbol of glacial
action—that mighty power which has here written its primeval
history in the three parallel roads in front of us. Like the clue
which Ariadne gave Theseus to the Labyrinth, it turns up Glen
Roy; and now seen faintly, now more clearly, over the peat-
haughs in the bottom, at length expands into the three Roads
so deeply cut on our left, and only a little less strongly repeated
on the cliffs to the right. " Each of them is a shelf or terrace,
cut by the shore waters of a lake that once filled Glen Roy.
The highest is, of course, the eldest, and those beneath it were
formed in succession, as the waters of the lake were lowered.'
The germ of this elucidation is due to Agassiz, and Mr. Jame-
son has shown that it is fully borne out by the evidences of
great glacial erasion, some of which I have named ; while others
are to be found in the Great Glen of the Caledonian Canal.
This valley seems once to have been filled to the brim with ice,
which dammed back the mouth of Glen Spean, and caused the
waters of Glen Roy to escape into Strathspey, when the upper-
most terrace or road (1,140 feet above the present sea-level)
was formed. Next, the lake gradually sunk, as more of this
ice melted away, to its second level, the waters now flowing
into Loch Laggan. Finally, as the great glacier of the Caledonian Canal melted still lower, the waters of Glen Roy and the
neighbouring glens fell into their present channels, which, of
course they have been ever deepening. Science thus waves
her magic wand, and the mystery of the Roads "fades into the
light of common day." As in the Eastern fairy-tale, the possession of an old lamp could build up splended palaces in a.

E

night, so the fragment of ice under the traveller's foot points to the mighty power which, in a period of time scarcely appreciable to the æons of geology, could transform the face of this rugged country at will, bid lakes gather and streams run in unaccustomed channels, and then in a peaceful mood invite man—man, that pigmy and ephemera—to speculate here on her bygone paroxysms and perversities.

The simplicity of this explanation, however, does not find favour with all geologists. As philosophers may be roughly divided into Aristotelians and Platonists, so those who refuse to see glacial action in the present aspects of Scotland are compelled to invoke the aid of the sea. The present condition of the landscape round Glen Roy, say these, does not answer to the theory of ice-barriers. Beyond the Roads themselves, which the sea could produce as easily as could a lake, the indispensable barriers, it is asserted, have left no wreck to tell of their existence. No trace exists of the once mighty mounds of rock, or sand, or gravel, which must have restrained the lacustrine waters. To this reasoning any one who has followed my footsteps, much more any one who has inspected Glen Roy for himself, will at once reply that the difficulty only exists on paper—*solvitur ambulando*. If the mounds themselves, which once acted as barriers to the lake, do not remain, their ruins, as I have striven to show, tell the tale in mute yet scarcely mistakable accents. " There can be no doubt," says Professor Nicol,* " that the sea was at one time there, over all the mountains and up every glen. Besides, there are other proofs of the presence of the sea. Above all, I find in Strath Spey, not thirty miles from Glen Roy, terraces less extensive indeed, but similar in all essential points, and in a locality where lakes cannot have existed. I can therefore no longer doubt that these famed roads are—as Darwin and Robert Chambers

* *The Geology and Scenery of the North of Scotland*, p. 76. Edinburgh : Oliver & Boyd, 1866.

affirmed—old sea margins." This reasoning is simply begging the question. It is probable, nay, it is almost certain, that every upholder of the ice-theory would allow that the mainland of Scotland had been more than once submerged and again elevated. But, over and above these theoretical submersions, the whole interest of the locality centres in its wonderful moraines and other evidences which point unmistakeably to a glacial age. On the view that the sea caused the roads of Glen Roy, all these heaps and mounds, the *débris* of a former world, remain unaccounted for. Perhaps the conclusion of the Duke of Argyll,* which embraces both theories, is the one to which most scientific students will at present give in their adhesion. With regard to the glacial origin of lake-basins, he lays it down that, being nothing but submerged valleys, they are due in part to glacier-action, although the other half of their creation is to be sought in the subterranean action of subsidence. As for the general fact of submergence and re-elevation, this, he adds, is perhaps as certain as any feature of geological science. He instances the raised beaches of the Isle of Jura and elsewhere ; but at Glen Roy, supposing the Parallel Roads were due to maritime forces, the glacial phenomena, which we have seen are so abundant, obtrusively demand a different explanation.

The reader, however, much more the actual observer, has probably by this time settled his own theory; the sun is slanting over Ben Nevis, and it is time to retrace our steps. All the glory of a stormy autumnal evening, broken clouds of red and gold, is being buffetted about the great mountain's head by a violent west wind, and their vivid colours are strongly relieved against the snow. It is a lonely walk to the little inn ; but every bank, every striated rock-surface, has its associations. Even when darkness falls, the unusual spectacle on every side, the ghostly forms of glacial scenery, keep the mind actively

* *On the Physical Structure of the Highlands* (British Association, Sept. 1876.)

employed. There is much comfort to be derived from visiting such a scene as this, which robs departure from it of its
sadness. Just as many people find the planning and selection
of a holiday quite as enjoyable as the actual visit, so the
memories and reminiscences of it in after years are often
even more pleasurable than the days spent amidst fatigue and
rain in order to obtain its coveted rest and refreshment. And
of all holidays a sojourn amongst mountains is most grateful to
jaded bodies and worn-out energies. Not only is the air
fresher and more invigorating as it rushes through the defiles
between them, and bears down health and coolness from the
higher tracts above their peaks, but the eyes are greeted with
an ever-changing feast of colour floating over their shoulders,
while the sylvan scents of firwood and all the wild odours of
heather and sweet gale enchant with their *copia narium*. As
for the higher aspects of mountain scenery, its moral and
æsthetic teachings, the modern High Priest of Beauty has
dilated on them in eloquent words which every disciple loves
to recall, but dares not imitate. Suffice it to say that every
murmur from the dripping mountain-pines, and the resounding
airs round each Scotch Albunea's house, which delight the
wanderer's ears as his eye dwells with rapture on the butter-
wort's purple flower, or watches the white vapours curl above
the dark and distant caldron into which the torrent wildly leaps
in its headlong chase to level ground—that sights and sounds
even more commonplace than these are amongst the hills trans-
muted into magical effects of calm and refreshment. Each
one's fardel of cares drops off; earth's vain ambitions and
money's false glitter fade away before the stern might of the
hills; the soul must needs rise higher wherever the eye is
turned; every tinkling rivulet brings down a message of peace.
Of course to the botanist, the ornithologist, or the geologist,
mountain scenery, as I have striven to show, reveals new
worlds of interest. No one need wonder, therefore, that

Switzerland offers such attractions to the weary ; the misfortune is that fashion drives its votaries thither, and business only relaxes its hold of its slaves in autumn, instead of winter and spring, when the birth of the new roses and gentians brings regeneration to tired human nature. In its own way, and to those who desire an easy retreat from troubles, Scotland possesses irresistible attractions ; but in too many cases the cost of travelling and the stereotyped high hotel charges deter the would-be visitor. Donald would make his fortune sooner throughout the whole country if he could forget that insidious proverb which bids him make hay while the sun shines. Before the commencement of a new tourist season it may be as well for him to take to heart the truth that it is better to make friends of fewer visitors, and to see them oftener and for longer periods at a time, than it is to welcome invading hordes of tourists for a night, and find next morning, as he presents his bill, that they fly Scotland for ever.

Sunshine at the Land's End.

THE great charm of English scenery consists in its unity in variety. Hills and dales, and softly-curved rivers flowing into a pleasant monotony of prospect, succeed one another, as the traveller passes through the length and breadth of the land, only interrupted here and there by moor or mountain, plain or fen, and everywhere fading off before any large extent of land is overpassed into a margin of grey sea. No wonder that every nook and corner of

" This isle
The greatest and the best of all the main "

is dear to the lover of nature. Amongst the exceptions to the generally even character of English scenery the Land's End district is pre-eminent. The absence of trees and hedges, the stern grandeur of its cliffs, the short turf glittering with a blaze of flowers from the blue vernal squill to the purples and yellows of autumn, the troubled waves that are ever chafing round this peninsula, together with the rich remains of antiquity it contains; megaliths, churches, wayside crosses, etc., are features which cannot be elsewhere paralleled in England. It may be briefly described as a patch of grey granite reaching from St. Ives on the northern coast to Penzance on Mount's Bay—the toes of a somewhat gouty foot, whose heel is formed by the Lizard. A thin line of slate breaks out here and there on the ruins of this little peninsula, which may be likened by a simile chosen from a native delicacy, to several bites taken at random by a hungry schoolboy from the edge of a huge Cornish pasty. The district swells every here and there to rocky elevations, none of any great altitude (the hill on the north-west of Towednack, 805 feet above the sea is the highest of these), but all of them singularly interesting from their wild and weatherworn appearance. When these are not known as *cairns* (huge upheavals of granite), they are generally crowned with *cliff-castles*, of which Treryn Dinas, near the Logan Stone, is an example familiar to most Cornish tourists.

Penzance will be found the best headquarters from which to explore this remarkable district. Apart from its own attractions of equable climate, and the almost tropical luxuriance of its vegetation, it can supply vehicles of all kinds with drivers able to point out the objects of interest in the neighbourhood. The stranger will not have been many days here before he notices the furious driving of everything upon wheels; this imparts considerable liveliness to the streets. In the market-place stands an old stone cross, and not far off are several sentry boxes, occupied by dames selling tripe. As this dainty is fixed on wooden skewers, and frequently half-roasted in the sunshine, so abundant at Penzance, Cockney tourists must beware of mistaking it for cat's-meat. Together with pilchards, tripe seems to form the staple luxury of the town. Add to these features groups of Newlyn fishwives, bearing on their shoulders huge baskets by a broad strap crossing their foreheads, a general odour as if everyone lived on fried fish, an enormous quantity of very yellow buns in the shop windows, coloured thus with saffron—a curious mixture of maritime and fashionable life, and you will gain a good notion of Penzance. It would be wrong to forget its pasties—the national dish of the county. They are composed of anything and everything that can be eaten and digested, insomuch that an old proverb says "the devil dare not come into Cornwall for fear he should be made into a pasty!" The most celebrated of these varied delicacies is undoubtedly the *stargazy-pasty*, formed of pilchards radiating from the centre of the dish, where their heads emerge in a bunch from the crust, much as the feet of pigeons do in the pies of more civilised regions. The great charm of Penzance, though, is its unrivalled situation, sloping upwards from the centre of the crescent-shaped Mount's Bay, with wooded heights, and pretty villas behind it, while to the west the white-washed cottages of Newlyn nestle under the cliffs; and on the east, rising grandly from the sea to catch every gleam of sun, every changeful hue that clouds can impart, the visitor finds an endless charm in St. Michael's Mount,

"The great vision of the guarded mount,"

where Milton fondly dreamt his Lycidas might sleep. No one who has ever visited Penzance can forget the kindly nature of its inhabitants, and the warm welcome they give a stranger. We will apply specially to them the quaint eulogy Borlase bestows upon the whole county:

"As to the manners of the inhabitants they are generally allowed to be civilised and courteous to strangers, and this is no novel character, but stands recorded as anciently as the times of Augustus Cæsar, and is attributed by Diod. Siculus to that frequent intercourse with merchants of foreign countries, which the traffic for their tin could not but occasion."

Many routes are recommended to travellers in the Land's End district by which its wonders may most easily be seen. Undoubtedly the best plan is to walk round the cliffs from Penzance to St. Ives, resting the first night at the Land's End Inn. Thus the cliff scenery may be thoroughly explored, and a divergence made, when necessary, to any inland object worth notice. Supposing, however, that a visitor takes a carriage and goes "the Madron round" to see its church and ruined baptistery, the Lanyon cromlech, the Mên an tol, and Chysauster village, which can easily be accomplished in an afternoon, he will have seen crucial specimens of all the land sights of the peninsula. Then he can make another excursion to Botallack,

if his journey by rail through the chief mining district of Cornwall about Camborne and Redruth, leads him to wish to descend
a mine. The Land's End district proper, embracing that headland, and all that lies at the south of it, still remains. As a
stranger is always extremely puzzled how to see this tract of
country, with its numerous objects of interest, with the least
amount of toil, we shall make no apology for drawing out the
most eligible route, briefly describing at the same time a few
of its beauties from an artistic point of view, in order that
home-keeping people may be able to form some conception
of the charms of this extreme corner of our land.

We will drive from Penzance to the Logan village, some
eight miles, choosing a day when the soft, summer sunshine
sleeps on the changing corn-fields and flourishing market-
gardens that hem in Penzance. This district supplies Covent
Garden with the earliest vegetables of the year, and from the
fertility of the soil and the kindly climate, is the garden of England. Fuchsias grow here into trees ; scarlet geraniums twine
up to the top of the second floor windows. We pass through
rich elm avenues, beside clear-flowing brooks, tufted with lady-
ferns and hart's-tongue ; then high banks and stone walls succeed, festooned with ivy and honeysuckle, where ferns, and
stonecrop, and fox-gloves, and blue scabious run riot in their
luxuriance. Few birds are visible in this district, rooks seem
especially scarce ; but we have seen several of them amicably
feeding with gulls in an arable field, not twenty yards from the
highway, and quite undisturbed at our appearance. Trees dimin-
ish as we reach the high ground over Penzance, but the living
mosaic of flowers that decks the short, sweet turf of the uplands quite makes up for their loss. Anon we dive into a quiet
combe, and a wood-pigeon lazily flaps across it to a clump of
firs on the opposite hill-side. Grey masses of granite protrude
from gorse-bushes, covered with stains of red, yellow, and
brown lichen, with which Nature, to compensate for their

nakedness, has kindly clothed them.   All is fresh and beautiful
exceedingly under the deep blue canopy of sky.   In the barest
valleys, where the huge granite blocks are thinly hid by bracken
and dog-roses, tall spires of fox-gloves impart a surprising tinge
of richness to the prospect, which is much heightened by the
brilliant colours of the ground-vegetation.   There is none of
that sense of barrenness and desolation so common on the
Yorkshire hills, even in the most solitary parts of this district.
From hill-sides glittering with bracken, (have you ever observed
the effect of sun on bracken?), and purpled over with heather,
we suddenly come upon a patch of arable land, in the centre
of which is a mound of earth blazing with scarlet poppies.
Instead of burning their weeds as farmers do in other countries, the agriculturists here leave them in a mass to decompose,
first sprinkling it with a layer of salt from the pilchard cellars,
and then planting cabbages on it; or, if in an outlying field,
leaving it, as in this case, for the poppies to overrun.   Grass
fields, instead of this mound, have invariably a rough granite
block erected like a pillar in their centre, for the kine to rub
against.   Unwary travellers may easily regard these as Druidi-
cal monuments when they first meet them, looking like specks
of grey light on the intensely green herbage of spring.   This
charm of warm colouring is one of the first impressions a trip
to Cornwall leaves upon the mind.

    Another feature which greatly contributes to the distinctive
character of Cornish scenery is the granite fences.   They are
to Cornwall what her hedges are to Devon.   Stone walls are
common enough in Wales, Derbyshire, and elsewhere, but nowhere else can they be found consolidated by mosses and vegetation into the strength of almost living rock.   In fact, these
fences are everlasting.   Like all good things, their first cost in
labour is considerable, and a new granite wall, all rough edges
and sharp angles, is neither picturesque to the eye nor comfortable to sit down upon.   But soon its projections are

weathered and softened down, and then mosses settle in this crevice, and lovingly fill up that gap, while lichens, red, orange, and purple, star its uniformity with their beauties. Anon ferns spring up here and there, polypody being sure to be first. Now the fence has lost its obtrusive ugliness, being tufted with heather here and there, and everywhere seamed with velvet moss, while honeysuckles, and ivy, pink, white, and yellow stonecrop, smother it annually with a richer covering overhead, till the wayfarer believes, were it not for a glimpse of granite breaking through now and then, that he is once more between the earth banks and hedgerows of Devon.

Trees disappear as we near St. Buryan's, whose tower, ninety feet high, is a conspicuous object from every part of this district. From its summit another magnificent Cornish church-tower is to be seen—Probus, forty-one miles distant by road. There is a good deal worth notice at St. Buryan's, beside the tower. Inside are curious monuments, a very fine wood screen and bench end carvings. A lich stone and gate stand at the entrance of the yard, and in it is one of the most characteristic crosses of the county. It stands on a broad base of five steps, with a representation of the Crucifixion on one side, and five bosses, symbolical of our Lord's wounds, on the other. Inside the porch here and at St. Levan's (as often in the rural churches of South Wales) are stoups for holy water.

The road to the Logan Stone from this village commands splendid views of coast and combe. Penberth, with its clump of fishermen's cottages, is eminently picturesque. The Logan itself is reached by a scramble over huge masses of granite, through Treryn Dinas, an old line of defence which may have been originally fortified by the Kelts, and which, doubtless (like the Dane's Dyke at Flamborough and many other similar positions), supplied succeeding ages with a fortress. Of the Logan Stone itself, we shall say nothing. Show-sights are generally disappointing, and this has been described over and over again.

A glance at the surrounding features will satisfy the visitor that it is a natural curiosity, the usual effect of weather on granite. He may see the process of its formation in every cliff of this coast.

An artist's eye dwells with peculiar fondness on the rich colouring of the sea near the Logan. On its eastern side the waves are a rich blue fringed with white foam, where they chafe on the stern rock-wall that fronts them. Dark masses of sunken granite, shading into the characteristic light grey hue of this rock as they near the surface, diversify the blue expanse here and there as storm-clouds fleck an azure sky on a gleamy day. On the other side of the rocky headland the contrast is wonderful, like the sudden changes of April weather. A small crescent of white sand, backed by grand granite cliffs, encloses the greenest sea to be found anywhere in Britain. It is positively a fairy sea, lovely as ever poet's imagination shadowed forth. The beach is formed entirely of minute shells (150 varieties, it is said, may be picked up), and their lustre, with the reflection and gloom of the surrounding cliffs, it is which produces this translucent sea. Every now and then as the sluggish Atlantic heaves or sinks here like the breathing of some vast monster, glimpses are disclosed of peaks and rock summits with unfathomable-looking wells of beauty by their side, till fancy prompts a plunge into their depth, whispering of marvels hidden there more entrancing than Mr. Matthew Arnold's merman's cave—more awful than those encountered by Schiller's diver.

Visitors will turn their backs reluctantly on this cove, glowing with enchanted colour, yet the walk over the cliffs to St. Levan is in its way equally charming. Carriages should be left behind at Logan village, and ordered to drive inland to Sowar, a melancholy-looking farm-house and buildings, while you walk around the coast to them. In this way the finest cliff scenery of Cornwall will be seen. It lies between the Logan and

Land's End. Paths wind over each headlong and dip into the valleys, conducting the stranger at every stage to new beauties. The whinchat sits on the furze bushes, a gull or two float lazily round each point ; here and there you startle a magpie, or come upon a family of wagtails flitting up and down a streamlet. Every bank is thinly clad in smooth, velvety turf, starred with stone-crop and centaury. In damp weather numberless small snails appear on this herbage, and are believed to add greatly to the succulence and sweetness of the mutton produced by the district. Heather fringes granite on every side, and on the left, far below, murmurs the unwearied surge. An enormous expanse of sea is to be discerned from this elevated station, flecked with many a sail, all of them, however, in the calmest weather, keeping a prudential distance from the shore. Soon we come to St. Levan's Church, perhaps the most lonely-looking edifice in England. Its grey walls and tower are weathered and lichen-clad, the summer wind sighs in the long grass of the yard, gravestones and enclosure are being rapidly overgrown with rank vegetation ; not a living thing is discernible around, and a ring of blue sea encircles the prospect. When the village is reached we find everything, even down to pig-sties built of granite, cows, pigs, and men alike seem sleepy and contented—the lotus-eaters of Cornwall set down in the dreamiest of atmospheres, far from cities and railroads and turmoil. The stone crosses in its churchyard and the brawling jesters carved on a bench-end, which you can see through the open door, present a curious contrast, and much enhance the singular interest attaching to the place. After a mile more the road dips to Porthgwarra Cove, a little colony of fishers. A tunnel cut through the granite leads to their boats. Standing above it another phase of sea-scenery delights us. The clearest of water sparkles and gleams below us in the tiniest of bays ; you see every parti-coloured pebble fathoms below ; while above, an ever-shifting network formed of the sun's rays on the broken waves, expands and contracts itself, and flows out into long streamers of shaking light and dancing shade, like a natural kaleidoscope. Of course this effect can only be seen when the sun is brilliant; but once seen is never forgotten. On either side the cliffs rise in grand precipices, furrowed and eaten out into caves, where day and night in summer,

> "The blind wave feels around its long sea-hall
>   In silence,"

and the huge rollers of winter strike and boom, and flash out again in showers of smoke-like foam. There is no more characteristic coast along the whole margin of our island than this.

Ascending the next hill, we come to the grandest cliff of the district—Tol Pedn Penwith. It rises two hundred feet, a sheer, almost unseamed wall of granite, soon, however, giving place to the typical forms the rock generally assumes in this corner of England. A capital example is to be found here—the chain-ladder. It is formed of huge cubical blocks, piled perpendicularly one on another, as if some young giant—son, may be, of that friend of our childhood slain at St. Michael's Mount by Jack the Giant-Killer,—had amused himself in infantine fashion building up a pebble-wall. In reality, weather and natural decay have decomposed the softer veins of the mass (where felspar perhaps predominated), and reduced it to this remarkable semblance of stratification. The roof of a cavern here has fallen in, whereby a singular hole called the Funnel, is left for visitors who care for the services of a guide and for show-sights. Another splendid sea-view is obtained from the fields over this headland. On it are erected two beacons to warn mariners of the Runnel-stone, a dangerous rock a mile from the the shore, which has proved fatal to many vessels. Visitors who do not care to walk the remaining four or five miles round the coast to the Land's End, may here rejoin their carriages by striking inland to Sowar. There are, however, several features of interest on the cliffs. We may briefly mention Bosistow Logan rock, Nanjizel Bay with the curious archway of Zawn Pyg, and Cairn Evall. All pedestrians should make a point of seeing them.

We will now leave the inn lately built at the Land's End on our left (as it does not stand on that promontory, but on a near neighbour), and scramble over a rough granite-strewn footpath to a commanding rock at the extremity of the land. It is impossible to reach the verge, owing to the granite dipping every here and there to the sea-level, and projecting in other places in rather a disappointing manner, but only after the fashion of other celebrated points, of which Flamborough Head is a signal instance. Its chalk, however, falls like a tame hill-side ; here stern peaks of granite, edged with green prismatic blocks, black and hungry-looking, and dripping with foam till they resemble the jaws of a maddened wild boar, eternally champ the surf, and seem to grin with a cruel impotence of wrath on the passing ships. Woe betide the venturous man who should attempt to bathe near these rocks. In the calmest weather you can see the currents swirling round each jutting mass, and sweeping off into still deeper water clots of churned foam, diverging rings of surf ; anon comes a vast pulsation of the mighty sea-bosom ; and, without a moment's warning, a sheet of green water is projected over the low-lying reefs, and streams off in silver showers adown every cranny, till once more the surrounding surface is treacherously calm. There is something irresistibly seductive in the sight, leading the eye to linger on the graceful curves and bright colours of the water, and with something of the giddy attractiveness of a precipice, tempting the swimmer to let himself down to its cool, gently-heaving expanse. There is nothing in the shape of beach or cove in the neighbourhood, no foil to mar the grandeur of the prospect. He must be insensible, indeed, who does not sit silent a space, charmed and awe-struck at the magnificence of sea and land alike.

Nowhere can waves, with all their varied loveliness of colour and outline, be better studied than at the Land's End. At one time soft as Correggio's tints, next moment wild with the green splendour dear to Claude, always solemn as the colouring of Titian, never the same even in their changeful combinations, no wonder that our greatest poet-painter has attempted to fix their evanescence for us. Those who do not know Turner's picture will gain a conception of it from his interpreter's winged words :—

" This is a study of sea whose whole organization has been broken up by constant recoils from a rocky coast. . . . It is a solemn green grey (with its foam seen dimly through the darkness of twilight), modulated with the fulness, changefulness, and sadness of a deep wild melody."* And then Mr. Ruskin proceeds to point out the confusion of tide, currents, and wind in its composition. In short, the picture is an idealized view of what, on a small scale, may be seen here any day in summer.

From the curious white scabious and snowy centaury which grows on these rocks, let us raise our eyes to the noble prospect. Long banks of mist-like gloom, with a high projection here and there, fade into light clouds on the horizon in front. A glass resolves these heights into the peaks of the low-lying Scilly Isles. Forty in number, and composed of the same granite as the point on which we stand, they represent the western extremity of the fabled land of Lyonnesse, which tradition, if not geology, reports to have sunk about the era of the Norman Conquest. On the left, Pordenack Headland closes the view— a wild promontory, with a mile of rock-scenery between us and those singular, isolated masses of granite in front—Enys dodnan, the Armed Knight, and the Dollar. Not far from us a quaint block hung (as they all are here) with yellow and white lichens, .

* *Modern Painters*, vol. i. p. 373.

forms a whimsical resemblance to Dr. Johnson's head. Cormorants and gulls sit on the jutting rocks below; seals are to be seen in the troubled waters around. The prospect on the right is bounded by Cape Cornwall with a deserted mine, whose tower looks like a pillar of white light against the green turf. Higher up are the works of the St. Just Consolidated Mine, and on the hill inland the neat, whitewashed houses erected by the Trinity Board for the lighthouse keepers; all these features presenting a glowing feast of colour to the eye. Whitesand Bay is under them, with the Irish Lady, a conspicuous rocky mass, standing out amongst the waves. The slate reappears at Cape Cornwall with its characteristic conical top; a mile off are the two Brisons, as fatal rocks as any on this dangerous coast. Wide-spreading sheets of surf surround them on the calmest of days. A mile in front of the Land's End itself, on a low reef, is erected the celebrated Longships Lighthouse, whose ruddy light is generally the first welcome to England the homeward bound ship receives. The sea, which is dark and treacherous-looking round the coast, is blue here, and leaps up to-day in playful jets of foam. When there is anything of a gale blowing, although its height from the sea is about 127 feet, the waves break over the lantern of the lighthouse, "in a green, mountainous giddiness of wrath," to quote Mr. Ruskin once more.

Far out at sea an attentive observer may notice a speck of surf in the blue expanse. Through a glass eddies of swirling water may be descried, spuirting up every now and then into silvery spray. This is the Wolf Rock, nine miles from the mainland, an awful object to mariners in its grim isolation. A lighthouse is now being built on it from Penzance. The blocks are squared and fitted into each other on shore, and during the fine weather in summer transported to the rock. Although the work has been in hand for several seasons, the men are always obliged to work in safety-belts. Indeed, only six courses of

F

masoning were completed up to the middle of July, 1866.*
Great damage was done to the foundations last winter, and sad
to say, the conviction is strong in the minds of all engaged on
the rock that the Atlantic on that occasion made a battering-
ram of some strong ship, scarcely a chip of which was left to
suggest her fate.

The proprietor of the famous " First and Last Inn in England "
(which is a mile off at Sennen), has built a new hotel at Land's
End. The visitor may generally find fair accommodation at
it during the summer months. We were there in July, a few
days after the *Great Eastern* with the cable (now prosperously
laid) had passed by. The visitors' book is full of original
entries, people becoming unrestrained in their fun in proportion
as this inn is removed from civilisation. One party stated
themselves in it to be "poor lunatics travelling with their
keepers for change of air." We add a portion of their testi-
monial to show the slang of the period :—

" We can testify to the elasticity of the bedrooms, for, in one
small room, five poor unfortunates hung out, and one of them
had room to snore. 'Toke' and 'skilly' as good as unan-
nounced pauper casuals have any right to expect. Landlord
a brick; did not come down in time to give us our bill. P.S.
—Bill came at the last moment."

Everyone will turn away with regret from the Land's End,
Britain's *angusto limite mundi*. The mind is over-awed at
the enormous scale of nature here, the boundless sea, far-reaching sky, and stupendous cliffs. Danger lurks everywhere, but
sleeps in the sunshine for the nonce. Imagination may revel
in the buried marvels of Lyounesse fathoms under the waves.
And now as the long amber tracts of light glitter in the sunset,
the characteristic swells of the Atlantic roll in from the west,
like lengthening ribands of gloom, with enormous intervals
between. Onwards they come, and break "a breath of thunder"

* This lighthouse has since been finished.

on the outlying rocks; and then the leaping surf subsides
into floating foam-flecks, the silvery streams pour back from
the jutting peaks, and a wild scene of whirling, confused, and
terrified billows succeeds, till once more the agitation gives
place to the glow of tide and currents, and once more the open
sea beyond sleeps with gently heaving bosom, like

> "The prophetic soul
> Of the wide world, dreaming on things to come."

And then evening floats up from the east, and creeps over the
vast expanse; the bright tints fade from the sky, and amongst
the conflicting hues of purple and gold and grey, the ceaseless
murmur of the waves, the long sunny day dies from our coasts.

There are many more points which ought to have been
touched upon, had we been writing a history of this district
instead of lightly sketching its summer beauties. The curious
similarity many Cornish remains and customs bear to the
legends, superstitions, and antiquities of Brittany should particularly be noticed, in connection with which may be remembered the wild story given by Procopius of the burial of
Bretons in Cornwall. The ecclesiastical history of the county,
indelibly stamped on its topography and church architecture,
is also extremely interesting. Like Lincolnshire, the preval-
ence of dissent in Cornwall illustrates, for the thoughtful mind,
many problems in modern religious thought. According to
his experience of the natives, the visitor may settle for himself
whether there are still more saints in Cornwall than in heaven,
as the old proverb declares. Nor have we entered upon the
unique botanical treasures to be found in this corner of
England—its mineralogy, economical resources, archæology.
These are worthily handled elsewhere. Though sorely tempted
to speak of Arthur, the glory of the district, "that valiant
warrior and true Christian," and to enter into the fables which
have crystallised round the now exploded Druids, we forbear.

They are written in the books of Borlase and Mallory. It has been a loving labour to dwell for a short time on the quiet home-scenes of the Land's End, which, if less stupendous than Alpine peaks, not so far-spread as Norwegian feld and fiord, have yet their own refreshment for the seeker of beauty. We would fain photograph for the pleasure of others, as well as of ourselves, these floating reminiscences of the Land's End, ere they pass away as the ghost-like ships that, on a sunny day, are wafted on without perceptible motion, from peak to peak of this rocky coast. They are but faint outlines at the best, echoes of the glorious harmonies of nature which a careful observer may always find here, confused somewhat as

> "In some flooded cave
> Sobs the strong broken spirit of a wave;"

and dimmed with the mists of absence, and also may be somewhat heightened by treacherous memory; but, such as they are, put on record to interest those precluded from visiting these remarkable shores, but who yet love the beauties of their native land.

Into Ballad-Land.

"I love a ballad but even too well."—*Winter's Tale.*

A DISCRIMINATING traveller cares little for the loveliest country unless it possess associations. Even Switzerland would lose much of the interest with which we now regard it, did not a halo gleam over its mountains, flung there by the struggles of patriotism and the poetry of Byron. Without that glow it would have been as void of sentiment, save to mere Alpine climbers, as are the huge rocky fortresses of South America. Lincolnshire has become much more tolerable to imaginative folk since Tennyson glorified its marshes and water-courses. When people of cultivated minds, therefore, take a holiday, they should be especially careful to choose some district which possesses historic or romantic memories. Thus, to go no farther afield than Yorkshire, besides its sands and breezy upland walks, Whitby is redolent of St. Hilda and the penance of Ralph de Percy and the youth of St. John of Beverley; of King Oswi and Wilfrid and Bishop Chad; of Cædmon and the Princess Elfleda; of Scandinavian pirates and Saxon ecclesiastics; of the great Council which settled the Easter controversy, and the celebrated school of learning which shines through the darkness of early English Christianity; while its pretentious northern neighbour, Saltburn, does not possess a single attraction for the antiquary. It consists of a few houses, a big hotel, and a modern church. With some the ideal element so preponderates that all they care for in a place is its associations. Thus, when fresh from mental excursions into the fascinating dreamlands of the *Odyssey* and the *Arabian Nights*, such minds look with scorn upon the humble efforts of geographers who would settle exactly where the Lotophagi lived, or in what sea lay the Isles of the Children of Khaledan. We must plead guilty to something of this feeling ourselves. On one occasion, when sitting at dinner next a hard-headed, matter-of-fact wrangler, to whom "a primrose by a river's brim" was certainly but "a yellow primrose," it received a rude shock. We had eagerly asked him about a celebrated curiosity in the next parish (of which he was incumbent), known as Arthur's Table, and were informed—"It is but a rude heap of stones spread over a bare hillside; if I had a mason or two and a few cartloads of boulders, I could put you together a much finer Round Table in an afternoon."

One autumn, when we had been more than usually haunted with memories of the past, and when many an echo of poetry floated round the fancy, "there came a day as still as heaven," a day like that on which they found the babe Arthur,

> "Upon the sands
> Of wild Dundagil, by the Cornish sea."

To take our lute and wallet and wander forth like a troubadour of old in quest of beauty, was clearly a necessity at such a time. An unresisting impulse bade us roam

> "Under groves that looked a paradise
> Of blossom, over sheets of hyacinth
> That seemed the heavens upbreaking through the earth,
> And on from hill to hill and every day."

Therefore, we translated the language of romance into the matter-of-fact realities of the nineteenth century by shouldering a knapsack, and preparing, stoutly shod and with a trusty staff, to walk into fairy-land. It lies all around us, we discover, when our eyes have once been purged by fancy's Euphrasy. Should we go south to those deep forest glades,

> " Through whose green boughs the golden sunshine creeps,
>   Where Merlin by the enchanted thorn-tree sleeps ? "

Alas! the "gurlie sea" must in that case be crossed, and no
Phantom Lover appeared to offer a speedy passage,

> " I have seven ships upon the sea,
>   The eighth brought me to land,
>   With four and twenty bold mariners,
>   And music on every hand."

It seemed more feasible to walk northwards to that other
Elf-land which an equally potent mage, Thomas the Rhymer,
visited with its Queen,—

> " After kissing her rosy lips,
>   All underneath the Eildon Tree."

And this was the manner of his progress—

> " She's mounted on her milk-white steed,
>   She's ta'en True Thomas up behind ;
>   And aye, whene'er her bridle rung, .
>   Her steed flew swifter than the wind.
>   *   *   *   *   *
>   He has gotten a coat of the even cloth,
>   And a pair of shoes of velvet green ;
>   And till seven years were gone and past,
>   True Thomas on earth was never seen."

Was it not there, too, that Bonny Kilmeny was rapt from earth—
that sweetest of all pure damsels—and when at length she
begged once more to see her friends, in this wise the fairies
granted her boon—

> " With distant music soft and deep,
>   They lull'd Kilmeny sound asleep ;
>   And when she awakened, she lay her lane,
>   All happed with flowers in the greenwood wene.
>   When seven lang years had come and fled ;
>   When grief was calm, and hope was dead :
>   When scarce was remember'd Kilmeny's name,
>   Late, late in a gloamin' Kilmeny came hame ! "

There, too, of late years dwelt a more lovable and more powerful bard and musician than either of the above, who created a whole company of imaginative worthies, " that great magician," according to the Chaldean M.S., which hath his dwelling in the old fastness, hard " by the river Jordan, which is by the Border." He transfigured a dull, foggy country into an enchanted land, peopled with airy castles, fantastic pageants, lovers, knights, and dames innumerable. His stirring strains have soothed many a sick-bed, and his potent spells have endowed many a gallant youth with patriotism, generosity, and self-denying heroism. Year by year his creations still flood the land with a gold-bearing stream of Southern and transatlantic visitors. Every hillside in that Border region has its legend, not unremembered by Sir Walter, every stream there flows straight from Fairy-land. Imagination sees on its wildest moorland a company of brave soldiers, a hawking party, or a runaway pair of ill-starred lovers. Thither must we turn this golden weather. There is no time like late autumn, even towards the end of October, for a walking tour ; whereas in summer it is always more or less burdensome to carry a knapsack, in these frosty morns and keen afternoons, it seldom becomes an incumbrance, even after twenty miles' walking. Away, then, from the clamour of the forum, the rattle of spinning-jennies ! Leave behind politics, school-boards, and cares, public, social, or domestic. In that clear atmosphere of the Borders we shall only breathe woodland scents, the fragrance of fine birch and heather ; no sound save the grouse's crow and the streamlet's murmur will fall upon the delighted ear,—

> " Jam mens prætrepidans avet vagari,
> Jam læti studio pedes vigescunt."

As we cannot climb Jack's beanstalk in order to find the entrance to Enchanted Land, and the celebrated horse of the *Arabian Nights* is not in our stud, which, whenever a man mounted and turned a key in his neck, transported him whither he would, it is needful to resort to the far more prosaic plan of taking a railway ticket in order to carry out our plans. But first calling to mind how Lord Soulis on leaving home was wont to throw his chamber's keys to Redcap, his familiar—

> " He took the keys from the rusty lock,
>   That never were ta'en before;
> He threw them over his left shoulder
>   With meikle care and pain,
> And he bade him keep them fathoms deep,
>   Till he return'd again."

We make over our keys of office to our better half, but, wiser than Bluebeard, hand them over unreservedly, well knowing it is better not to arouse female curiosity by making exceptions. If he had said nothing of the mysterious chamber which contained her murdered predecessors, his wife would never have cared to go near it.

It is not till Durham that the outskirts of Ballad-land are touched. The castle and cathedral at once transport the traveller to the past; and is not Brancepeth Castle, the stronghold of the Nevills, nigh the town? A breeze from the far-off days of chivalry seems to blow here, and we weary ourselves with thinking what gallant pageants and what vicissitudes of fortune those marvellous Norman pillars of the Cathedral nave have seen. At Newcastle the country connected with the Battle of Otterbourn is entered. It was fought by moonlight, August 15, 1388. The exact scene is some thirty miles from Newcastle on the River Reed, which comes down from Carter Fell, but it was in a skirmish before the walls of that town that Hotspur's lance and pennon were taken by Douglas.

> " It fell about the Lammas tide,
>   When the muirmen win their hay,
> The doughty Douglas bound him to ride
>   Into England, to drive a prey;
> He chose the Gordons and the Græmes,
>   With them the Lindesays light and gay.
> *   *   *   *   *   *   *   *

> "The moon was clear, the day drew near,
>   The spears in flinders flew ;
> But many a gallant Englishman
>   Ere day the Scotchmen slew."

Froissart commemorates the death of the brave Douglas "who went ever forwarde lyk a hardy Hector, wyllynge alone to conquere the felde and to discomfyte his enemyes ;" and we may be sure that ballad poetry has not forgotten him—

> "Oh bury me by the braken bush,
>   Beneath the blooming brier,
> Let never living mortal ken
>   That ere a kindly Scot lies here."

He was, however, carried to Melrose Abbey, where his tomb is still shown. Away to the left runs the Roman Wall from which in the Northumbrian ballad of "The Death of Featherstonhaugh," Will of the Wa' obtained his nickname—

> "Hoot awa', lads, hoot awa',
> Ha' ye heard how the Ridleys, and Thirlwalls, and a',
> Ha' set upon Albany Featherstonhaugh,
> And taken his life at the Deadmanshaugh ?
>   There was Willimoteswick,
>   And Hardriding Dick,
> And Hughie of Hawdon, and Will o' the Wa' ;
>   I canno tell a, I canno tell a,
> And mony a mair that the deil may knaw."

In Newcastle Jail Jock o' the Syde was immured when so gallantly freed by the Laird's Jock, the Laird's Wat, and Hobbie Noble :

> "He is weil kend, Johne o' the Syde,
>   A greater thief did never ryde ;
>   He never tyris
>   For to break byris."

The ballad-singer expands into a grim burst of humour as the boon comrades burst in upon Jock in his dungeon, who was to be hanged in the morning—

> "Now sune they reach Newcastle Jail,
>   And to the prisoner thus they call ;

> Sleeps thou, wakes thou, Jock o' the Syde,
>   Or art thou weary of thy thrall?
>
> Jock answers thus, wi' dolefu' tone;
>   Aft, aft I wake—I seldom sleep;
> But whae's this kens my name sae weel,
>   And thus to mese [soothe] my woes does seek?"

And again—

> " Sae out at the gates they a' are gane,
>   The prisoner's set on horseback hie;
> And now wi' speed they've taen the gate,
>   While ilk ane jokes fu' wantonlie:
>
> Oh, Jock, sae winsomely ye ride,
>   Wi' baith your feet upon ae side:
> Sae weel ye're harneist and sae trig,
>   In troth ye sit like ony bride!"

Up the Tyne, too, is Cholerford brae, where on the night of his
release "the water ran like mountains hie;" but the prisoner,
mounted behind the Laird's Jock, safely swims it, while the
twenty pursuers dare not attempt to follow, and one ludicrously
begs from this side—

> "The prisoner take,
> But leave the fetters, I pray, to me."

Past Alnwick, Dunstanbrough, and the Farne Islands, so dear
to ornithologists; past Bambrough too and Holy Island, all
fragrant with old-world memories, we are swiftly borne on to
Berwick. Here we will don our knapsacks in earnest. It
was ever a turbulent town, "a Berwick Christmas" being a
synonym for a riotous festival, and was not often so peaceable
as when Lord Eurie held it in the time of Henry VIII.

> " Since he has kepte Berwick-upon-Tweed,
>   The town was never better kept, I wot.
> He maintained leal and order along the Border,
>   And still was ready to prick the Scot."

A walk round the ramparts shows the unrivalled situation of
the town, which was so often a bone of contention between the

two kingdoms, at the mouth of a considerable river, full of fish, whence ingress and egress might readily be obtained. The old bridge, built in Elizabeth's time, must have been crossed on many a wild errand by the adventurous of both nations, while its neighbour, the railway viaduct, flung high aloft, speaks of nothing but amity and peace. Sunrise from the town walls is a fine sight, as the misty light glimmers onwards, bringing into prominence the gurly yellow waves chafing in the offing. Halidon Hill may be seen from the opposite side of the town. The quaint old wynds are very curious to a Southron. On the bell tower of the castle the alarm beacon used to be kindled, but the railway station stands where the castle itself was situated.

The Tweed is so beautiful throughout its course, and flows through such a land of glamour, that it is well for a pilgrim to pursue its windings. Numberless poets have chanted its praises both by day and night. It is the "silver Tweed," when the sun glitters on its streams, but its charms are multiplied at night, when it

> " Is heard to rave,
> And the owlet to hoot o'er the dead man's grave."

Then (as Alexander sings),—

> " Oh, ha'e ye seen the Tweed while the moon shone bright
> And the stars gemmed the sky wi' their siller light?
> If ye ha'e na seen it, then
> Half its sweets ye canna ken.
> Oh, gae back and look again
> On a shining night ! "

And again,—

> " Oh, hae ye seen the Tweed when the moon's gane down,
> When the sun caps ilk hill wi' a gowden crown?
> Oh, ye'd pause in fixed delight
> As bursts upon the sight,
> " Neath the Eildons, spreading bright,
> The landscape roun' ! "

Apart from association, much of the Tweed's beauty among rivers is due to its curving, well-wooded banks—much more, perhaps, to its shallowness in proportion to its width, which lends it an irresistibly seductive summer-murmur. In autumn the russet woods which overhang it form a veritable golden gate to the rich feast of beauty which the pilgrim of song has before him. Beyond the modern and melancholy Twizell Castle the Till is crossed, deep and sullen-looking, with a trout leaping here and there, but not unsuited in character to the slaughter which took place on the neighbouring Flodden. Well may the Scottish lassie here take up her lament,—

> "Oh, the haymaking's pleasant in bright, sunny June,
> The hay-time is cheery when hearts are in tune ;
> But while others are joking and laughing sae free,
> There's a pang at my heart and a tear i' my e'e.
>
> At e'en i' the gloaming adoun by the burn,
> Fu' dowie and wae, aft I daunder and mourn ;
> Amang the lang broom I sit greeting alane,
> And sigh for my dear and the days that are gane."

And still more plaintively in the well-known "Flowers of the Forest,"—

> "Dool and wae for the order sent our lads to the Border !
> The English, for ance, by guile won the day.
> The flowers o' the forest, that fought aye the foremost,
> The praise o' our land, are cauld in the clay.
>
> We'll hear nae mair lilting at the ewe-milking,
> Women and bairns are heartless and wae,
> Sighing and moaning on ilka green loaning ;
> The flowers o' the forest are a' wede awae."

"Norham's castled steep" comes speedily into view, standing grim and gaunt and massive against the sky. Though reputed "the dangerust place in England," it was taken by the Scots just before Flodden. The feudal spirit still lingers in the peasantry of this district ; one told us with much scorn, speak-

ing of a *novus homo* with abundance of wealth who had settled
in the neighbourhood, "he hasna muckle bluid." From the
curious conical hill on which the ruins of Wark Castle are carelessly flung, to whiten like Time's bones in the distant sunlight, Kelso is soon reached—a place of many memories. But
it should, at all events, be borne in mind, that at Wark took
place the memorable circumstance which led to the institution
in 1349 of the Order of the Garter.

Scott spent some time with his aunt at Kelso, after leaving
school at Edinburgh, and it was in her garden, under a wide-
spreading plane-tree, that he first read Percy's *Reliques*. There,
too, he made the acquaintance of the Ballantynes, who were
to colour his future life so deeply. It rains here, but we will
push on with poetic snatches to console us,—

> "Sic a day o' wind and rain,
>   Oh, wae's me for Prince Charlie!"

And, after all, the Douglas maxim ought to be the motto of every
pedestrian—"Better to hear the lark sing than the mouse
cheep." A rift in the clouds on our leaving pours a flood of
soft light over the old Abbey's mouldering walls by the Tweed,
and we look back upon the place with some regret on bidding
it farewell—with some such feelings as were those of the Border
widow on burying her slain husband,—

> "But think na ye my heart was sair,
>   When I laid the moul' on his yellow hair?
>   Oh, think na ye my heart was wae
>   When I turned about awa' to gae?"

She could easily, however, procure a new one, if another ballad
may be believed,—

> "Hoot, hoot, the auld man's slain outright!
>   Lay him now wi' his face down: he's a sorrowful sight,
>   Janet, thou donot!
>   I'll lay my best bonnet,
>   Thou gets a new gude man afore it be night."

A boy, riding a grey pony, " Donal," as he affectionately calls him, "doesna ken" much about things in general, but guides us to Sandyknowe, the *locus classicus* of Scott's child-hood, where, in all probability, his taste for the eerie and the picturesque first developed itself. The old house is now pulled down and stables are built on its site; but close at hand is Smailholm Tower, where the lad would often roam to indulge in the day-dreams which he afterwards clothed in such splendour for the world. Turner's picture somewhat idealises it, as is his wont, and thereby mars its loneliness. A lakelet in front is ruffled with the wind from the adjoining moor, but the stern crags are cheerful with wild pink and heartsease blossoms, and are mantled with ivy and polypody. A "cuddy" grazes hard by, but all else is desolation; naked, swelling moorlands leading up to the marked triple outlines of the Eildons. Smailholm itself bears all the characters of the numerous peels of the Jumna, set up against the Sikhs and Mahrattas, and shows how curi-ously, in far distant quarters of the world, the instinct of self-preservation has prompted the same means of defence—the massive tower and doorway planted high in the side—against robber-chieftains and midnight marauders. Further on, the mist-veil lifts in the manner so exquisitely described in the " Bridal of Triermain," and the Tweed winds out like a stream of flashing silver from the golden woods and blue hills beyond. The Mertoun groves are below us, and far away in the dim grey distance of the Cheviots gleams the Waterloo pillar. Then we approach · Wallace's statue, and dip down to Dry-burgh. Its ruins are small, and deeply embowered in woods. Perhaps they are almost disappointing, save for the sentiments which must fill each poetical pilgrim as he stands before the Haliburton transept. There are the plain granite slabs which mark where Sir Walter Scott, his wife, and son, and Lockhart, his son-in-law and biographer, lie among numerous older memorials of the dead, in the burying-place of his ancestors.

There, too, imagination may busy itself with the life of one whose name alone is carved on a stone, thus :

```
+ ELΘSE
  TARGA
```

Did a stormy, eventful career end in this sign of hope and reconciliation? or is it a record of peaceful, lifelong devotion, the gravestone of an abbess or a sister? Does an unrequited love there leave its memory in stone? None can tell. All is voiceless and silent now ; and Heloise Targa's sorrows are as if they had never been, till the day dawns that she thus hopefully looks on to.

On the Leader, Cowdenknowes, at once recalls the ballad,—

> " Oh, the broom, and the bonny, bonny broom,
> And the broom of the Cowdenknows,
> And aye sae sweet as the lassie sang
> I' the bought, milking the ewes."

And the *dénoûement*, which showed "the bonny May, with yellow hair and grass-green sleeve," who her lover was,—

> " I am the Laird of the Oakland hills,
> I ha'e thirty plows and three,
> And I hae gotten the bonniest lass
> That's in a' the south countrie."

Having "seen Melrose aright" (by moonlight, from the window of our room in the adjoining Abbey Hotel), next morning is devoted to examining the rich carving and details of the ruined pile. The rose window which represents the Crown of Thorns is duly admired, and the antiquary may note a few inscriptions, as the motto of the last abbot, *Durum patienter frango*. Another stone bears "Heir lyes the race of the Hous of Zair." Most of the sculptured emblems are of a very funereal character. One stone is specially noticeable : an hour-glass, a bell, a death's head and cross-bones are cut on it, with the warning—

"FUGIT HORA, DISCE MORI."

From these gloomy thoughts we will advance to the Rhymer's glen, where

> " True Thomas lay on Huntlie Bank ;
> A ferlie he spied wi' his e'e ;
> And there he saw a lady bright
> Come riding down by the Eildon Tree."

The tree has long since perished, but the place is marked by a large stone ; the neighbouring brook, too, is known as Bogle Burn ; adjoining is Abbotsford. It has often been described, and there is no need to attempt it here ; but the charm that hangs round it is indescribable, and must be felt to be realised. It is a poem cut in stone. The visitor is struck with its being much smaller than he had been led to expect. The library, though containing 20,000 volumes, appears circumscribed, and the gardens are formal. It is in the armoury and Sir Walter's study that most people linger longest, and here what perseverance can effect is an impression very strongly borne in upon the mind. Outside, the ripe yellow leaves dropping without a breath of air from the trees which Scott planted, seem on this lovely autumnal morning in exact unison with our saddened thoughts as we leave this curious monument of Scott's constructive genius.

Up the vale of the Gala, near Stow, is Thirlestane Castle, commemorated in the ballad of "Auld Maitland," when the southern invaders

> " Lighted on the banks of Tweed,
> And blew their coals sae het,
> And fired the Merse and Teviotdale
> All in an evening late.

G

> As they fared up o'er Lammermore,
>   They burned baith up and down,
> Until they came to a darksome house,
>   Some call it Leader-town."

Returning, we must cross the Tweed and cry to the ferryman
with the Jacobite song,—

> "Come boat me o'er, come row me o'er,
>   Come boat me o'er to Charlie;
> I'll gi'e John Ross anither bawbee,
>   To ferry me o'er to Charlie!"

By the mill stands a blue-eyed girl, who at once brings Burns to
our mind,—

> "Oh, ken ye what Meg o' the Mill has gotten?
>   And ken ye what Meg o' the Mill has gotten?
> She has gotten a coof wi' a claut o' siller,
>   And broken the heart o' the Barley Miller."

It does not do to admire her too openly.   Does not the same
poet tell that she's coy as well as inconstant?—

> "Aye vow and protest that ye care na for me,
>   And whiles ye may lichtly my beauty a wee;
> But court na anither, though jokin' ye be,
>   For fear that she wyle your fancy frae me!"

Joanna Baillie may help us to the finale of the romance, on
her lover's side at least,—

> "Then out spake the wily bridegroom,
>   Weel waled were his wordies, I ween)
> I'm rich though my coffers be toom,
>   Wi' the blink o' your bonnie blue een.
> I'm prouder o' thee by my side,
>   Tho' thy ruffles and ribbons be few,
> Than if Kate o' the Craft were my bride,
>   Wi' purples and pearlings enew."

And Burns will end our romance with her own sentiments;
very proper ones too for a young wife,—

"Oh, gear will buy me rigs o' land,
   And gear will buy me sheep and kye,
But the tender heart o' leesome love,
   The goud and siller canna buy.

We may be poor, Robie and I,
   Light is the burden love lays on ;
Content and love brings peace and joy ;
   What mair ha'e queens upon a throne ? "

Selkirk is beautifully situated, could the obtrusive factories on
its outskirts be expunged. The cobblers of Selkirk were distinguished men of old,—

" Up wi' the souters o' Selkirk,
   For they are baith trusty and leal ;
And up wi' the men o' the Forest,
   And down wi' the Merse to the deil ! "

Outside Selkirk is Philiphaugh, the field so fatal to the hopes
of Montrose. He galloped to it from his quarters in the town,
when surprised by the noise of his infantry being slaughtered
outside. The battle extended over a long stretch of country,—

" On Philiphaugh a fray began,
   On Hairhead Wood it ended. "

But the scene of the final struggle is marked by a monument.
His conqueror, Sir David Lesly, is amusingly commemorated in
ballad lore by a verse with *variorum* readings,—

" When they came to the Shaw burn,
   Said he, ' Sae weel we frame,
I think it is convenient
   That we should sing a psalm ! ' "

or, as others have it,—

" That we should take a dram. "

Somewhere near the Tinnies, above Hangingshaw, if any have
a mind to search for hidden treasure, is a well or pond, in
which the attendant of the Earl of Traquair is reported to
have flung the money which his master was bringing for the

payment of Graham's troops, when the pursuit of Lesly's dragoons became too hot to be pleasant.

"Sweet Bowhill," the seat of Scott's great friend, the bold Buccleuch, is well hidden amongst its wild park scenery, and the exquisitely-coloured foliage of its old beeches. A mason at work hard by tells us with a sad face he "weel minds Sir Walter : he was very free, and wad talk to ony o' us." The fine sheep in the park are grand specimens of breeding; and a noble black bull, with shining muzzle, long curved horns, and crisped black coat, chews the cud with placid indifference, as we "boo" at him. (*N.B.*—A stout fence intervenes, or we should think twice before venturing on such a liberty.) Soon "Newark's riven tower" comes in sight, charmingly situated on an eminence overhanging the Yarrow, looking across to Foulshiels Hill, itself "renowned in Border story," the very heart of a country rich with poetic associations. Newark was once a hunting-box of James II., and as such is celebrated in one of the introductions to *Marmion*. Many of the prisoners taken after Philiphaugh were butchered in its courtyard in cold blood. The cottage in which Mungo Park was born stands nearly opposite. Yarrow, with its steel-blue streams, breaking into foam every here and there over submerged rock-ledges, as it hurries swiftly down the valley, is one of the chief rivers of Ballad-land. Its murmurs are resonant of many a sad love-song, many a beautiful lay ; for where is the minstrel who has not been touched by the fate of the "Flower of Yarrow?" Thus Logan sings,—

> " The tear shall never leave my cheek,
>   No other youth shall be my marrow—
> I'll seek thy body in the stream,
>   And then with thee I'll sleep in Yarrow.
> The tear did never leave her cheek,
>   No other youth became her marrow ;
> She found his body in the stream,
>   And now with him she sleeps in Yarrow."

And even more beautifully an anonymous ballad-writer,—

> " O gentle wind that bloweth south
> From where my love repaireth,
> Convey a kiss frae his dear mouth,
> And tell me how he fareth.

> *   *   *   *   *

> Oh came ye by yon water-side ?
> Pou'ed ye the rose or lily ?
> Or came ye by yon meadow green,
> Or saw you my sweet Willie ?

> She sought him up, she sought him down,
> She sought him braid and narrow ;
> Syne, in the cleaving of a craig,
> She found him drowned in Yarrow."

Who could forget the cadences of Wordsworth's " Yarrow Unvisited ? "

> " Be Yarrow stream unseen, unknown ;
> It must, or we shall rue it ;
> We have a vision of our own,
> Ah ! why should we undo it ?
> The treasured dreams of times long past,
> We'll keep them, winsome marrow !
> For when we're there, although 'tis fair,
> 'Twill be another Yarrow ! "

And its charming pendant, " Yarrow Visited ? "

> " But thou that didst appear so fair
> To fond imagination,
> Dost rival in the light of day
> Her delicate creation :
> Meek loveliness is round thee spread,
> A softness still and holy ;
> The grace of forest charms decay'd
> And pastoral melancholy."

We must add one more stanza to complete the subject, from " Yarrow Revisited," and that under very painful circumstances in the autumn of 1831,—

> " Flow on for ever, Yarrow stream,
>   Fulfil thy pensive duty,
> Well pleased that future bards should chant
>   For simple hearts thy beauty ;
> To dream-light dear, while yet unseen,
>   Dear to the common sunshine,
> And dearer still, as now I feel,
>   To memory's shadowy moon-shine ! "

Of course Sir Walter has touchingly alluded to these scenes in *Marmion*,—

> " Thus pleasures fade away,
> Youth, talents, beauty thus decay,
> And leave us dark, forlorn, and grey ;
> Then gaze on Dryhope's ruin'd tower,
> And think on Yarrow's faded Flower."

The Flower of Yarrow, who has evoked so much tender enthusiasm, was Mary Scott, daughter of Philip Scott, of Dry-hope Tower. She really married a Border laird, commonly known as Auld Wat of Harden. He appears to advantage in the ballad of "Jamie Telfer." His son is sore stricken in a skirmish which arose on a case of cattle-lifting,—

> " But he's ta'en aff his gude steel cap,
>   And thrice he's waved it in the air,
> The Dinlay snaw was ne'er mair white
>   Nor the lyart locks of Harden's hair.

> ' Revenge ! revenge !' auld Wat 'gan cry ;
> ' Fye, lads, lay on them cruellie !
> We'll ne'er see Tiviotside again,
>   On Willie's death revenged sall he !' "

To him also is attributed the remark, on seeing a haystack in one of his raids over the Border—"By my soul ! had ye but four feet, ye should not stand lang there !" Another tragic deed connected with Annan's Treat, west of Yarrow Kirk, is duly mourned in " The Dowie Dens o' Yarrow : "

> " Yestreen I dreamed a dolefu' dream,
>   I fear there will be sorrow !
> I dreamed I pu'd the heather green,
>   Wi' my true love on Yarrow !
> *   *   *   *   *   *
> She kissed his cheeks, she kaim'd his hair,
>   She searched his wounds all thorough,
> She kissed them till her lips grew red,
>   On the dowie houms of Yarrow."

Returning to Selkirk, two miles below Newark, we pass Carterhaugh, the plain so renowned in the ballad of " Young Tamlane." It stands by the conflux of Ettrick and Yarrow. Miles Cross, where Janet awaited the coming of the fairy train, was nearer Bowhill. " Fair Janet " herself is a pretty picture, with " green kirtle kilted a little abune her knee," " wearing gowd on her hair " (*i.e.*, having yellow hair), pulling " the red, red rose " by the well, or

> " Prinking herself and prinning herself
>   By the ae light of the moon,"

before she rides to Carterhaugh to meet her lover. As for Tamlane, the fairy lover, the "elfin grey" as he is called, he tells her how, when a boy of nine years, he was stolen by the little people,—

> " There came a wind out of the north,
>   A sharp wind and a snell,
> And a deep sleep came over me,
>   And from my horse I fell.
>
> The Queen of Fairies keppit me,
>   In yon green hill to dwell,
> And I'm a fairy, lyth and limb,
>   Fair ladye, view me well."

He is not ill-pleased to stay in Elfin-land, but even there *surgit amari aliquid* in the cup of bliss,—

> " Aye at every seven years,
>   They pay the teind to hell ;
> And I am sae fat and fair of flesh
>   I fear 'twill be mysell ! "

The scene which follows, when Janet's devoted love rescues him, is one of the most curious scraps of fairy lore to be found in all literature. Having concealed herself on "good Hallowe'en" at the ringing of the bridles of the fairy troop, she springs out upon and successfully possesses herself of Tamlane. The wrath of the Fairy Queen at this exploit is amusing,—

> "'Had I but kenned, Tamlane,' she says,
>   'Before ye cam frae hame,
>   I wad hae ta'en out your heart o' flesh,
>   Put in a heart o' stane;
>
>   Had I but had the wit yestreen
>   That I ha'e coft* the day—
>   I'd paid my kane† seven times to hell
>   Ere you'd been won away!'"

The old Tower of Hangingshaw, on the banks of Yarrow (long since demolished), is popularly considered to have been the scene of "The Sang of the Outlaw Murray."

> "Ettricke Foreste is a feir foreste,
>   In it grows manie a semelie tree;
>   There's hart and hynd and dae and rae,
>   And of a' wilde bestis grete plentie;
>   There's a feir castelle, bigged wi' lime and stane,
>   Oh gin it stands not pleasauntlie!'

The story is too long to quote, but finally James IV., his sovereign, says to him,—

> "Wilt thou give me the keys of thy Castell,
>   Wi' the blessing of thy gaye ladye?
>   I'se make thee sheriffe of Ettricke Foreste
>   Surely while upwards grows the tree;
>   If you be not traitour to the King,
>   Forfaulted sall thou never be!"

His answer shows to what the intense affection of the Scots to the heads of their clans was due,—

* Coft, bought.   † Kane, rent paid in kind.

" But, Prince, what sall cum' o' my men ?
    When I gae back, traitour they'll ca' me.
I had rather lose my life and land
    Ere my merryemen rebuked me.

Will your merryemen amend their lives ?
    And a' their pardons I grant thee—
Now name their landis where'er they lie,
    And here I render them to thee ? "

Thus the outlaw acquires "fair Philiphaugh," (which is still possessed by his representative,) Newark Lee, Hangingshaw, and
other lands, and the ballad ends,—

" He was made sheriffe of Ettriche Foreste,
    Surely while upward grows the tree ;
For if he was na traitour to the king,
    Forfaulted he sall never be."

We must next stretch southwards over the moorland to another
scene celebrated in song, Hassendean (or Hazledean), whence
the maid eloped

" O'er the border and awa'
    Wi' Jock o' Hazledean."

A lovely and characteristic view spreads before us, rolling dun
coloured moors, chequered here and there with a browner
patch of fern, or a few warm tufts of late blooming heather.
The cawing of rooks floats to our ears through the fresh morning
air from a distant "clachan," while close at hand, on one side
of the track, a " wimplin' burn " endeavours to be a great one ;
and two old crows sit on a rail close to the road, trying their
best to puff themselves out to the magnitude of ravens.   A
cross track winds down the valley to the left, with memorials of
what winter is in these wastes by tall posts, their upper parts
painted black, planted alongside of it every hundred yards or
so in order that the traveller may find his way over the snow.
At present, far below, the white sheep are dotted about, and
the shepherd wrapped in plaid and wearing the universal

Balmoral bonnet, walks round attended by his colley. Like all the countrymen hereabouts, he has the *rutilæ Caledoniam habitantium comæ*, which Tacitus notes and ascribes to their German origin. The distant Cheviots fill up the background of the picture in grey and blue tints, with here and there a green field running a short way up their sides, and wisps of mist straying ever their flanks; overhead grey skies, with a drifting mist-rack torn into ragged edges, speak of coming storms; while on the right an eye of sunshine lights up a brae or falls in a yellow glory over a stubble field. Adjoining it a reaping-machine is at work upon some barley thus late in the year.

At Minto we roam into the kirk, where if there be no "kist fu' o' whistles," there is at all events a modern warming apparatus. A labourer who was employed with it, tells us "we ha'e Sacrament twice a year noo, we did but use to hae it ance," in a tone which seemed to imply a protest against the novel practice, and which we could not help contrasting with the state of things in England. It is to be hoped that Scotch sermons are not so long now as those the old ballad represents.

> "There is a preacher in our chapell,
>   And a' the live-lang day teaches he :
> When day is gane and night is come,
>   There's ne'er a word I mark but three.
> The first and second is Faith and Conscience,
>   The third—Ne'er let a traitour free."

From a kirk the transition is easy to a school. Not being altogether strange to school inspecting in the sister kingdom, during this ramble into Ballad-land we also made our way to a parish school. A careworn master gravely bade us welcome, and informed us he was "the dominie." We answered we had supposed in our ignorance that functionary was the minister's clerk. "No, a dominie is jist a schoolmaster;" and recollections of Dominie Sampson then rose to substantiate his statement. The schoolroom was long, low, and dirty; a row of fading geraniums occupied a bench which ought to have been used by the children. Being harvest-time, only about eleven urchins were present. Discipline seemed somewhat lax ; one kept his cap on while we were there. What would "my Lords " have said to all this in an English school? Discarding official questions, we asked the weary-looking master in a friendly way what he taught. His answer showed that we had fallen upon a walking cyclopædia. No wonder he looked pale. "I jist teach Latin, Greek, French, mathematics, sketching, and painting."

" And what are you paid for all this? "

" I never had more than four shillings a quarter for each pupil. Average attendance? Say forty-four out of a popula-tion of four hundred. In Latin I take them on to Horace. Then most of the hinds' sons go to a university, and there follow up their Latin and Greek."

Smarting with memories of our own youth at the Perth seminaries, we inquired " Have you a pair of taws? " (a terrible instrument made of leather as thick as the trace of a carriage, with fringed ends, applied in Scotland to the palms of the idle in the shape of "palmies ").

" Have I taws? Oo ay ; but I dinna ken where it is. I sae seldom use it. I mostly sharpen my razors upon it!"

After that we gave him up. The idea of proposing high moral motives to such urchins as our friend taught was absurd. The good old plan of beating boys has not yet been proved inferior to the lofty, moral, persuasive method of modern times. Crabbe's philosophy is still sound,—

> " To tell a boy that if he will improve,
> His friends will praise him and his parents love,
> Is doing nothing—he has not a doubt
> But they will love him, nay applaud, without ;
> Let no fond sire a boy's ambition trust,
> To make him study—let him see he must ! "

Far over the Teviot in front gleams Carter Mountain, on
which is the Reidswire, where a skirmish took place at one of
the Border Courts in Elizabeth's time, which is handed down
by a ballad.   The character of such a meeting when Sir John
Carmichael and Sir John Foster, being the respective wardens
for the two kingdoms, met to redress mutual grievances under a
hollow truce, is graphically told in the following lines from it,—

> " Yet was our meeting meek enough,
>   Begun wi' merriment and mowes,
> And at the brae, aboon the heugh,
>   The clerk sat down to call the rowes [rolls],
> And some for kyne and some for ewes,
>   Call'd in of Dandrie, Hob, and Jock—
> We saw come marching ower the knows,
>   Five hundred Fenwicks in a flock—
> With jack and speir, and bows all bent,
>   And warlike weapons at their will :
> Although we were na weel content,
>   Yet, by my troth, we feared no ill.
> Some gaed to drink, and some stude still,
>   And some to cards and dice them sped."

Leaving the great chain of the Cheviots with their dark fells
and lonely dales in Dumfriesshire, we reach the district so
pathetically regretted in the ballad which relates Lord Maxwell's farewell, on having to flee the country after murdering
his enemy, one of the Johnstones, " Lochmaben's gate sae
fair," " Langholm where birks there be," and " Fair Eskdale."

> " The wind was fair, the ship was clear,
>   That good Lord went away ;
> And most part of his friends were there,
>   To give him a fair convey.
> They drank the wine, they didna spare,
>   Even in that guid Lord's sight,
> Sae now he's o'er the floods sae grey,
>   And Lord Maxwell has ta'en his good-night."

Still passing westward in Liddisdale, at Suport, is localised
that wild chant "The Fray of Suport," which is perhaps the

most spirited of all the Border ballads. An Englishwoman's cattle have been harried, and she calls her friends and neighbours to immediate pursuit, in verses of great power. One must suffice,—

> "But Peenye, my guid son, is out at the Hagbut Head,
>   His een glittering for anger like a fiery gleed ;
>   Crying, Mak' sure the hooks
>   Of Maky's-muir crooks,
>   For the wily Scot takes by nooks, hooks, and crooks,
>   Gin we meet a' together in a head the morn,
>   We'll be merry men !
>   Fy, lads ! shout a', a', a', a', a',
>   My gear's a' gane !"

It was here too that the gallant Hobbie Noble, whom, we have seen as one of the deliverers of Jock o' the Syde, was betrayed to the English to be hanged at Carlisle,—

> " At Kershope foot the tryste was set,
>   Kershope of the lilye lee."

By "Cannobie Lea" and the Esk, which the young Lochinvar crossed, "where ford there was none," we draw near to "merrie Carlisle." It is worth noting, on the way, that Lady Heron's song was ingeniously altered by Scott from a much older version called " Katharine Janfarie." The affray that ensued on this lady's abduction was said to have taken place where the Cadden joins the Tweed,—

> " Oh meikle was the blood was shed
>   Upon the Cowden brae,
>   And aye she made the trumpet sound,
>   It's a' fair play ! "

At Netherby Hall, by the Esk, in the old debateable land, a man of ballad tastes naturally remembers the unfortunate end of Hughie the Græme, one of the numerous thieves of the clan. He was hanged at Carlisle,—

> " Gude Lord Scroope's to the hunting gane,
>   He has ridden o'er moss and muir,
>   And he has grippit Hughie the Græme,
>   For stealing o' the Bishop's mare."

Sir Walter Scott could not precisely identify him, but suspected him to have been one out of some four hundred Borderers "wanted" about 1553 for divers murders and maraudings. Indeed, it would be difficult as well as invidious to select him from his kith and kin, who, along with many more, are thus enumerated :—"Ritchie Grame of Bailie, Will's Jock Grame, Wat Grame, called Flaughtail, Nimble Willie Grame, Mickle Willie Grame," &c., &c.

What memories crowd upon us at Carlisle ! In very early days tradition connected it with King Arthur. As the Laureate, however, does not introduce the city in his "Idylls" (doubtless because Sir Walter had already associated it with the Flower of Kings in his "Bridal of Triermain"), this is often forgotten. Yet the King's Round Table may be seen near Penrith, as well as at Winchester. The present generation of readers should compare how much finer is the moral character of King Arthur under Mr. Tennyson's hands than in Sir Walter Scott's conception of him.

One of the most gallant of Border exploits was performed at " Carlisle fair and free," in 1596, when Lord Buccleuch, with two hundred men, one night surprised the castle (in which the Warden of the Marches, Lord Scroope of Bolton, was sleeping at the time), and utterly forbearing to take plunder or hold the place, contented himself with rescuing a prisoner whom Scroope, he conceived, had unjustly seized. The ballad of "Kinmont Willie" abounds with flashes of humour in telling the tale. Kinmont himself, when rescued, calls :—

> " ' Farewell, farewell, my gude Lord Scroope !
>   My gude Lord Scroope, farewell ! ' he cried,
>   ' I'll pay you for my lodging maill [rent],
>   When first we meet on the Border side.' "

And still more amusingly, when he is borne, heavily-ironed, down the scaling-ladders on the shoulders of Red Rowan, "the starkest man in Teviotdale : "—

> " ' Oh mony a time,' quo' Kinmont Willie,
>   ' I have ridden horse baith wild and wood ;
> But a rougher beast than Red Rowan
>   I ween my legs have ne'er bestrode.
>
> ' And mony a time,' quo' Kinmont Willie,
>   ' I've pricked a horse out o'er the furs [furrows],
> But since the day I backed a steed,
>   I never wore sic cumbrous spurs ! ' "

Haribee Hill, outside Carlisle, has witnessed the death of many a Border rover ; the common gallows used to stand there. The Rickergate, a street in the city, is commemorated in " Hobbie Noble" in a picturesque verse,—

> " They ha'e ta'en him up the Rickergate ;
>   The wives they cast their windows wide ;
> And every wife to another can say,
>   ' That's the man loosed Jock o' the Syde ! ' "

A few more poetic memories still detain us in Liddisdale, where the Liddell, tracked by the dark spires of fir-trees, runs alongside of shady fells, with dark ravines cut through their brown sides by the torrents of ages. At the site of Mangerton Castle, for instance, below Castletown, it is difficult to avoid sympathising, if we are troubled by unpunctuality at home, with one commendable custom of the place,—

> " It was then the use of Pudding-burn house,
>   And the house of Mangerton, all hail,
> Them that cam' na at the first ca',
>   Got nae mair meat till the neist meal."

At the Hollows, a few miles from Langholm, is the roofless peel of Johnnie Armstrong of Gilnockie, another celebrated personage in Border legend. The temptation is great to quote his justification of himself when hailed as a traitor. That the

lines were often upon Sir Walter Scott's lips may be some
excuse,—

> " ' Ye lied, ye lied now, King,' he says,
>   ' Altho' a King and prince ye be !
> For I've luved naething in my life,
>   I weel dare say it, but honestie—
>
> ' Save a fat horse and a fair woman,
>   Twa bonny dogs to kill a deir ;
> But England suld ha'e found me meal and mault
>   Gif I had lived this hundred yeir !
>
> ' She suld ha'e found me meal and mault,
>   And beef and mutton in a' plentie ;
> But never a Scot's wyfe could ha'e said
>   That e'er I skaithed her a puir flee.
>
> To seek het water beneath cauld ice
>   Surely it is a great folie—
> I have asked grace at a graceless face,
>   But there is nane for my men and me ! ' "

His end shows how extremes meet.   With his companions he
was tried for cattle-lifting; and though no fact could be proved,
he was conveniently condemned according to Scotch law, "by
repute and habit"—*i.e.*, because of his general bad character.
Upon this he seized and broke up a heavy oak chair whereon
he sat, and handing its fragments to his comrades, begged
them to stand by him, and he would fight his way out with them
safely; but they held his hands and besought him "to suffer
them to die like Christians!"

Another nook of Ballad-land in Dumfriesshire should by no
means be neglected.   The little river Kirtle earned itself a sad
notoriety a few years ago by the Kirtlebridge railway accident,
but it has long been celebrated in song.   The ill-fated loves of
Helen Irving and Adam Fleming, and her death through a
shot which she intercepted, fired by a jealous rival from the
other bank of the Kirtle, form one of the most exquisite of the
Border ballads.   Who does not love its pathetic cadences ?

> " I wish I were where Helen lies,
>   Night and day on me she cries ;
> Oh that I were where Helen lies
>   On fair Kirkconnell Lea ;
> Curst be the heart that thought the thought,
> And curst the hand that fired the shot,
> When in my arms burd Helen dropt,
>   And died to succour me ! "

The fine lines of another ballad answer well to her traditional beauty,—

> " The red that's on my true love's cheek,
>   Is like blood-drops on the snaw ;
> The white that is on her breast bare,
>   Like the down o' the white sea-maw."

Many a modern poet has tried his hand on the legend, but its finale cannot be better told than by Wordsworth, who has changed Fleming into Bruce,—

> " Now ye who willingly have heard
>   The tale I have been telling,
> May in Kirkconnell Churchyard view
>   The grave of lovely Ellen.
> By Ellen's side the Bruce is laid ;
> And, for the stone upon his head,
> May no rude hand deface it !
> And its forlorn *Hic Jacet !* "

But here we must stop. Though it be delightful to tarry a while in Ballad-land, and we find ourselves echoing simple Mopsa's sentiment, " I love a ballad in print o' life," it does not follow that we believe her reason for it, " for then we are sure they are true."   It is time to return to the realities of life, and to thank our readers for following us thus far in our poetical pilgrimage,—

> " O dulces comitum valete cœtus,
> Longe quos simul a domo projectos
> Diverse variæ viæ reportant.'

H

Better still, let us part in the hearty manner of the country
through which we have been wandering,— ·

> " And there's a han', my trusty frien',
>   And gie's a hand o' thine ;
>   And we'll tak' a richt gude willie waught,
>   For auld lang syne ! "

There is no more pleasant land for a walking tour than the
Border.   Go where the traveller will (as we trust we have shown
him), are memorials of a glorious and romantic past.   In this
part of the country, too, civility and moderate charges repel the
accusation of rapacity which is so often urged against the Scotch
innkeeper.   Indeed, the best receipt for a walking tour in this
country of glamour, if a man wishes to learn the kindliness of
the natives and to see their land to perfection, is to bid him
lose himself as soon as possible and wander from the highways,
making friends with every one he meets.   A king of the country,
"the gaberlunzie man," has ere now set him the example.   In
this manner only is it possible to pick up legends or local
anecdotes, and to discover untrodden but interesting scenes, as
yet undreamt of by the guide-books.   Such a traveller may yet
light on folk-lore and supernatural beings, brownie or warlock,
maintaining a precarious and alas! a short-lived existence
against the opposing forces of railroads and post-offices.   If he
attempts at night to exorcise such an evil spirit from his quarters,
let him be sure to speak in Latin, and, above all, to have the
last word with the ghost.   This is as important as when a man
argues with his wife.   No sounder cure than such a walking
tour as we have sketched, through lands redolent of love and
song, can be suggested to a disappointed lover.   By a natural
process of homeopathy it will soon give him relief, pointing out
how many others have loved and lost and—lived, before him.
If he leaves home, like the swain who was drowned in Annan
Water, so sad that

> " The waistcoat bursted off his breast,
>   He was so full of melancholy—"

he will certainly return from his raid into Ballad-land in far different flight to another hapless lover, Lord Randal,—

> "Mother, make my bed soon,
> For I'm sick at the heart, and fain wad lie down."

He will bring back a store of sunny recollections and bright dreams, a plenteous stock of health, and a lighter heart wherewith to engage afresh with the stern stuff whereof modern life is made up. And, as he turns his back upon Ballad-land, he will watch, with all the fond longings of a lover, the curves of the fast-receding hills and their many-changing lines—purple, deep blue, and grey—till outlines and shades alike wax faint and fainter still, and at length disappear into the clouds, often to be reproduced hereafter in bright visions, coloured by fancy and contentment.

On Ottery East Hill.

Up, up the hill-side let us resolutely push; between the diminutive stony fields, roughly fenced with a few brambles, some big stones, or it may be a log laid on the bank; leaving far below the tall elms cut into bottle-brushes, a custom which so greatly defaces South-East Devon—scarcely finding time for more than a glance at the old-fashioned three-toothed plough drawn by a donkey, an ox, and a sorry jade, which is slowly scratching the pebbly surface of one patch at our side. Onward again; till at the edge of cultivation the last signs of man are reached, a low, white-washed cottage sheltering under the brow of the hill. Its domestic arrangements are primitive enough; an open umbrella hanging from the roof forms a convenient receptacle for the wardrobe as well as any superfluities of the family. The children do not know what coal is, as wood from the strip of pine-forest hard by is always burnt on the large open hearth. Wordsworth's Lucy might here have obtained in perfection those mystical nature-teachings which he promised her; these urchins, for their part, daily attend the village school two miles below. We knock at the half-open door with its tufts of "bloody warriors" (Devon for "wall flowers;") out walk a grey cat and a couple of fowls. Father is probably driving the plough, and mother taking him dinner, so we enter. A chubby boy is fast asleep in the inner chamber, whose door also stands invitingly open; with the gentle flush of childish slumbers upon his cheeks and the rounded features of innocence, he is a veritable Sleeping Beauty; but, sooth to say, his face is too dirty to tempt us to awake him with the orthodox kiss. So we slip a penny into his open hand, and retire, enjoying the thought of his wonder on awaking, much as Goldsmith rejoiced while putting his last guinea in the sleeping beggar's pocket. These children's harvest ripens at Midsummer, when they gather the whortleberries which abound on these heights, and sell them to the visitors at Sidmouth or Budleigh Salterton. Higher, higher yet! We are now fairly on the waste, struggling through golden-blossomed furze, which is so bright that it seems to wink in the sun's eye, now up a bare gravel slope, now through deep bushes of heather, not without many a prick and stumble. A rabbit darts into a hole, but no other living thing comes in sight. Gentle foretastes of the breeze at the top fan our cheek. One more push for forty yards, and the fresh keen breeze fully greets us. At last we are on the long flat ridge of Ottery East Hill, with a wide panorama of hill and dale below, and far away to the left a glittering blue patch of sea.

The vegetation up here is very striking ; primroses and dog-violets, the dainty wild strawberry, the shyly-opening wood-sorrel are left below us at the side of the red water-grooved tracks winding between the little strips of cultivation. As far as man presses upon the wild, they lovingly follow his footsteps. The ferns, too, have changed ; *Adiantum nigrum*, the plumed male fern, and *Asplenium Trichomanes* have lingered in the grateful moisture below. The curiously dissimilar fertile and barren fronds of the *Blechnum spicant* may be found instead of them up here under any protecting mound of earth. Those trusty companions of the water-loving ferns, the *Chrysosplenium*, or golden saxifrage, and the *Adoxa Moschatellina*, are also chequering the damp moss-tufts in the deep lanes far beneath. A keen eye may notice vegetation varying according to its regular laws even in these comparatively pigmy altitudes of a few hundred feet above the sea-level. Below lies that net-work of lanes which forms a bewildering maze on each side of

the range to the stranger, and to the lover of the hill presents
that aspect of multiplicity, and yet uniformity, which lends a
special charm to this district of England.   We are standing on
the summit of a level ridge which extends some four miles,
stretching to the south-west, and ending abruptly over Sidmouth, while its other extremity loses itself in the pinewoods
and gently-falling "combes" above Honiton.   From the vale
below, this singular ridge forms the strongest contrast to a
Spanish sierra; it resembles rather a long knife-blade, not
picturesque save when traversed by atmospheric effects, but
striking from being unlike anything else in England.   A poet
might compare it to a couching lion regarding the fertile valleys
below.   It is not without

> " The silence and the calm
>   Of mute insensate things,"

while its very uniformity enables memory to reproduce it the
more easily afar from the nameless charm of its presence.   As
the bright spring sunshine travels over its face, notice the wealth
of colour which it awakes beside us.   The heather shakes its
withered white bells over the grey reindeer-moss which carpets
the pebbly ground, save where the warmer hues of yellow and
brown stones interrupt its continuity, the larger of these bearing
many a ruddy or golden rosette of lichen.   Then succeeds the
whortleberry with its brilliantly red unopened blooms and faint
green leaves, and then another blinding wall of furze blossom.
Beyond that lies a patch of pale yellow bents, with many flints,
white, grey, and red, scattered amongst them ; here runs, perhaps, a trail of ivy ; while there is a cluster of mossy spear-
heads, more beautiful, if you look microscopically into them
than even the red-stemmed Scotch firs behind us.   Each tiny
shaft might be made of delicate pink glass, while their golden
spear-heads, like those of the insolent Gauls of old, might be
defying the skies to fall, and they would bear them up.   On
the other side of this common, the russet leaves of stunted

beech-trees which have triumphed over wintry winds glow with
colour, while ivy hangs in wind-torn festoons from the higher
ones, backed up by stunted larches; and then comes the sea of
Scotch firs which everywhere on these heights surges more or
less on to the heath. That murmur which is so dear to mountain lovers sighs eternally through them, now flooding the red
stems and writhing branches with a full tide of aërial music,
now whispering gently higher up in the grey-blue foliage,—

> " Powerful almost as vocal harmony
> To stay the wanderer's steps, and soothe his thoughts; "

and now again in low, deep swells recurrent, like the beatings
of the great world-heart. Who would not throw himself down
on the heather here, and indulge a momentary day-dream?

But, even in Devon, spring sunshine, though bright, is fleeting, like an old acquaintance in a hurry, who grasps your hand
and speeds on his way. It is time to turn from artistic studies
to the physical characteristics of the district. A glance at the
barren table-land on which we stand, and the fertile vale below,
shows that water has mainly caused their configuration. We
trip over a fossil sea-egg *(echinus)* which tells the same tale.
To the north-east a hill of marvellous blue tints, with lofty
scarped sides, closes the view. It is the termination nominally
of the Black Down Range, and those white-scarped walls are
the entrances to the celebrated scythe-stone quarries. But
geologically* the hill on which we stand, and, indeed, the whole
of the high land between the Golden Cap, near Lyme Regis,
and the Haldon Hills (the first range on our left beyond the
estuary of the Exe) forms a portion of this Black Down range.
This East Hill, together with its brother, the West Hill, which
rises opposite on different sides of the Otter river, belongs to
the green-sand formation. It underlies the chalk of that grand

---

* See a Paper on the Geology of this district, by the late lamented Rev.
R. Kirwan, in Rev. Dr. Cornish's *Short Notes on Ottery St. Mary*.

headland, Beer Head, behind us, the last point westward where chalk is seen, and consists of sandstone, with green earth, chert, and flints. Through its entire extent this area exhibits extensive marks of denudation. Thus the table-land from which we look possesses but a scanty covering of soil. There is a substratum of tenacious yellow clay, or sometimes the sandstone rises almost to the surface with a thin covering of flints and rounded pebbles, that tell their own tale, with a scanty surface vegetation. In the valleys around the hills of this greensand formation that is below us, are the red marls and conglomerates of the new red sandstone, fertile in elms and corn-fields, while the surface soil of this East Hill has been washed down the sides, resting but little on the slopes high up, but remaining deeper below, and lying rich, deep, and productive in the descents and "combes" which lie yet lower down. This accounts for the barren plateau on which we are standing, with its fern, heather, and furze, while pastures, corn-fields, and orchards are piled, as it were, one on the other below us ; and the boundary line, being nowhere strictly drawn between desolation and productiveness on the East Hill's slopes, runs picturesquely like a dark rim along its flanks, matching, in some sort, the fringe of Scotch firs which crowns it every here and there, and shows to the dweller in the vales patches of blue sky between the boles.

This contrast of hill and dale, fertility and barreness, makes up an epitome of Devonshire scenery. All the characteristics of the county are here presented to the eye, save the dark slate rock walls which, on the north and south-west, confront the sea. The features on which depend so much of the picturesqueness which we are wont to associate with Devonshire are here especially prominent—the wealth of wild flowers, the deep winding lanes, the moss-grown orchards, small enclosures, and huge rough banks. Far away under the West Hill runs a broad silvery band, the Otter river, through deep green meadows, intersected also by many shining streaks to which they owe their emerald hue, the cunning system of irrigation in vogue in the West of England. A wood, in which beech-trees grow in great beauty, and whose dales are carpeted with ferns, lies in Harpford Parish, to the left; whitewashed farms and grey hamlets are well represented. The red Devon cows pasture here and there; the donkeys, so much used by the cottagers on the heights, browse by our side. Vale after vale lies before us with the crest of the hills rising beyond. Over the estuary of the Exe, on the left, are seen the Haldon Hills at a higher elevation than the long, swelling heights of Woodbury. They terminate in the wooded projection of Mamhead. Beyond the Haldon range run the faint blue peaks of Dartmoor, the twin points of Hey Tor being distinctiy visible; while glimmering through the haze and closing the extensive panorama are the shadowy outlines of two Cornish giants, Rough Tor and Brown Willy. These natural features remind us how severely Westcote is exercised in his *View of Devonshire* (1630), on the derivation of the county's name. He summarily rejects the fancy of those who would name it from the Danes (*quasi* Daneshire); though there are modern etymologists who still connect the Den at Teignmouth with those invaders. The "combes" everywhere met with in Devon suggest to him that their ancient name, *Diffinent* or *Dennan,* appears in the county's name, while another natural feature, the rivers (in Keltic, *Afon*), contends with this view, as from them might be derived De-afonshire or Devonshire. He leaves the difficulty, however (as we may too), "with him who, like Nævius, can, *cotem novacula scindere,* cleave hard stones with razors." The rough uneven surface, again, leads him to compare it with Ithaca in Homer and Horace, *non est aptus equis,* &c., or as the proverb, which he quotes, runs—

> The country is best for the bider
> That's most cumbersome to the rider.

The enormous *haiæ* or hedges of the county, many of which are visible from our points of observation, which spring from broad and high banks, some wide enough for a waggon to run on, are characteristic things in the landscape. They are very old, and are mentioned as far back as King John's days in the Charter for Disafforesting Devon. Many villages and bartons take the name of Hayes from them, and the surname Hedge-land is not uncommon in the two western shires.

To the west Berry Head closes the view. Let us thread the pine plantations behind us, and in a couple of hundred yards a richer country, its "combes" opening to the south, spreads out; Portland gleaming on the distant horizon, and terminating in this direction the field of vision. It is a sad sea to our mind, this Bay of Sidmouth; vast, monotonous, fading into the blue sky-line, streaked with oily tidal lanes, but flecked by no white sails to tell of man's energy. The silent highway of commerce to the New World lies far to the south of it. Outward-bound vessels after making Portland stretch across to sight the Lizard, and then, skirting Mount's Bay, leave our shores by the Longships Lighthouse. There is no pier at Sidmouth, and it is an inconvenient place for small craft, so that but few pleasure boats are seen on the Bay. A great element in our love of the sea is thus wanting at Sidmouth. For it is the sense of victory won and safe transit over the sea being now secured which chiefly endears to us islanders our natural barrier of waves, whatever the sentimentalists may say. The Laureate depicts the tortures inflicted by the monotony of the Tropic Sea on his "long-bearded solitary" Enoch Arden, who morn after morn marked the sun's beams rise on one hand over it, to set each eve on the other over a shining expanse never relieved by the sight of a sail. But Sidmouth Bay is not quite so bad. As we look, from a grey cloudbank glimmers a white speck, and as suddenly fades back into nothingness. That glimpse is enough to reassure us, and the eye returns with a longing gratified to the wooded hill-sides and fertile vales in front. There the little river Sid cuts it way through holly, ferns, and bracken. Wolfersly, said to have been the lair of the last wolf in this district, lies in one direction ; Penhill stands above it. The green plovers are so tame that you can discern their crests as they daintily pick their way over the herbage on the right. Even thus early in the year the wood-pigeon's coo falls with its inexpressible home-like associations on the ear. A dozen fir plantations and as many lanes lead each into its own little world of peace below us, where as Herrick (himself a Devonshire parson) sang,—

> " The damaskt medowes and the pebbly streames
> Sweeten and make soft your dreames."

Now a couple of jackdaws launch themselves overhead into the blue cloud-depths beyond, while the bleat of lambs, the banging of a gate, the roar of a distant train float upwards from the world of man. Verily, Devonshire is the pearl of English counties, so far as regards soft pastoral beauty, aërial distances, and the rounded hills which so insensibly please the eyes and through them soothe the mind.

But it possesses other interests to which we will now turn. What can be learnt of the ancient inhabitants of these vales? Not much beyond the scattered scraps of information which may be picked out of the early writers as to the names of the tribes, the stature and complexion, &c., of the men. As for particulars of their domestic life and social state, which would be so interesting, we are left to collect what little can be recovered of these, by our knowledge of the Kelts elsewhere. They were a people, Aristotle tells us, brave even to rashness. It is fair to assume that here, as at other places in England, the Romans inherited from them the occupation of that chain of conical hill-tops which stretches in front of us. Four such summits at least are visible, stretching away from Black Hill near the sea, through Woodbury and Cadbury to Hembury

Fort, and so into the heart of the fertile country round Taunton. Barrows or cemeteries may have been occasionaly found in such situations, but it is impossible to doubt that these hill-tops, succeeding one another from the shore inland, each with its crown of fir-trees, were military posts. Indeed, on some of them (as at Woodbury and Hembury) the line of the Roman *vallum* may yet be traced. In one of his " Prose Idylls " Canon Kingsley supposes, somewhat fancifully, the character of the treacherous, shrinking, tortuous Kelts to be expressed in the deep winding lanes which so greatly abound in the West of England. These were probably after all inherited by the Aryan immigrants from the aborigines whom they dispossessed, and it may be exterminated, tribes which used flint arrowheads, and secluded themselves in caves and thickets from nature's inclemency and the now extinct monsters of their time.* The chief fault of the Kelts was not cowardice but rather fickleness, instability of will and counsel. Other strong camps are found further westward, guarding the narrow gorge of the Teign, which Mr. Merivale regards as the scene of the final combat between Roman and Damnonian ; while on the open side of Hamilton Down on Dartmoor is the old British village of Grimspound. This with its low enclosure, where assailants must at once have come to close quarters with its defenders, is enough of itself to vindicate the Keltic character for courage.

When we search yet deeper into the ethnology of the extensive view now spread before us, one stratum below the Kelts we reach that primitive people whose remains are found from Caithness to the English Channel associated with rude stone weapons and the bones of the cave bear and woolly rhinoceros; men who rose successively, according to modern archæology, through the various grades of civilisation represented by beautifully polished flint and jade weapons, to the knowledge of the

* See Professor Lightfoot, Excursus on the "Galatian People," pp. 14 and 235, in his *Epistle to the Galatians.*

use of bronze and then to that of iron. On the concluding swells of this East Hill towards Honiton, tumuli may be seen in which remnants of these buried civilisations yet sleep. Indeed, few districts in England are richer in pre-historic antiquities than the one on which we stand. Walking eastward, we look into a series of fertile "combes" bending towards the sea, and on the high table-land which breaks down into these wooded valleys may be noticed many small mounds crowned with trees. We know that the natives of the Bronze Age were wont to bury their dead on lofty hills, and these tumuli have been conclusively proved by the late Mr. Kirwan's researches to have been places of sepulture, and probably to have belonged to that epoch. The record of his investigations is very interesting.* In 1868 he opened three of these funeral mounds with the utmost care. They were about ninety feet in diameter and eight or nine feet in height, of a conical shape. On the original level of the ground was found a deposit of charcoal enclosed in a circle of large boulders in one case. Then came a layer of calcined bones, and above them clay and burnt earth ; in one case a cairn of flints was built over them, and then the surface earth had been piled over all. Cremation was the mode by which these dead persons had been disposed of. Each of the three tumuli also contained treasures of great worth in the eyes of an archæologist ; not, indeed, the "crocks of gold" which the country people believe are concealed in them, but infinitely more valuable articles, judging them by their scientific interest. In the first tumulus was discovered a cup some three and a half inches high and three inches wide, of a bell-shaped pattern tapering downwards to a cone. It would hold about a gill. Its ornamentation is extremely simple and in admirable taste, consisting externally of four series of rings, while the inner margin of the rim is indented with two parallel chevrony zigzags that

* See *Transactions of the Devonshire Association for the Advancement of Science aud Art.* *1868.*

run beneath a single horizontal enclosed line. On the outside is a handle, but too small for the finger; it was probably secured round its owner's neck by a string passed through this projection.

This very rare and curious relic is formed, it is now almost conclusively settled, of Kimmeridge coal, and it has probably been turned on a pole lathe. We had an opportunity of inspecting it soon after its discovery, and were much surprised at its lightness and delicacy, to say nothing of its admirable preservation. What a train of far-reaching thoughts, too, did it arouse, thoughts which pierced the mists that surround the dawn of authentic history, and then recoiled upon themselves in baffled awe !

In the second mound was discovered a curious "incense cup" of pale brown clay, some two inches high and three inches wide, ornamented with rectangular compartments enclosing the well-known "herring-bone" markings .Even the bottom of it was covered with marks of this kind arranged in a rude cruciform fashion. It contained apparently the calcined bones of an infant, which was possibly buried here along with its mother. Suttee and infanticide are abominations supposed to have been practised in pagan Britain, therefore it is not necessary to suppose that the baby was dead when thus buried together with its mother. In his researches amongst the kitchen-middens of Caithness, Mr. Laing found a couple of human jaw-bones under circumstances which raise a strong presumption that these primitive races were cannibals, if not always, at least under the pressure of starvation. The third mound on being opened displayed fragments of a cinerary urn of the usual wide-rimmed type, together with a food-vessel of singular shape. No bones were found, no skulls over which Science could wrangle whether they were of the brachycephalic or dolichocephalic variety. That these interments were not Roman, the absence of the coins and pottery usually found in their graves naturally

suggests, while that they were not Saxon is still more conclusively proved by the absence of the ambre or glass beads, the
brooches of gold, silver and copper, so frequently associated with
Saxon sepulchres.　Many bronze celts have been found on this
Broad Down and the neighbourhood; and vague as is the testi-
mony they afford (for they might not belong to the same period
as the above "finds"), they are all the collateral circumstances
which we possess in order to form a judgment on the nation
and age of those here interred.　They belonged so the pre-historic population of the county, and that is all we can at present
affirm.　When the members of the British Association held a
pic-nic on Broad Down, and deserted their tent and the generous
hospitality which the county afforded them therein, to be suddenly sobered as they gazed upon these relics of a nation
which has long since passed away from human ken, Archæology
could but stand sadly by and lay her hand on her mouth.
Each age is a marvel to its successors, and we shall be no exception in the eyes of posterity.

> "Scilicet et tempus veniet, quum finibus illis
> Agricola, incurvo terram molitus aratro,
> Exesa inveniet scabra rubigine pila,
> Aut gravibus rastris galeas pulsabit inanes,
> Grandiaque effossis mirabitur ossa sepulchris."

From these sombre thoughts a sunbeam recalls us to a bright
point in the landscape below, as it glints on the spirelet which
tops the north tower of St. Mary's Church at Ottery.　It is set
in a pleasant haze of white houses, bursting foliage, and drifting
smoke, suggestive of many homes, each with its own garden,
closing in upon the Minister.　A network of gleaming lanes,
too, can be seen running down the hill-sides to converge on the
old grey church, which seems to attract to itself all the life of
the district.　If we transport ourselves to its quiet precincts,
the studiously plain architecture of this early English church,
with its transceptal towers, from which Bishop Quivil in the
latter years of the thirteenth century probably borrowed the

idea for his cathedral at Exeter, will at once remind us of the
connection of Ottery with Normandy, though even on the
Continent Le Mans is the only other church with this arrangement—the quaint schoolroom and uneven roofs of the "King's
New Grammar School" hard by, as its founder Henry VIII.
designated it—the pre-occupied air of the little town, with the
mediæval names still clinging to its streets—all this we take in
at a glance.   Unlike Ilfracombe churchyard, no tablet inscribed
with the names of centenarians is seen in the churchyard,
though Ottery can boast of many parishioners who have
attained the respectable age of ninety.   Inside, through the
dim religious light, may be discerned some forty painted
windows, all aglow with Scriptural imagery, while the eyes travel
up fair white columns to a roof blazing with gold and colours,
and then descend to the fan tracery of the Dorset aisle, and a
certain Captain Coke's statue, in trunk hose, highly painted,
concerning whom many legends are told.   Sleeping, too, in the
soft sunshine, each under a floriated canopy, appear the re-
cumbent figures of Sir Otho de Grandisson and his wife
Beatrix ; her dogs, to symbolise faithfulness, lying at her feet.
Here, too, is an epitaph on a young wife who died in the first
week of her marriage.   It is said that Southey laid his hand on
it when he visited the church, and unhesitatingly pronounced
it to be the composition of William Browne, the author of
Britannia's Pastorals, a Devonshire poet of no mean fame.
The reader shall judge for himself whether it has the true ring
of poetry,—

> "If wealth, wit, beautie, youth, or modest mirth
>   Could hire, persuade, entice, prolong, beguile
> Death's fatal dart, this fading flowre on earth,
>   Might, yet unquailed, have flourished awhile ;
> But mirth, youth, beautie, wit, nor wealth, nor all,
> Can stay, or once delay, when Death doth call.
>
> No sooner was she to a loving mate
>   From careful parents solemnly bequeathed,

The new alliance scarce congratulate,
   But she from him, them, all, was straight bereaved :
Slipping from bridal feast to funeral bere,
She soon fell sick, expired ; lies buried here.

O Death, thou mightest have waited in the field
   On murd'ring cannon, wounding sword and spear,
Or there, where fearful passengers do yield
   At every surge each blast of wind doth rear ;
In stabbing taverns or infected towns,
On loathsome prisons, or on princes' frowns.

There not unlook't for many a one abides
   Thy direful summons ; but a nuptial feast
Needs not thy grim attendance ; maiden brides
   In strength and flower of age thou may'st let rest,
With wings so weak mortality doth fly,
In height of flight Death strikes ; we fall and dy."

These fine verses may be compared with another epitaph
given in Prince's "Worthies of Devon." The gem must be
allowed to shine in Prince's own setting. One Edward Gee,
parson of St. Mary, Tedbourne, wrote the epitaph in memory
of his wife, Jane, who deceased September 21st 1613 ; it may
still be seen, we believe, in that church. After lamenting in
lugubrious verse that he had never been enrolled in Hymenæus's
books, &c., the disconsolate widower concludes—

" Thy features, O my Jane, out of my heart shall slide
  When beasts from fields and fishes all out of the sea shall glide ;
  Henceforth I will no more alight upon a fair green tree,
  But as a turtle which hath lost his dear mate I will be."

"Notwithstanding which resolution" (adds Prince), "'tis
said he left behind him at his death, which happened about the
year of our Lord 1618, a widow named Mary to turtle it after
him, as he had done before."

It is time, however, to return from these reminiscences of the
church, which from the top of the East Hill catches our atten-
tion, as the sun dwells on its vane. The curious connection

above spoken of between Ottery and the Continent claims a moment's consideration. It is expressed by the royal arms of France and England emblazoned on stone scutcheons over the church's altar, and right nobly supported by the armorial bearings of the Grandissons, Montacutes, and Courtenays. There the lions of England, borne by Edward III., who assumed the title of King of France about 1337, hold a proud position next the golden lilies of France, the bearings of Isabel, daughter of Philip IV., in whose right her son, Edward III., made claim to that kingdom. The Manor of Ottery was granted by Edward the Confessor in 1061 to the Cathedral Church of Rouen, in Normandy. In *Domesday Book* it is described as being held of the King by the Church of St. Mary at Rouen, and is valued at a rental of sixty-six marks. John de Grandisson, Bishop of Exeter in the time of Edward III., had long desired to found a college of monks, and, having settled on Ottery as a most convenient site, after some negotiations bought the manor and advowson, and proceeded to the carrying out of his devout purposes. The purchase was concluded in June, 1335. For this corporation, which he prescribed should consist of a warden and thirty-nine members, he drew up most minute statutes. With an eye to domestic thrift, he lays down when and where the wax for the candles may be bought at most advantage. The very strokes of the bells are numbered; and he says, with some humour, "inhibemus ne nimis prolixe pulsentur, nec iterum post officia vel in aurora, *sicut solet Exonie;* quia nihil prodest animabus 'æs sonans aut cymbalum tinniens,' et tamen multum nocet auribus et fabrice ac campanis."* A similar instance of the good Bishop's dry humour comes out in the injunction that all the college should be indoors after the last stroke of the "ignitegium," or curfew (this bell, we may add, is still rung at Ottery during the winter half of the year); "et propter pericula incendii et ignis que frequenter contingunt, pre-

* Statuta No. 76, ap. Oliver's *Monasticon Dioc. Exon.*, p. 270.

cipimus quod omnes ad lectos simul vadant et lumen simul extinguant, *ne forsitan aliquis soporatus, quod absit, socios combureret et seipsum.*"* The first writer of eclogues in the English language, William Barclay, was one of the prebendaries of the church, and is remembered for his translation into our tongue of the celebrated *Navis Stultifera* of Sebastian Brandt.

This college was dissolved by Henry VIII., and the church, &c., made over to a church corporation of four governors (similar to that of Crediton), which remains substantially the same at the present day. The great tithes passed to the Dean and Chapter of Windsor, but now belong to the Ecclesiastical Commissioners, while, until a few years ago, the vicar was presented by the Lord Chancellor. A more anomalous state of things can hardly be imagined, considering the size and population of Ottery St. Mary.

Running the eye over the large tract of tilth and woodland before us, one or two great names emerge from the past and challenge mention. This is, to begin with, the country of Sir Walter Raleigh, " the glory not of this county only, but the kingdom," as Prince patriotically asserts.† Far to the left, under the shelter of an extensive wood, lies his birthplace, Hayes Farm. It is a long, low, whitewashed building, evidently of great antiquity, but contains no relics of the Raleighs. Their pew, with its fine oak carving, may, however, be seen in the adjacent parish church of East Budleigh. At Colaton Raleigh, too, which is the next village to Newton, down the Otter river, in the valley before us, is an old manor-house belonging to the family, and tradition tells that there the first potatoes ever grown in England were planted. More than one house at Ottery St. Mary is popularly connected with Sir W. Raleigh ; but that which possessed the best claim to have been his residence was the chief of a block of five tenements in the centre of the town, which were unfortunately destroyed by fire on May 15, 1805.

* Stat. 51.   † *Worthies of Devon*, p. 666. Ed. 1810.

Old inhabitants describe it as rising high above the adjoining houses with stone mullioned windows, and a projecting open porch having a bench on either side within, and a chamber over it with battlemented parapet.   Polwhele (*History of Devonshire*, 1793-7) speaks of it as a mouldering structure, "with one turret still existing, and the house has altogether a monasterial appearance."   It was, in short, like a multitude of the old houses that yet exist in this part of the country.   Many will remember another curious old house in the same town, burnt in the great fire of 1866, which was inhabited by a local worthy, named John Reed, a postmaster known far and wide for his uprightness and consistency of character.   He used to declare that the sanctum in which he was continually to be found with his long clay pipe was, appropriately enough, the very room in which Raleigh's servant threw a measure of beer over his master, on first seeing him smoking.   It is, at all events, pleasing to his surviving friends to associate Reed's name with the legend. These sojournings in Devon were probably the happiest days of Raleigh's unquiet life.

In the school-house, before mentioned, adjoining Ottery Church, was born another dreamer, whose wanderings, however, were in the shadowy realms of poetry and metaphysics, Samuel Taylor Coleridge, the first to confer literary lustre upon a name still worthily represented at Ottery St. Mary.   His father, the parish vicar and schoolmaster, was himself no mean scholar. He published a Latin Grammar, now probably as little known as the manuals of Roger Ascham.   Tradition also tells of the sonorous accents in which he would quote from the pulpit Hebrew prophecy in the original.   But the father is eclipsed by his son's fame, "S. T. Coleridge, Esq., Gentleman, Poet, and Philosopher in a mist."   We ourselves have often slept in the room where he first saw the light.   Save the fact of his birth at Ottery, but little remains to connect Coleridge's name with his native country.   We habitually refer him rather to the green

Quantock hills and the moist valleys of Westmoreland, to the cloud-cuckoo-land of his own ideal Pantisocracy, and perhaps above all to Highgate, with the benign friends who there cheered the closing scene of the large-browed seer.

One or two of the large farms round Ottery are sufficiently memorable to find a line in this survey. Cadhay is a fine old stone hall with quadrangle, the ancient seat of the Haydons. Thorn was the inheritance of Gaulterus de Spineto in the reign of Henry III. Sunk in a depression below us is another old house, garlanded with ivy, and Virginian creeper containing a dining-hall which well deserves inspection. This is Knight-stone, once the residence of the Shermans. Far to the left, beyond the river, may be seen a row of pollard limes, which are just swelling into a myriad of ruby-budded shoots, and every here and there unfolding leaves which only Millais could paint. They extend along the front of Bishopscourt, once, says Lysons (ii. 378), the abode of Bishop Grandisson himself. Enlarging our view, many goodly names rise before us. Beginning on the right, for instance, in Luppit parish, near Honiton, was Mohuns Ottery, the seat of the Carews, who were amongst the oldest of Devonshire families. In the sixteenth century this house was described as impregnable except by cannon, and filled with magnificent furniture. Soon the eye reaches Fenny Bridges over the Otter, where, July 27, 1549, a sharp skirmish took place between the Cornish insurgents, Lord Russell and the Carews, in which either side suffered equally. The little meadow wherein the rebels were encamped is dear to the trout fisher, and the stream of human interests which used to flow along this road from the West of England and return thither from London, has been diverted from it by the rail, leaving Honiton and its melancholy-looking inns to testify to the mutability of fortune. From Fair Mile, where stood in old time "a gallows at the hill-top," we may gather the need of this object of terror as the eye passes on to Straight-wood

Head, from Westcote's words :—We will haste from Strich-wood, *alias* Straight-wood Head, as speedily as we may, for many have feared and shunned it, and others have paid heavily for their passage or before they were suffered to pass; for in former times it was very infamous for sheltering of thieves " (p. 231). Hard by Fenny Bridges may be noticed the quaint modern parsonage of Affington, built in strict mediæval fashion, with its adjoining little church. A sad interest attaches to these, for it was here that the good Bishop Patteson, recently murdered by the South Sea Islanders, held his first cure. From this little patch of grey, as it seems from this height, the eye falls on the dark masses of fir-trees in Escot Park, where Locke would often wander, and, as tradition tells, laid out several of the clumps and other sylvan beauties of that charming piece of landscape gardening. In the west are the wild moors and woodlands which surround Bicton House, whose elms are gigantic even amongst the elms of Devon. And so the mind returns from the varied survey to the termination of the range on which we stand towards Sidmouth, the Beacon, as it is called, from its prominent form and the stories which connect it with the distant heights, as forming the first in a series of beacons which flashed onwards news of any descent made on the coast, and which, if they were not lighted on the occasion of William's landing at Torbay, we may be certain announced to " the wide vale of Trent " the approach of the Armada.

In this wide expanse of country, however, there is one characteristic feature of which nothing has yet been said. Every farm-house, every hamlet below us is surrounded, nay smothered, in its orchards. They climb every hill and descend into every " goyle " adjacent to the dwellings of man, and em-brace, as it were, the farms with the spreading wings of plenty. For they are symbolical of substance and happiness in this county, where so many quarts of cider per week still supple-ment the labourers' wages. We can see one of these orchard-strips just below, hanging over the whitewashed farm beneath. The trees lean towards each other at all angles, and lovingly commingle their boughs ; while every here and there one or two gnarled trunks totter away from their fellows, as if over come by their own cider. It is to the monks that we are indebted for apple-trees as well as for the introduction of so many of our culinary plants. The first orchard in Devon is recorded to have been planted by the Cistercians at Buckfastleigh. No mistletoe, strangely enough, will be found in any Devon orchard. For some unknown reason it does not grow in the county, though legends say that its absence arose from the Druids cursing Devon and forbidding their sacred plant to grow in it. A curious story is told of an orchard on the confines of Devon and Somerset, half being in each county, and only separated the one from the other by a deep ditch. Its owner has tried in vain to propagate mistletoe in the county, under Druidic ban, while it grows in almost troublesome profusion in the opposite part of the orchard.* In its absence the Devonshire apple-trees are hung with beards of white and grey *usnea*, and show many a splash of yellow lichen on their boles. Their spreading tops occasionally may be noticed compact and matted together with lichen, till the mind wonders how sun can ever pierce the entanglement. Yet in another three weeks these orchards will be gorgeously clad in pink and white clouds of beauty, the whole county being girt, as it were, with the cestus of Pomona, till a stranger doubts no longer what is the time of the year in which to see Devon to perfection. Yet autumn broods over this land with a touching and tender melancholy which enhances its red-soil tints and lends a dreamy attraction to the fruitage weighing down these old apple-trees ; and as we grow older ourselves, the beauty of Nature, just passing her prime, appeals even more powerfully to the heart than did its budding spring.

* See *Notes and Queries*, IV., vol. x., p. 495.

Hurrying along to the sea with that impetuous course which earned the river its name, meaning swiftness, the Otter gleams like a glittering serpent below us as it rushes through meadows full of red Devon oxen and Southdowns. Drayton, misled by the spelling of Otry (instead of Autrie, meaning "rapid," its ancient title), erroneously says,—

> " Otry, that her name doth of the otters take
> Abounding in her banks. "*

This rapidity of its stream greatly enhances the natural beauties of red sandstone cliffs with hanging trees and bushes which bound one side of its channel. Among the many beautiful streams of the county the Otter possesses a character of its own. Frequent diversities of scenery occur beside it, which modify its current and occasionally cause it to run in a deep, silent trough; but for the most part its shallowness, and the numerous beds of many-coloured gravel over which it passes, insure its being always attended by its own music. To the angler it offers many a nook and "stickle" full of trout, while the naturalist is delighted at the numbers of birds which everywhere haunt its banks. According to the legend, it was in this corner of England that Brute and his Trojans, when expelled by the Saxons from the interior,

> " Found refuge in their flight, where Axe and Otrey first
> Gave these poor souls to drink opprest with grevious thirst ; "†

but the Otter's chief poet is Coleridge, who very affectingly recalls it in after-life, and faithfully paints its general features,—

> " So deep imprest
> Sink the sweet scenes of childhood, that mine eyes
> I never shut amid the sunny ray ;
> But straight with all their tints thy waters rise,
> Thy crossing plank, thy marge with willows grey,
> And bedded sand that veined with various dyes

---

* *Polyolbion*, song i.   † Drayton, *ut supra.*

Gleam'd through thy bright transparence. On my way,
Visions of childhood ! oft have ye beguiled
Lone manhood's cares." *

In one of the above-mentioned red cliffs a little below
Ottery St. Mary, is a cave known as the "Pixies' Parlour." Its
situation is very pleasing, with the river murmuring below, trees
clothing the bank beside it, and streamers of ivy depending
around it in fine contrast with the ruddy sandstone. The
pixies are of course the fairies of Devon, of whom, in old days,
many a story was told, which have to be sought, now that railroads and schoolmasters have become more general, in the
pages of *Notes and Queries*. Few indeed, we should imagine,
are the mothers at the present day who place a Prayer-book
under their children's pillows as a charm to keep away these
"good folks." On this little cave and the surrounding landscape Coleridge wrote an irregular ode in which he makes the
pixies,

" With quaint music hymn the parting gleam
By lonely Otter's sleep-persuading stream ;
Or where his waves with loud, unquiet song
Dash'd o'er the rocky channel froth along ;
Or where, his silver waters smoothed to rest,
The tall trees' shadow sleeps upon his breast."

The poet's own initials, amongst a multitude of others, may
still be seen cut in the soft sandstone—"S. T. C. 1789."

One curious fact connected with the power that a swift, if not
wide, stream possesses as a barrier to stop the dissemination of
plant-life should be noticed before leaving the rich meadows
which below Ottery border the river. The Otter seems here
the natural line of demarcation between the bare chalk and
flints of the hill on which we stand, with its rich red marls
which have been swept into the valley below and the deep
black bog earth of the West Hill opposite, with it heatherclad
slopes. On the former, or east side of the river, primroses

* S. T. Coleridge, "Sonnet on the Otter."

grow everywhere in profusion, running down to the water's edge, and starring its thickets and nestling round every tree-stem; while it is only by much searching that any are to be found in the hedgerows and on the hills contiguous to it on the west. The foxglove, which there grows luxuriantly, is com-paratively rare on the East Hill, while the blue bell (or wild hyacinth), which lower down the river on the left absolutely gives the predominant hue to the meadows in spring, is seldom found on the opposite banks. An extreme sensitiveness to unkindly conditions also distinguishes the ferns in this district; they are distributed in patches, and sometimes in an elevation of thirty feet one species wholly disappears and gives place to another, to be succeeded by a third, it may be, in a hundred yards. This would be a delightful region for such a poet-naturalist as the American Thoreau to investigate. Its anomalies and characteristic beauties would have ample justice done to them by a mind so much alive to the charms of a familiar district, and so lovingly attracted to its flowers and animals.

But the pride of the day is declining, and weather is very treacherous close to the Atlantic. Already the granite peaks of Dartmoor are veiled in mists, and, while we look, from the rounded summits of the white cloud-range which rises out of that rainy district, ray-like streams course through the heaven towards us and "the useful trouble of the rain" begins in earnest. No one need wonder, seeing how often it rains here, that the ferns are so luxuriant, the foliage so abundant and deeply tinted, at a time when farmers in the Midland Counties are hailing with joy any signs of green in the grey boughs. Far overhead a couple of seagulls are wheeling in wide circles and screaming to each other, as if they scented a storm. A mighty gloom, too, falls upon the fir-trees, and that hoarse murmur, which the poets dwell on as portending bad weather, swells from their great Æolian harp. We must hurry downwards. This western climate is lovely in spring when it is wreathed in smiles ; but for good, steady, soaking rain, when it once falls in earnest, few districts in England can compare with Devonshire. And now the whole landscape is blotted out, so that garrulousness has no further excuse to dwell on its beauties. Albeit it sound ungrateful, we cannot help adding as *l'envoi*—Praise Devon, but live in Yorkshire !

In Assynt.

THE first view of Sutherlandshire is apt to be disappointing. It is often gained by the traveller along the western route in this wise. The *Clydesdale* rounds Ru Coygach to roll a good deal in the sea that sets into the Minch; but as soon as the entrance to Loch Inver is gained, the steamer is less buffeted by the fast-running swells. More especially is this the case when it leaves Sheep Island behind—a bare, oblong rock tenanted by a few of the animals which give it a name. Once in Loch Inver itself, eager eyes are directed towards the shore from the dank and dripping steamer. The cold, dark Laurentian rocks are seen edged with foam. All above is smothered in mists. It is impossible to discern anything which is forty feet above the sea-level. The Captain politely points out the quarter where Suilven should gloom against the sky, and Quinaig majestically wear her diadem of quartz, and, beyond all, Ben More raise his mighty mass. Alas! the keenest gaze cannot pierce their mist veils, and nothing can be more tantalising than the various criticisms on the rival mountains uttered by those round the visitor familiar with the view. But there the mists are, aud they impress him as at the outset of his tour he stands, his "sea-gown scarfed around him," with the conviction that no one should go to Sutherlandshire who cannot give the climate plenty of time to recover from these frequent fits of sulkiness. Like a spoilt child, even in summer Sutherland-shire hides her face, it may be for days, and then, without the least apparent motive, the mist-clouds rise, the sea brightens out against the great brown mountains, and the beholder is delighted at the change. The Highlanders themselves do not try his patience so much as the coy moods of their mountains.

But let us take a different scene. It is eleven o'clock on a balmy July night, and Loch Assynt sleeps far spread below in lustrous beauty, watched by Quinaig on one hand, like a lion couchant, and on the other flanked by dark rock walls, rounded and tufted with bushy trees every here and there, till they give way to heather on the higher altitudes. These crags culminate in Canisp and Suilven, whose massive heads peer over the nearest range of cliffs. A strange amber light diffuses itself everywhere—such a light as Poole would paint for the setting of an enchanted land, and Turner might have despaired of ever reproducing in all its copiousness of aërial transparency. The setting sun has flooded the opposite heights with a deep golden glow, which fades to rich saffron, and then to this singularly warm twilight, which is seldom or never seen away from the Northern mountains. A few black cattle and many heaps of peat speck the valley below. Every rocky shelf around is brought into vivid distinctness. The perfect stillness is almost oppressive. No swallows are found here; no swifts dart screaming overhead as they would in England. The distant rumble and screech of the locomotive is here unknown. Not a murmur from the great world invades the landscape's peace. Only a thin light hum rises and falls in the air, a gnat thirsting for your blood, for here these troublesome insects abound. Fortunately the " clegs " (or still more fell gadflies) have ceased to be aggressive at sundown. You draw out your watch; it is eleven, but quite light enough to enable a letter to be read. So you linger drinking in draughts of balmy air and mountain beauty. Their summits are now purple, while gloom gathers below, and gradually creeping upwards, displaces the purple tints with cold grey outlines. And now like ghosts of their daylight-selves the mountains stand clear-cut against a starry sky. Small wonder is it that, after several such evenings, the visitor bears away lively reminiscences of Sutherlandshire.

Thanks to the careful regulations and wise policy of the Duke, Sutherlandshire, when once reached, can offer fair accommodation to tourists, together with plentiful, if homely fare, and rooms of perfect cleanliness. To such minute matters of detail does the Duke's supervision extend, that it is a capital crime for an innkeeper to cheat or overcharge a visitor. Consequently, no one need go north with the melancholy forebodings which Boswell entertained when he dined for the first time with Johnson—"I supposed we should scarcely have knives and forks, and only some strange, uncouth, ill-drest dish." The result is sure to agree with the model biographer's experience, who found everything "in very good order." The larger holdings are mostly let on a nine-years' lease, while smaller farms are held on a yearly agreement. This enables a prompt change of tenants to be effected, should any house be troublesome for poaching. By these and similar measures keepers find their office a sinecure, so far as detecting poachers is concerned. None of those lawless midnight brawls occur which disgrace more thickly populated districts of England. A couple of keepers are enough for a stretch of land thirty miles across; and the Duke is known familiarly as the "good Duke," "the best of all the Dukes we have had." The cordiality of the relations subsisting between him and his numerous tenantry greatly adds to the pleasure of residing in his domains. Yet few tourists, pure and simple, find their way so far north. Naturalists and, above all, fishermen, form the bulk of the visitors. The talk is everywhere of "flees" and "sawmon powles;" of lochs and burns, and fishing-days and spates. The salmon-rivers are let; but all lochs and burns and rivers may be whipped by trout-fishers, with a few exceptions, which may be learnt from the different landlords of the inns. Trout appear at every meal, and salmon is so often served that the guest is involuntarily reminded of the apocryphal story of maid-servants and apprentices, who used, in the good old times in England, to covenant specially with their masters that they were not to be fed on this fish more than three days in the week. Sooth to say, of all dishes, salmon is the one which soonest palls on the appetite, whereas, when sharpened by exercise, hungry fishermen can always eat trout. This is fortunate, as the parish of Assynt possesses some three hundred lochs in its 97,000 acres, and many of them abound with trout.

The eastern side of Sutherlandshire is the scene of the Duke's experiments in clearing the moor and establishing farms. Assynt, on the opposite shore, is as great a contrast to these trim square fields as can be imagined. Rough moor and heather-tufted rock alternate with lochs, which lie under some of the wildest and most imposing mountains of Scotland. Everywhere in Assynt four of these, Suilven, Canisp, Quinaig, and Ben More, are conspicuous; that is to say, when not hidden in mists. These are the oldest mountains in the British Isles ; the three former being composed of Cambrian conglo-merate and sandstone, Quinaig being capped with silurian quartzose, while Ben More is made up of silurian quartzite and traps.* The strip of the Laurentian system on the coast is overlaid by silurian beds as the traveller advances inland, and the two result in a bare, bleak country, treeless, almost devoid of bushes, intersected by a streak of limestone, which runs up into gigantic terraces and buttresses at Stromechrubie by the back of the little hotel of Inchnadamph. These bony processes, as it were, of the country are clothed with a scanty covering of appropriate vegetation—heath and bog plants, with a few rare ferns in the sheltered recesses, down which burns flow to the lochs. It is a country which must be very much loved or very much detested. The ordinary tourist, away from the comforts of hotels and railroads, falls under the latter category. We

* Lyell's *Elements of Geology*, 2nd ed. p. 89.

have never heard that the enterprising Mr. Cook ever "person-
ally conducted" his myrmidons here, though he marshals them
at the North Cape, to see the midnight sun.   But to the artist,
the lover of nature in her sterner and grander moods, and above
all, to the naturalist and angler, Assynt is a delightful reality at
the time of visiting it, while afterwards it fades into a dreamland of stately mountains and lochs studded with water-lilies.
Thither we mentally retire when the facts of common life
obtrude themselves too much, when troubles and business, and
the hurry of daily existence, weigh down the spirits.   It is
astonishing what fine stags can often at such times be stalked
on the lonely corries which the golden eagle sweeps across from
Quinaig, where he yet lives and thrives—how we can watch him
swoop down upon the alpine hare, which, aware of the shadow
dimming the sunlight overhead, darts rapidly into his cave in
the crags, and escapes the royal bird ;—and how we can battle
successfully with monster salmon on the Inver, or catch trout of
grand weight on Loch Awe.   Thus it is that fancy compensates
for the monotony of work, and in every beautiful spot that we
visit grows the " bright golden flower " of blissful content,—

> " More med'cinal than that moly
>   That Hermes once to wise Ulysses gave,
>   Of sovran use
>   'Gainst all enchantments, mildew blast, or damp.
>   Or ghastly furies' apparition."

For this flower of simple happiness transmutes the dullest scene
into an enchanted land.   Certainly it grows abundantly, if a man
can only find it, on the bare crags of Assynt.   If any prosaic
reader desires the names of some rare plants at which he may
"peep and botanise" in Assynt, he will find them in the note.*

* *Cornus suecica, cherleria sedoides, saxifraga stellaris, luzula spicata,
arctostaphylos alpina, azalea procumbens, epipactis media, galium boreale,
dryas octopetala.* Ferns—*cistopteris fragilis, asplenium viride, pol. lonchitis,
oreopteris, lunaria,* &c.

Little has been written respecting the district of Assynt itself, but two or three books may be recommended to those who would have a general knowledge of Sutherlandshire. First must come *A History of the Earldom of Sutherland*, by Sir Robert Gordon, written in 1630, but not published until 1813. It contains a celebrated passage on the fauna of the county, but many of the creatures' names require an antiquarian to identify them. "All these forrests and schases are verie profitable for feiding of bestiall, and delectable for hunting. They are full of reid deer and roes, wulffs, foxes, wyld cates, brocks, skuyrrels, whittrets, weasels, otters, martrixes, hares, and fumarts. In these forrests and in all this province, ther is great store of partriges, pluivers, capercaleys, blackwaks, mure-fowls, heth-hens, swanes, bewters, turtle-doves, herons, dowes, steares or stirlings, lairigigh or kuag (which is a foull lyk unto a paroket, or parret, which maks place for her nest with her beck in the oak tree), duke, draig, widgeon, teale, wildgouse, ringouse, routs, whaips, shot-whaips, wookcok, larkes, sparrowes, snyps, black-burds or osills, meweis, thrushes, and all other kinds of wild foull and birds, which ar to be had in any pairt of this kingdome " (p. 3). Save the vermin in this list, the "weasels, martrixes," &c., the generality of these birds and beasts yet flourish in Assynt, though their numbers and distribution have, of course, been greatly affected by the system of preserving game. The chronicler occasionally deals in the marvellous, as when he tells us of certain forked-tail deer inhabiting a mountain called Arkill, and still more amusingly (though the air of the county deserves the compliment), "ther is not a ratt in Sutherland, and if they doe come thither in shipps from other pairts (which often happeneth), they die presentlie, how soone they doe smell the aire of that countrey, and (which is strange) their is a great store and abundance of them in Catteynes, the verie next adjacent province" (p. 7). For sea-birds and fishing, Wilson's *Voyage Round the West Coast of Scotland* is useful.

K

He was a brother of Professor Wilson, an ardent sportsman and amusing writer, and, landing occasionally on his upward voyage, found time to fish and make observations on natural history, Another book, more valuable in its day than at present, but still useful from the many acute remarks of its enthusiastic writer, is Mr. St. John's *Tour in Sutherlandshire* (2 vols. 12mo., London, 1849). The book also is somewhat of a misnomer, as only three parts of the first volume are devoted to extracts from a journal describing a ramble through Sutherlandshire ; the rest consisting of field notes, remarks on deer-stalking and fishing. Still it takes the reader back to the time when Assynt was infinitely more primitive than it now is, and it was easier to find a man who had been to the North Cape than one who knew anything of this charming district. In those days, say forty years ago, the osprey might be seen. It bred in several localities near Kylescu and Scourie, and especially Loch Assynt, where, two years before Mr. St. John wrote, it had been shot, and that by no less a sportsman than himself, though no one would guess it from his words (vol. i. p. 119) :—"At Loch Assynt on a peninsula (once an island, and now occasionally so), there are the ruins of an old castle. On the summit of the highest part of the wall is an immense pile of weather-beaten and bleached sticks, which, two years ago, formed an osprey's nest ; but unluckily this most interesting bird has been killed or driven from its picturesque and exposed dwelling-place." The fisherman yet looks up with regret to the platform on which a cartload of sticks used to form the osprey's nest, and listens to the recitals of the natives on the picturesque manner in which the ospreys used to dash into the lake in front while feeding, and then reflects with something of the feeling which prompted the celebrated exclamation, *Et tu, Brute !* that their destroyers were two of the most eminent sportsmen and naturalists of the time. To such lengths will a longing for specimens carry collectors ! And now the ornithologist's malison is said !

A curious feature of Assynt is the Loch Muloch corrie, or Gillaroo Loch, as it is sometimes called, from being tenanted by the variety of trout called gillaroo. The peculiarity of this fish consists in a thickening of the gizzard, apparent on dissection, and which is said to arise from its feeding largely on pond snails. To an ordinary eye the fish do not differ from the common trout of the country, but a gillie or experienced fisherman will at once detect the gillaroo. This loch lies high up on the limestone hills over Inchnadamph, and if a guide be not taken, can only be found by a compass. The best way is to ascend from the road by Loch Assynt up the course of the Trailigill burn, and when some two miles have been conquered, then to strike over the swelling wastes of heather to the right. The burn itself is a typical mountain stream, now leaping down a dark, narrow chasm into a deep pool edged with stunted elders, now spreading out over boulders and gravel, now brawling over rock-shelves with brilliant golden blossoms at the side and little trout glancing over the shallows, but never forgetting its mission to gain the lower ground and carry down to Loch Assynt the drainage of the hills. The heather slopes above are indented with singular cup-like hollows, supposed by some to be the site of a camp or a village, but we think that a dispassionate examination will show them to be natural features. Every here and there a lonely shealing, or a shepherd's hut, is passed. A few hens stride over the " midden " in front, where pestilential odours poison the sweet mountain air ; some cabbages in a plot, overrun with weeds and fenced in rudely with stones and hurdles, are growing on one side. On the other is a decrepit peat-shed. The cottage itself is low, of rough stone, roofed with peat and heather, fastened down with straw bands, and there are sure to be two or three bare-legged lads and lassies in front playing with a kitten. As for sanitary arrangements, there are none, but the fresh air and pure water around forbid disease. At a little distance nothing more picturesque than such a cottage can be imagined, nothing more suitable to the *genius loci*, with its thin column of blue "peat reek" ascending against the purple slope of the hill.   There are other institutions and customs of the Scotch equally fair—at a distance.   Wearily do we plunge through the heather which rises almost up to the middle in some sheltered corries, and at length discern a colley far in front.   Soon a second appears, and then their owner, a thin, spare man, clad in jacket and homespun trousers and wearing a huge "Tam o'Shanter" bonnet.   Nothing loth, both of us "foregather," turning to have a look at Assynt spread far below, and the huge tops of Canisp and Suilven peering over nearer mountains beyond. We admire his colleys, a sure way to win the shepherd's heart, and are told how they sleep with the children and have the re-mains of their porridge, and are in every respect treated with consideration as being valuable allies.   What would a shepherd's life be worth on a wild December afternoon, when the east wind carries the sleet straight into his face, had he not Donald and Wallace?   They are eminently "douce" dogs, too, and every Sabbath accompany their master to kirk in a very different frame of mind to their ordinary alert and frolicsome mood.   Is this an hereditary result of the long Gaelic sermons to which their progenitors listened?   All the shepherds and gillies here are allowed by the Duke to fish for trout—a kindly as well as a politic measure, the only restrictions being that they are not to fish a stream before a gentleman if he is seen advancing down it, nor are they permitted to fish within sight of a high-road.   The privilege is greatly valued, as may be supposed, and is the means of many a salmon being spared on the breed-ing-beds and many a callow brood of grouse being rescued from Wallace's maw.   We part with mutual good wishes and stumble upon the Gillaroo Loch, exactly where we had settled it ought to be, thanks to the compass.   Its shores are shallow, and the centre is a good deal choked with weeds, but, by leapiag from rock to boulder, we get out some way, and, letting out much line, just manage to secure one fish for a specimen. Then the sun blazes out, as it only does on these Highland hills in July, and we give up fishing as useless, making a *détour* to avoid the steeper parts of the craggy hill-side overhanging the little inn at Inchnadamph, and so down an abrupt descent leading to the burn, stumble upon Harry Malcolm, the keeper.

All who are fond of natural history and sport naturally like a chat with a keeper. No one else is brought into such familiar relations with the birds and beasts on the hill-side. The Scotch poacher is a pleasant companion owing to his enthusiasm and anecdotes. Kingsley depicts him exactly—

> " I'm aff and away to the muirs, mither, to hunt the dun deer,
>   Ranging far frae frowning faces and the douce folks here ;
>   Crawling up through burn and bracken, leaping down the screes,
>   Looking out frae crag and headland, drinking up the summer breeze."

But he has not the time requisite to make the acquaintance of the wild creatures at home. He must kill and be off with his booty, instead of lying motionless in a heather clump at early dawn, and watching at leisure the many animals which love to roam at night stealing homewards to their dens. Edward, the Banff naturalist, in his nocturnal rambles, only coincides with the conviction possessed by sportsmen and observers all over the world, that he who would see the lower animals in their most fearless and congenial moods ought to watch for them at night or early morn. Malcolm's intelligent face shaded by an old solar-topee matches his wiry and athletic form ; and both together assure a casual visitor to the kingdom of the birds, now as fairly baffled with regard to the right track as Execestides himself,* that he will readily point out the direction in which the shortest path lies, and give information on the many interesting birds and beasts of this district. Accordingly we sink into the heather and gain the following facts from our chat

---

* See Aristophanes, *The Birds*, 11.

with him :—" Eagles ? Yes, there are golden eagles now, a pair of them on Quinaig in front, but they are not often seen on this side. Sometimes, however, they sweep overhead at a great height in circling eddies, and, of course, they are on the look-out for a dead sheep or weakly lamb. The blue (or alpine) hare is also a favourite dish; their persecution has developed in this hare a need of a den for retreat, which ordinary hares never think of. Thus they seize upon any hole or cranny in the rocks around us, and, when attracted, flee into it, when they are at once safe. I have seen a golden eagle blockade one, so eager was it, but the hare would not venture into the open until the eagle somewhat reluctantly took wing. Eagles abounded much more even in 1846 when I came here as keeper. At that time it was possible to see nine in the air at once. I shot three in one day, and no less than sixteen in three weeks. Now eagles and peregrine falcons are strictly preserved by the Duke. The favourite prey of the peregrine is the grouse, and the opinion has prevailed that by striking down the last and therefore the weakest of the covey, the bird was assisting nature in exterminating or reducing to very small proportions the grouse disease. My district ? It is twenty-two miles long and some fifty miles in circumference. It was swarming with vermin when I first came. But blood-money was promised us, and the scheme was but too fatal. For every eagle we shot or trapped £1 was allowed; for every dog-fox, 10s., but for the vixen, £2; every cub (till August 12, when they were supposed to have become adult foxes), 10s.; hawks, buzzards, &c., brought in 1s. each. The grey or scaul crow was worth 1s., but the raven 2s. 6d. Have kept tame eagles, which would sit on my arm, but would never let me see them feed, as they would spread their wings and turn round as often as I sought to see what and how they eat. They could not bear dogs or strangers, and often attacked them. I came in for their anger at times, and had to kick them off in self-defence. Finally, they took to evil ways—chicken-killing and the like. I could not bear to shoot them, so set my dogs on them and drove them off to the mountains. The deer are generally feeding in the corries on the other side of Ben More at this time of the year, but you may see them coming down to Loch Assynt at times. Last summer a fine stag used to feed among the cattle evening after evening in the meadow at the head of the Loch. The herd-boys amused themselves by stalking it, and trying who could approach nearest. It was almost always seen on the Sabbath evening, but was at length shot. The badger is very scarce now, if not exterminated. I killed the last which has been seen hereabouts, and it is now stuffed in the museum at Dunrobin." And so, taking a "richt gude willie waught" with the keeper, we rise refreshed and pursue our stroll.

If anyone should wish to know more of the birds and beasts of Sutherland than these scraps, picked up during a noontide halt, he may be confidently recommended to two excellent papers on them published in the Natural History Society of Glasgow's *Transactions*, by Mr. E. R. Alston and Mr. J. Harvie Brown. From these papers it may be gathered that 115 species of birds breed in the country; but their numbers, and their abundance or scarcity in different years, present many curious problems to the ornithologist. Thus there are no blackbirds at Inchnadamph, near Assynt, though they are common some fourteen miles off at Loch Inver; instead of them we saw ring-ousels pilfering the black currants which grow in the inn-garden. The rook too is uncommon, and local in Assynt. We saw not a single swallow or marten during our stay. The wild cat is certainly not extinct on the higher crags, nor the common marten, though they escape the notice of casual observers. The curlew breeds on the moor near Loch Awe; we were attacked by the parents and a brood of five, all of whom screamed and whistled as they flew near us in a very insulted manner. The lesser black-backed gull is a positive

nuisance to the angler on Loch Assynt, from the manner in
which she swoops down upon him and abuses him in the
choicest of bird-Billingsgate. It is very pleasant to see birds
thus tame and fearless of man, and speaks volumes for the
treatment they obtain at the hands of the few natives. The
Isle of Handa on the west coast of the country forms, it is well
known, the breeding-place of thousands of gulls and such like
birds.

On the edge of Loch Assynt, the ruins of Ardvreck Castle are
very conspicuous. Sir R. Gordon, himself, a younger son of
the family of Sutherland, born in 1580, gives a good account of
the solitary incident which has rendered this ruin famous, the
capture of the great Montrose. In general, his history is weary
reading, but the episode of Montrose is a purple patch in the
dull chronicle. How would the reader enjoy page after page of
the following character? "Tormat Macloyd, Laird of Assint,
was one of the sons of Rory Moir Macloyd of the Leenes.
Tormat Macloyd of Assint had three sons : Angus (who was
called Old Angus, who travelled into France and Italie ;) John
Reawigh, who possessed the Cogigh ; and Tormat Bane, who
went to Rome with his brother Old Angus," &c. &c. David
Leslie had sent his officers, Hacket and Strachan, to capture
Montrose ; and having defeated his little band on April 27,
1650, they pursued him and the Earl of Kinnoul, who had together made their escape into Assynt. The whole of that night
and the next two days the fugitives held on, though sorely in
want of food, when (and here the chronicler shall tell his own
story, his book being exceedingly rare) "the Earl of Kinnoul,
being faint for lack of meat and not able to travel any further,
was left there among the mountains, where it was supposed he
perished. James Graham had almost famished, but that he
fortuned in this miserie to light upon a smal cottage in that
wildernesse, where he was supplied with some milk and bread.
Immediately after the fight, Captain Andro Munro did write to

Neil Mackleud, Laird of Assint, who had married his sister,
desiring him earnestlie to apprehend any that should come in
his countrie, and chiefly James Graham. The Laird of Assint
was not negligent, but sent parties everywhere. Some of them
met James Graham, accompanied only with one Major Sinclare,
ane Orknay man. The partie apprehends them both, and
brings them to Andwreck (the Laird of Assint his chief residence.) James Graham made great offers to the Laird of
Assint, if he would goe with him to Orknay, all which he refused, and did write to the leivtenant-generall. James Graham
was two nights in Skibo, and from thence he was conveyed to
Brayn, and so to Edinburgh. Being presented there before
the parlament, he was sentenced to be hanged publiclie at the
merkat crosse of Edinburgh, and to be quartered; his head to
be put above the tolbuith of Edinburgh, where his vncle (the
Earl of Gowrie) his head was formerlie placed, the year one
thousand sixth hundredth; his four quarters were appointed to
be sent to Glasco, Stirlin, Saint Johnston, and Aberdeen, there
to be hung vp; and his bodie to be buried in the Borrow-Mure,
where the most odious malefactors are vsuallie hanged and
buried: all which was dewly performed. He was executed the
twentie one day of May, one thousand six hundredth and fiftie
years. He hade bin formerlie forfalted and excommunicated.
The ministers dealt verie earnestlie with him to acknowledge
his offence, that he might be absolued from the dreadfull sent-
ence of excommunication, which he refused to doe, and so
died obstinat. He had sent a seditious declaration into Scotland the preceding winter, full of arrogance, sedition, and vain
glorie; and he hade caused printe ane historie of his proceed-
ings formerlie in Scotland, full of lies and untruths. One of
these was put vpon either of his shoulders when he was vpon
the scaffold, which were both formerlie burnt by the hand of
the hangman. Thus perished James Graham (sometime Earl
and Marquis of Montros,) when (in his own conceit) he was

at the top of his glorie; a man certainly indued with great gifts, if they had bin rightlie imployed."*

Of the many lochs in Assynt there are two which, from their beauty and the abundance of trout in them, are specially dear to fishermen. Loch Beannoch Beg is some four miles from Loch Inver village over the moorland. The walk may be enlivened by a glance at the wild duck with her young ones flapping down the shallows of the river, by putting up a little family of grouse, and collecting the characteristic plants of the locality. This Little Beannoch is a circular sheet of water surrounded by dark rocks, and full of water-lilies, which rise and fall on the mimic breezes of a summer day, and lend animation to what would otherwise be rather a dreary spot. The fish are of good size and flavour, but difficult to catch, as there is no boat, and when hooked from the side they at once make for the lilies. Here a pair of black-throated divers build regularly on an islet; the female scorns to fly away from her dusky fledgeling, but contents herself with swimming to the opposite side as the angler fishes onwards, and utters loud guttural barks at the intruder. On a rock which projects slightly above the surface, a lesser black-backed gull with her young one take their stand, in no ways alarmed at the fishermen's approach. Long may it be ere these interesting birds are destroyed or driven irom their secluded loch!

The other, or Large Loch Beannoch, is considerably larger, and contains several islands, some of which are well wooded for this county, and on the birch-trees of one of these, often at a height of not more than six feet, is a heronry. The nests are built of sticks and heather; and as there is a boat here, the ornithologist can approach and notice the ungainly attitudes of

* P. 556. Two MSS. of this chronicle are extant : one in the possession of the Duke of Sutherland, the other in the Advocates' Library. The author is described as having been "warm in his enmities and friendships," which is borne out by the above extract.

the old birds, as they alight to feed the little ones ; but their
screams are so harsh that he will soon be glad to leave them
and row elsewhere to throw his flies in peace. Rocky points,
plumed with heather, jut into deep water ; shelves of nature's
cyclopean masonry crop out unexpectedly ; blocks, grey with
lichen or warm with velvety moss, show themselves here and
there above the surface ; lilies and water-plaintains float in the
mimic bays. Forests of tall green reeds, like the papyrus, bow
before the evening breeze at one end, where the scenery is
almost tropical from the luxuriance of these water-weeds, and
the angler momentarily expects to see the dark snout of a
crocodile peering at him, or a flock of rice-birds fluttering over
the reeds, until he raises his eyes to the barren background of
mountains. Stern and impressive are they, with no clumps of
palm seen against a deep blue sky, no impervious greenery
clothing their sides ; mists shroud the farther giants, and a few
wreaths of vapour soften the faces of the nearer brotherhood.
A corbie utters his ill-omened cry over a dying sheep, or an
eagle sails overhead to its eyrie. Reassured that he is in
"Caledonia stern and wild," the poetic child resumes his fishing.

It may be that the wind rises and the mists descend in alarm-
ing showers at first, but towards evening in decided dogged
rain. With old Roderick (well known at Loch Inver village)
as his gilly, the tramp home across the spongy heather may be
much shortened if the angler judiciously leads him on to speak
of witchcraft and second-sight. Think not, O tourist ! self-
confident in the abundance of thy gold and thy powers of
banter, to unlock his "buke full of brownyis and bogilis" by a
few scoffing inquiries. The Scotch peasantry distrust all
searchers into their tales of the dark art. The belief in these
lies deep in their own hearts, under their strong sense of religious awe, and unless they meet with a sympathetic nature
they are very chary of so much as naming any northern super-

stition. The same distrust and diffidence may be seen in the feeling of the ancient Greeks towards the Eumenides and the Mysteries, and it is instictively rooted in human nature. The first night on which Roderick carried our fish from Loch Bean-noch he was impenetrable to any questioning. Though an excellent fisherman, he is the exact type of a seer, with his reverent old-world beliefs and somewhat dreamy eye. Scott might have drawn his Allan Bane from him,—

> " A grey-haired sire, whose eye, intent,
> Was on the visioned future bent."

But in the steady drizzle he replied with an amazed negative to all our inquiries whether he knew no story of witches and war-locks, whose cantrips might beguile the way. Spaewives and women who will send favourable wind, Thomas the Rhymer or Merlin, Tamlane and the Fairy Queen—had he never heard of them? "'Deed, no, sir; I did never hear tell of them," and he looked at us with a serious look, as if he expected we were not altogether "canny." In despair, we told him of village queans turning into mawkins (hares), and *vice versâ*, of profes-sors of witchcraft we had known, of pentagons and horoscopes, and all the commonplaces of the wizard's art. He only listened in awestruck silence. But he became more at home when we related how we had once met a veritable witch on Tweedside, evidently proved to be such because she was walking without being wet through a violent thunder-shower; and how, next day, a terrified hare ran under the wheels of the carriage in which we drove hard by, and was killed. It was easy to con-nect the two occurrences, and a much slighter coincidence in old days would have sufficed to condemn the poor beldame. When Roderick found out, however, that we were to be trusted, a night or two afterwards hs treated to a choice display of witch-craft, and spoke with amusing force and evident conviction, the charm of which we dispair of conveying to our readers. He began by instancing the witch of Endor (being, like all

Scotch peasants, well-read in the Scriptures); and on our re-
joining that ventriloquism might account for the words of
Samuel, and reminding him that after all Saul is not said to
have seen the prophet, he answered earnestly, "The men of
those days were very big and wild fellows ; but there is witches
about still in many places."

Finding him now inclined to be communicative, we turned
the conversation to the Mhor Venn (or Big Witch), one of the
curiosities of modern Sutherlandshire witchcraft.   One Sarah
Benn (*alias* Big Benn or Witch Benn) seems to have lived near
Cape Wrath about the beginning of this century, and to have
been renowned for her many "cantrips."   The commonest of
these was to sail in an empty eggshell to Stornoway opposite.
At length, four young men seized her, and as they could not
hang her in the ordinary way (which is said to be impossible in
the case of a witch), they, with much cruelty, passed a rope
under her own door, and putting it round her neck on the outside, pulled it from within, thus strangling her on her own
doorstep.   "I did know one of them myself," added Roderick ;
"he was called Rory McLeod, an old white-headed man, and
he lived long after her murder ; but what was very remarkable,
none of the rest came to a quiet end—some were drowned,
some killed other ways whateffer."

We ventured to interrupt, and ask whether they were ever
tried for the murder.   Roderick's recital was so singular, was
told with such earnestness of belief, and is so amusingly repug-
nant to the boasted critical accuracy of the present day, that it
is worth while (at the risk of appearing to steal Mr. Black's
style) to set it forth as closely as may be in his own words.
Still it lacks the intensity of his utterance ; and the impressive
scenery in which it was told, of course, greatly enhanced its
effect.

"Old McLeod of Girvan, in Ross-shire, you must know, was
very intimate with the witches of his time, and especially with

the mother of the Mhor Venn; but how, I did not hear whateffer. Well; he was taken very ill. He had been a soldier,
and had had a piece of one of his ears shot off in the wars with
Napoleon. He was dying before long, and was so ill that one
of the McLeods was sent over to Loch Inver to tell of his approaching death. He had a fery long walk over the hills, and
it was a fery rough night,—

> " That night a child might understand
> The deil had business on his hand."

Well, sir, at Altnoi (that is, the Long Burn), half way between
Inchnadamph and Altnagellagach, some twenty miles up this
fery road, he walked over the bridge and heard some one saying, " We'll manage ye, Donald; we'll manage ye; we'll tak'
ye." He looked, and saw two witches sitting in the middle of
the road before him, moulding an image of clay, which was all
stuck over with pins;* but, somehow or other, they could
never get the tip of the ear, which had been shot off, you know,
to stick on to their image. Donald was a fery strong man whateffer, and rushed at them, and knocked them both over. Then
he seized their image, and ran with it home to Girvan to
McLeod; for, being witches, they could not cross the running
water of the burn. He took it up to the chamber where his
master lay, and gave it to him. First they drew out one very
big pin from his heart. I mind those big pins well. He was
at once much better. Then they took out the smaller ones,
one after the other, each giving him greater relief, till at length,
on the last one being removed, he was quite well.

" About the same time, McLeod one night sent a servant to

---

* This part of the story may be compared with the bewitching of Sir
George Maxwell, in 1656, when a young girl named Janet Douglas divulged
that a certain widow kept an image of Sir George, thrust through with
pins, in a hole behind her fire. She was burnt to death. Burton says
(*Anatomy of Melancholy* i. cap. 3), " The devil's instruments are many
times worse, if it be possible, than he himself, as Erastus thinks."

Dornoch on an errand. The man rather hung back. It was a wild night, and he would have to cross the Tain, which is always a mischancy river, with many dangers round it of ford and evil things. McLeod noticed his hesitation, and roared out at him, 'Tak' the grey horse, and the deil himself will not stap ye!' He took it with sair misgivings, and rode into the darkness till he reached the ford over the Tain. In the midst of this he found his bridle seized by two witches, one on each side. Says he (for he was fery bold), 'I have been waiting to see you of this long time.' Says they, 'And we are fery welcome to see you; all you have to do is to sign your name in blood in this parchment book in the name of the devil.' Well, he did not make more ado, but took a pin and pricked himself till the blood came, and then, laying the book open on the saddle before him, was about to write, when all at once he gave the grey a slap behind with his open hand; up he sprang, far in the air, and threw down both witches into the water, and then sprang round and sped home like the wind, while the man held the book tight under his arm. He was soon at McLeod's house, as you may suppose, and gives him the book. He opens it, and, believe me, sir,"—here it is hopeless to express the mysterious tones and agitated manner of Roderick as he held up his hand, with close-set lips and staring eyes—"believe me, sir, there was the names written therein of all the richest women of Ross-shire. Yes; he had them all down there ! McLeod next proclaimed on the ensuing Sabbath, in the kirk, that if any harm were done to him or his by witches, he should know who had done it; and sure enough no harm was ever done him. He was very intimate, sure enough, with the witches.

" Now, when the young men who had murdered the Mhor Venn were seized and taken to prison, nothing could save them. Being, however, clansmen of McLeod of Girvan, Ross-shire, they managed to send a man to tell him of their plight and ask his help. McLeod's son met them outside the window of the room in which his father sate, and after hearing the story, shakes his head and says nothing can be done. His father inside saw this, and hitching up his trousers—they all wore short trousers then—came out and said, 'Yes; it can be done, and it shall be done.' Accordingly he went to the court, and there produced the image and the book, and of course they got off at once."

How we longed that Sir Walter Scott had ever met Roderick! He would certainly have been immortalized. Finding him in the vein to continue these eerie recitals, we encouraged him to tell about the mother of the Mhor Venn. "She was sent to prison, sir, after this, to Dornoch, and for a whole year she neither ate, drank, nor spoke, but remained leaning on her stick, thus—" and he came to a halt in the rain, leaning upon the landing net. "It was a great wonder. Well, when at length nobody could make her speak, a young minister said, 'I am sure I can;' so he went, and what he said I never could rightly hear, but she spoke, and the first words she said were, 'Thou hast deceived me, O devil, saying that no one born of living woman could ever make me speak!' 'Oh, no! he has not deceived you,' said the young minister, 'for my mother died just before I was born on the island in Loch Ness.' So saying, he kicked away her stick, and she fell to the ground a heap of dust."

Having duly marvelled at this story (the *dénoûement* of which will remind the reader of one of Edgar Poe's *Tales of Mystery*), we hazarded the heterodox opinion that there were no witches in the land at present.

"Ah, but there is, though!" answered Roderick, with great animation; "there is witches in the Lewes, for all that! Now, my son Roderick—my youngest son, who is twenty-one next month—was last year at the herrin' fishery at Fraserburgh. One night he went ashore, and met a strange woman and man walking. They did stop, and did ask who he was and where he did come from. "From Loch Inver," says he. "And so do we," says they (which was singular as he did never set eyes on them before). "Come with us, and we will give you a drink"—of beer, or of rum, or of whisky, or of gin, I do not rightly mind which it was whateffer. You must know, sir, that each boat, at the herrin' fishery time, takes a woman on board to cook meat and wash for them; there will be many women go to sea in this manner. Well, they did ask my son at the tavern, "Did you have good luck with the herrin' to-day?" "No; very bad." "Did you yesterday?" "No; worse again." "Ah! but," says she, "you will have to-morrow." Well, sure enough, he did fill his boat next day with fery many crans of herrin', and did get £15 for his share that one day. It was a wonderful thing. But he did tell me that gold did do him no good; he had no idea how it did get spent whateffer. That day he did go looking about after the man and woman all over, but he did never see them again; I did not hear of his ever again seeing them.

"Roderick!" I said to him when he told me, "Roderick! I do hope you will never again have anything to do with these witches." "No, father; I fill never again, so long as I do live." He is away to Fraserburgh this year again.

"I did hear of another witch in the Lewes fifteen year agone. She lived at Stornoway; and did sell winds to sailors. One of our Loch Inver boats did not get away that autumn for weeks. The wind was always dead against them. Well; they did go to her, and what they paid her I did not hear, but she gave them a black string tied with three knots, and said, "Ye'll be getting awa' to-morrow. Now, if the wind is not strong enough, lose one knot; if even then it is not enough, lose the second; but, on your life! on your life! dinna lose the third!" Well, they got off sure enough next morning with a fair breeze; and then the skipper loosed one knot. On the boat sprang, and the wind rose. Soon he loosed the second, and they tore over the

L

waves, and were very soon over the Minch near Loch Inver.
They got to the entrance of the harbour, near the new stone
house—ye ken it? on the right—and the skipper says, "We're
a'richt now; if the deil himself withstands me I will lose the
third!" He did lose it, and though so near home, the boat
only got ashore in little bits! She was altogether broken up!
The men were all saved."

The little inn at Inchnadamph now came in sight, with its
few ash-trees shining in the general outlook of water and mist.
Roderick found time, however, to tell us that the former landlord once shot a hare, on a mountain side, overhanging a little
cottage near. The animal escaped wounded; but the woman
who tenanted the cottage, Elspeth McKenzie, became ill and
took to her bed. Daily she grew worse for some months, and
Roderick had himself seen her when "very ill whateffer." At
length she died, and the woman who came to perform the
necessary offices found her legs riddled with shot, the small shot
shining yet blue in them.

With such tales will an aged gilly beguile the way for the
angler in Assynt, if the sportsman possess the art of gaining the
man's confidence. These stories were told the writer in July
last, and testify to a marvellous mass of superstition and
tradition overlaying the Gaelic mind, on which the super-
structure of religion is built almost exclusively, in outlying districts, by careful study of the Word of God. It is this Bible
reading which has given the Scottish character the steadfastness
and gravity which it has possessed since the days of the Cove-
nanters.

The mention of Altnoi burn reminds us that another kind of
witchcraft flourished there this summer, as we were wont to
cross it, in order to fish Loch Awe, attended by a stalwart
young gilly of very impressible age, and halted at times to dash
the whiskey in our flask with the sparkling streams that eddied
over the brown rocks, and caused the golden gravel at their

edge to flash like uncertain fairy gold. It was certainly an uncanny spot to Ronald. His heart had been pierced, not by
any malignant twilight beldame, but by a comely lassie with bare
ancles and loosely snooded hair, who was daily busied "hag-
ging the peat" amongst the little stacks on our right. An
artistic eye could not help noticing the flashing of those ancles
against the black heaps of peat; but we soon saw poor Ronald's
cheek change colour as he saw her—perhaps ourselves having
been winged with a kindred flame in the south country—while
the lassie was evidently pleased to draw nearer by ten yards,
and exchange (as our erstwhile lover's eye told us) the least glance
of sympathy with the blushing Ronald. It was the fairy tale of
youth and hope told over again in the sunshine of this lovely
Highland strath, and the song instantly came into our mind,—

> "At kirk or at market, whene'er ye meet me,
> Gang by me as though that ye cared na a flee ;
> But steal me a blink o' your bonnie black ee,
> Yet look as ye were na lookin' at me,
> Yet look as ye were na lookin' at me."

We trust that teetotallers will now applaud us for the virtuous
action of stopping every time we passed and, even when the
flask was dry, drinking unconscionable draughts of the cold
water in the bed of the stream, while Ronald, on the stone
bridge above, had this time (as we ascertained by Tom of
Coventry's peeping craft) to reply, with many a wave of the
hand, to the blooming damsel's salutations some hundred yards
off in the wet peat hag. How opportune must he have thought
our thirst ! May Ourania Aphrodite be propitious to us in like
need ! How easy to picture, when far away, that they are now
happily married. Ronald had a few savings we discovered, and
though the girl's father, doubtless some neighbouring shepherd,
would deprecate a hasty match (every true love ought to be
crossed at least once), she would be sure to win consolation
from her mother, if the old Border song be true,—

> " Out spak the bride's mither,
>   ' What deil needs a' this pride ?
> I had na a plack in my pouch
>   The night I was a bride ;
> My gown was linsey-woolsey,
>   And ne'er a sark ava' ;
> And ye hae ribbons and buskins,
>   Mae than ane or twa.' "

At all events, these are pleasant dreams of what is going on in Assynt in November, when inns are closed, tourists unknown, every mountain smothered in snow, and the mail-cart, that with difficulty winds along the road at their base, to deliver the few letters that in winter cheer the natives, always has a saddle under the seat, so that when the driver is stopped (as not unfrequently happens) by snow-drifts, he may mount the horse, put the bag on his saddle-bow, and abandoning the "machine" till better times, make his way, half-frozen, to the nearest clachan for shelter. So we invariably stopped at Altnoi during our sojourn in the strath, and after a decent interval, unsuspected, went on watching Ronald's lips move, and helped by Clough to interpret their sentiment :

> " *Slan leat, caleg Looach !* "

" That was the Gaelic, it seemed, for ' I bid you farewell, bonnie lassie ! ' " (*The Bothy of Tober-na-Vuolich*). And then we mischievously whistled, hoping that Ronald did not know the Lowland song—

> " Alas ! my son, you little know
> The sorrows that from wedlock flow.
> Farewell to every day of ease,
> When you have gotten a wife to please !
>   Sae bide you yet, and bide you yet,
>   Ye little ken what's to betide you yet ;
>   The half of that will gang you get,
>   If a wayward wife obtain you yet ! "

With which Sutherlandshire idyll our reminiscences of Assynt may well end.

British Birds and Bird Lovers.

EVER since the study of nature revived in this century at the close of the Great War, the observation of our native birds and their habits has possessed peculiar attractions for all quiet-minded people. No more charming recreation can be conceived, when its prosecution calls men to the varied scenery of English woodlands, to the sides of ancient rivers, the summits of the Lake mountains, or even the solitude of the wintry shore. But without going further afield than the lawn or garden, it is quite possible to develop a whole province of ornithological research, which ordinary people for the most part systematically ignore. Still further narrowing the field of view, many invalids have found an occupation congenial to their infirm energies, and just sufficiently absorbing to rouse the interest of a jaded mind, in watching the idiosyncrasies of birds allured by daily doles of food to their window-ledges. Cordial intimacies, too, have in this manner been struck up between the wise-looking jackdaws of the Bodleian Library (the modern substitutes for Athene's owls) and their unplumed fellow bipeds in the college rooms which overlook that classic haunt. Nor is it only in novels that sempstresses and clerks have learnt cheerfulness, and maintained at a higher level the flow of sympathy and tender affections, by tending a lark or canary within the still more confined space of a cage. He was a true benefactor of the human family who in the sixteenth century (as Bechstein supposes) introduced this latter bird into England from the Fortunate Isles; no computation can gauge the additional store of contentment and kindliness which thereby accrued to mankind. Apart, however, from the country and the home life of the parlour, dwellers in cities may discover many traits of bird character evoked by civilisation amongst the street pigeons and gutter-haunting sparrows. An ornithological disciple of Mr. Darwin may thus deduce much amusing lore concerning the prominence which domestication affords to the evil qualities of the latter birds, while it fosters the peacefulness, trust, and graceful tenderness peculiar to the former. Curious speculations, not dissimilar to man's interminable disquisitions on predestination and free will, must also arise among the philosophical societies of bird life when they note the facts that *passer domesticus*, always a rogue at his best, rapidly deteriorates into a smoke-begrimed impudent but self-possessed thief in our great cities, evidently from his admiring imitation of the rough ; whereas in crowded Whitechapel, amongst costermongers, dog-stealers, and the like, or on the gilded eaves of the countess's boudoir, a pigeon never forgets its innate gentility. We must not, however, lose ourselves in ornithological metaphysics.

It is easy to see several reasons which account for the popularity of ornithology as a rural recreation. In the first place it can be pursued everywhere. Even the barest common has its birds, and yet there is just sufficient diversity amongst the birds which haunt similar localities in different counties, to interest the mind and induce philosophical reflection on the causes of this variation. Indeed the number of problems which the study of birds presents is another reason why it is so generally fascinating. The mere dilettante can amuse himself in solving these, while the professed student finds many which baffle his closest scrutiny. The migrations of swallows, for instance, were until recent years beset by the same haziness which attended them in Gilbert White's mind. People, sensible enough on other points, gravely affirmed that the approach of winter drove the *hirundines* to their hibernating quarters, hollow trees or the bottoms of rivers. The claims of overlapping species, of partial migration, of the abundance or paucity of allied species in different years, of the curious changes of colour in the plumage of many shore birds without their undergoing a moult, together with that special *crux* of most departments of natural history, what constitutes a species? are specimens of the speculations to which modern ornithology addresses herself. But even more difficult and delicate enquiries remain on such points as the presence of instinct and violition in bird life. The disappearance, whether partial or total, of different species from the several provinces of Great Britain, or even altogether from our islands, forms another interesting branch of study, and others might be indicated if the extent and variety of questions which imperatively demand an answer from the scientific ornithologist had not been sufficiently demonstrated. Perhaps the being brought face to tace with nature while prosecuting these and the like inquiries, and freedom from the drudgery involved in the use of the microscope indoors, enter largely into the pleasures of the bird lover. And yet ornithology demands in the open air minute and extended observation, large powers of discrimination and comparison, and an enthusiasm which never flags at disappointment. The ornithologist might almost be weighed against the comprehensive standard of virtues required of the angler in the seventeenth century. He must be untiring and eagle-eyed, sanguine yet disinclined to believe on insufficient premises, a clever anatomist, a well-taught disciple of the inductive method, skilful at forming a hypothesis, but slow to admit its truth without the most rigorous collection of instances and testing of their agreement. Such an admirable Crichton is the scientific ornithologist of the nineteenth century, and amongst our own countrymen such men can be counted on the fingers.

We must own to a strong sympathy for another kind of ornithologist, the practical worker of the parsonage lawn or the doctor's back garden. In many a country rectory Gilbert White's charming book and innocent life furnish a pattern for their contented and cultivated owners. Every ramble through lanes smothered in honeysuckles, and along the oak-tufted uplands to the distant farm-house or knot of cottages which demand his ministrations, provides the parson with an inexhaustible fund of recreation. The creative marvels of earth and air form an appropriate study wherein he meditates, in accordance with high episcopal advice, his sermon for next Sunday ; and the key note of happiness ringing everywhere around him, pervades his meditations on Redeeming Love with admirable effect. Though his eyes take in the trout that leaps under the willow, as well as the ferns nodding above it, and the butterfly borne on over the stream with somewhat fatal daring, his bosom friends are the birds. For him the kestrel hovers over the clover field, and the sparrow-hawk dashes over its hedge, like the pirates of the Chinese seas, never visible until they make their swoop ; the magpie chatters from her thorn bush, and the jay shows her blue feathers in the sunlight. Amongst the smaller birds, too, the finches and larks, his observations are just as carefully made ; the sky-lark transports his soul above to return on her lessening wings only to admire the more the beauty and prodigality of contrivance in the landscape spreading around. In such sort did that excellent prelate Bishop Andrewes " often profess that to observe the grass, herbs, corn, trees, cattle, earth, waters, heavens, any of the creatures, and to contemplate their natures, orders, qualities, virtues, uses, &c., was even to him the greatest mirth, content, and recreation that could be, and this he held to his dying day." * And the country parson keeps diaries and meteorological entries, in a somewhat erratic manner it may be, but still in a manner to qualify him to act as arbitrator on natural phenomena at the squire's dining-table or in the columns of the *County Jupiter.* All these little interests intensify his thankfulness and content, as the meadows waving with hay become still more beautiful to him when the wood-pigeon cooes

* Life by Isaacson, his Secretary.

over them from the plantation on the hill.   " Passing rich on
forty pounds a year," the good man's days are daily soothed by
his feathered favourites, so that of all the walks in life he chiefly
doats on the Happy Valley which bounds his own guileless
activities.

Nor is it otherwise with the village doctor, so much of whose
life is necessarily passed in the saddle or on the gig's seat
visiting a widely scattered circle of patients.   He observes as
carefully as the parson, but from the bent of his mind, induced
by his peculiar occupation, he proceeds a step further, to
theorise on facts.   As might be expected, the doctrine of the
survival of the fittest is a favourite with him, and he has worked
a good deal at natural selection, beginning at the few fossil
birds which are as yet known to science.   He is not even
alarmed at " sexual dimorphism," and " divergent varieties."
The parson is more attracted by the song, he by the sight of
birds ; where the former would lie on a bank listening and
watching, his impulse, as being more pressed for time, is to
shoot the bird.   He has a fair collection of stuffed birds which
(like the late Dr. Routh's books) has gradually overflowed his
study, extended into dining-room and passages, and is now
stealing into his bedrooms.   It is noticeable, too, that whereas
the parson from conservative tendencies clings fondly to the
old Latin names wherewith birds were classed by Linnæus in
the last century, the doctor, with wider and more liberal views,
prefers a brand new nomenclature.   He professes also to be
able to read with pleasure, after a long day of visiting and perhaps five hours in bed during the last three nights, an article in
the *Ibis* which to the uninitiated resembles a catalogue of
grotesque Latin names answering to nothing that he could recognise " in the flesh."   In the same manner have we known a
musical curate avow himself enraptured by merely poring over
the score of *St. Paul* in lodgings which were too small to admit
a piano.   The contemplative but ignorant lover of birds stands

aghast at this etymological development of modern ornithology. Every one knows the chiff-chaff's gentle note. The bird used to be called *Sylvia rufa*, and a pretty name it was, bringing before the mind's eye the dainty olive-green denizen of our woodlands. Open a new ornithological work, and it is now branded as *Phylloscopus collybita*, which suggests nothing so much as Bucephalus broken to harness but a confirmed crib-biter. For the rest, our worthy doctor is one day transported into raptures by being authorised to write after his name those mystic letters M.B.O.U., which might seem to outsiders an appropriate attempt to reproduce the booming of the bittern, but which really denote Member of the British Ornithological Union.

These rustic worthies may well be placed in juxtaposition with a portrait from the busy town. Let us take a lawyer, pent up by day in the Temple and returning fagged at evening to his house in the West End. It would not be thought possible for him to find opportunities for ornithology, or even time to indulge in its study, save during the few weeks which he snatches in autumn for the grouse. But our friend is an early riser, and only those who have tried* rising with the lark know what a *rus in urbe* may be found before nine A.M. in the London parks. Thrushes feed there late and early in the day, and even build in high trees inaccessible to boys. Chaffinches, gay as in a country orchard, may be seen there, and robins; indeed the latter penetrate, especially in winter, to the squares. There are rookeries at Kensington Palace and in Holland Park. The wood-pigeon's coo floats to the ears along with the distant roar of the awakening city, from the tallest trees in Kensington

---

* How very early this must be we have often experienced. In summer the lark warbles in the skies long before dawn. Milton has not left unnoticed this habit of the lark—

> " To hear the lark begin his flight
> And singing startle the dull night,
> From his watch-tower in the skies
> Till the dappled dawn doth rise."—*L'Allegro*, 41.

Gardens and Regent's Park. In this latter locality and in Hyde Park the blackcap sings during summer. In such situations too the swallow tribe may be noticed, being banished there and to the suburbs by the smoke and noise. The starling, however, makes its nests on the top of the tall West End mansions, and occasionally a few martins will build under the eaves of such houses. All these are favourites of our lawyer. He has ascertained that the birds indigenous to London may thus be catalogued, according to the frequency of their occurring :—Sparrow, redbreast, starling, rook, thrush, blackbird, blue titmouse. During the severe weather which closed 1874, fieldfares and redwings were picked up starved to death in the great West End thoroughfares. On one day at the beginning of January, 1874, our friend observed in the Temple Gardens as the snow was melting early in the afternoon a Royston crow, two redwings, two thrushes, a blackbird, several starlings and a moorhen. This was a red-letter day to the lawyer naturalist. The enumeration of these birds will surprise those who fancy that the practical study of ornithology is impossible in London, and nothing has been said of the many summer visitants which attentive observation will discover by their notes at early morning and after the park gates are closed at night. To ascend to a higher family than any which we have hitherto touched, some years ago a pair of sparrow-hawks reared their young among the coils of rope at the feet of Nelson in Trafalgar Square, and another pair for several seasons built and reared their young between the wings of the golden dragon which formed the weathervane of Bow Church, Cheapside.* By noting these birds our lawyer relieves the monotony of business and proves conclusively that a love of nature is not incompatible with life in a great city.

In the portraits of the country clergyman and doctor, the contemplative and scientific aspects of the ornithologist have

* For many of these facts see the *Field* for January 16 and 23, 1875.

been lightly sketched; may we fill in these outlines by taking
Christopher North and Charles Waterton, respectively, for the
concrete expression of the idea? The one of these is emotional, the other logical; or (as perhaps it may be better stated),
the one was a bird lover, the other an ornithologist. Intolerably
prejudiced and egotistical was Waterton, and yet he is exact,
painstaking, and persevering. Wilson, on the other hand, with
a vast flow of animal spirits, and a fund of rhetoric which
hurries him on *monte decurrens velut amnis*, grips your hand in
his own hearty grasp, lets you into his inmost thoughts, and
spirits you away with him on eagle's wings to the lonely moor
and the plunging surf off the Stack Rocks. There he will
pour out declamation by the hour on the falcon, and freeze the
blood with his delineation of the midnight murders of the
owl amongst that " feeble folk " the field-mice; but no one can
suppose the while that he is listening to exact science. Hear
him enlarge on the raven: " The raven, it is thought, is in the
habit of living upwards of a hundred years, perhaps a couple of
centuries. Children grow into girls, girls into maidens, maidens
into wives, wives into widows, widows into old decrepit, crones,
and crones into dust; and the raven who wons at the head of
the glen is aware of all the births, baptisms, marriages, death-
beds, and funerals. Certain it is—at least men so say—that he
is aware of the death-beds and the funerals. Often does he
flap his wings against door and window of hut, when the wretch
within is in extremity, or, sitting on the heather roof, croaks
horror into the dying dream. As the funeral winds its way towards the mountain cemetery, he hovers aloft in the air, or,
swooping down nearer to the bier, precedes the corpse like a
sable saulie. While the party of friends are carousing in the
house of death, he too, scorning funeral baked-meats, croaks
hoarse hymns and dismal dirges as he is devouring the pet-lamb
of the little grandchild of the deceased. . . . Dying ravens hide
themselves from daylight in burial places among the rocks, and

are seen hobbling into their tombs, as if driven thither by a flock of fears, and crouching under a remorse that disturbs instinct, even as if it were conscience. So sings and says the Celtic superstition, muttered to us in a dream—adding that there are raven-ghosts, great black bundles of feathers, for ever in the forests, night-hunting in famine for prey, emitting a last feeble croak at the blush of the dawn, and then all at once invisible." * Poetry here thrusts science to the wall.

Contrast this striking but fanciful description with the matter-of-fact, careful, and precise observations of Waterton. Even in the case of so common a bird as the chaffinch, he takes nothing for granted, and displays the accurate eye and suggestive habits of thought of the true naturalist: " I see the chaffinch at almost every step. He is in the fruit and forest trees, and also in the lowly hawthorn; he is on the housetop, and on the ground close to your feet. You may observe him on the stack-bar and on the dunghill; on the king's highway, in the fallow field, in the meadow, in the pasture, and by the margin of the stream. His nest is a paragon of perfection. He attaches lichens to the outside of it by means of the spider's slender web. In the year 1805, when I was on a plantation in Guiana, I saw the humming-bird making use of the spider's web in its nidification, and then the thought struck me that our chaffinch might pro-bably make use of it too. On my return to Europe, I watched a chaffinch busy at its nest; it left it and flew to an old wall, took a cobweb from it, then conveyed it to its nest and inter-wove it with the lichen on the outside of it. . . . Like all its congeners, it never covers its eggs on retiring from its nest, for its young are hatched blind. The chaffinch never sings when on the wing, but it warbles incessantly on the trees and on the hedgerows, from the early part of February to the second week in July."† Every one is familiar with the chaffinch, and yet

* _Recreations_, vol. ii. p. 151. (Ed. 1868.)
† _Essays on Natural History._ First Series, 6th Ed. p. 280.

who does not learn something from this sketch? How naturally, as it were, did the hypothesis of the spider's web being used for the chaffinch's nest come into the observer's mind. There is no attempt at fine writing, but these, and a few paragraphs which we have omitted, give a fair life history of the bird.

During the hard weather which closed 1874, bird lovers grieved over many birds which met their death by starvation. When a bird dies of old age, that curious instinct which is not wholly unknown in the higher animals, warns it to retire into a spot secluded from the busy life of its fellows. It is the rarest thing to find a dead bird save during a frost. Its rigours cause the weaker birds to forget the *convenances* of happier times, and the stronger instinct of self-preservation supersedes the love of a decorus death. Our northern visitors, the fieldfares and redwings, especially the latter, succumb first to cold. Redbreasts are also speedily affected, and are found before death hopping in yards, outhouses, &c., mere bags of bones. The migratory thrushes, during the severe spell of weather in December, 1874, were driven to the abodes of men, and were even picked up dead in West End thoroughfares. Multitudes of them in their enfeebled condition are knocked down by village boys in the country, and many more shot by the prowling gunners who at such a time appear to spring up from the earth. On the Continent bird lovers are more humane. During the severe December of 1874, a society formed at Halle gave three meals a day to many hundreds of birds at twenty-two stations in the neighbourhood of the town, believing that the expense will be repaid a hundredfold by the destruction of noxious insects.

Spite of their small size, the wren and the diminutive goldcrest seem able to endure the most inclement weather. The tomtits also rejoice in it, and their merry twitterings are the only sounds which break the silence of the snow-laden pine woods. Blackbirds soon perish in severe weather, privation of food conspiring with the external cold to enfeeble them. The thrush, by dint of an occasional snail dragged out of its hibernaculum, has a better chance of life. Few people are aware what havoc a severe winter makes amongst our garden friends. "I estimated that the winter of 1854-5 destroyed four-fifths of the birds in my own grounds, and this is a tremendous destruction when we remember that ten per cent is an extraordinary severe mortality from epidemics with man* Our British birds are commonly weather-wise, and a laggard swallow left behind by his brethren only serves as the exception to prove the rule. These departing flights of birds are seldom caught by inclement weather. Before it comes they take the wings of the north wind, and, after great parade and many preludes of flight from the top of the old barn or the tallest house of the neighbourhood, disappear one evening, and next day it is speedily found that summer has fled with them. We have, however, seen occasional stragglers among the *hirundines ;* a chimney swallow, for instance, which hawked round a church during the sunny hours of noon on three days, in the middle of November, 1865, and a swift in the middle of September, 1874, but a miserable end was in store for these lingerers, unless we believe the last century's theory of their sub-aqueous hibernation. Sometimes, too, sea-birds are driven inland by severe weather which has caught them on the coast, and then they perish miserably. Thus a Fulmar petrel was killed in a turnip-field in North Lincolnshire in 1867, which was unwounded, but from the buffetings of recent severe weather was apparently unable to rise from the ground ; and in 1865 the same fate befell a red-necked grebe (*Podiceps rubricollis*) in that district, which though a distinctly marine species, was knocked on the head in a small pond inland after inclement weather. "There is a common notion that animals

* Darwin's *Origin of Species*, 1st Ed. p. 68.

are better meteorologists than men," says Lowell, "and I have little doubt that in immediate weather-wisdom they have the advantage of our sophisticated senses, though I suspect a sailor or a shepherd would be their match." And then he goes on to instance thriftlessness on the part of American birds : " I have noted but two days' difference in the coming of the song-sparrow between a very early and a very backward spring. This very year I saw the linnets at work thatching just before a snowstorm which covered the ground several inches deep for a couple of days. They struck work and left us for a while, no doubt in search of food. Birds frequently perish from sudden changes in our whimsical spring weather, of which they had no forboding. More than thirty years ago a cherry-tree, then in full bloom, near my window, was covered with humming-birds benumbed by a fall of mingled rain and snow which probably killed many of them. It should seem that their coming was dated by the height of the sun, which betrays them into unthrifty matrimony."* Probably it is owing to our more genial climate that such mischances are rare amongst English birds. Just as Thoreau said, that if he fell into a trance in the midst of his beloved woodlands, he thought he could tell by the plants in flower around him what time of the year it was within two days when he awoke, an English ornithologist would be at no loss to decide without a calendar on the day and month during early spring, if he might only note the arrival of our immigrants.

In the case of our larger birds, the enthusiastic collector will have to resort, it seems likely, in a very few years, to the dealers. Extermination is rapidly overtaking many of them. The last kite seen in Lincolnshire was shot about 1860. We have only witnessed their magnificent hoverings and great stretch of wing in South Wales. Ravens are banished to the higher mountains like, Helvellyn, and to the most inaccessible sea

* See *My Study Windows* : Essays by Lowell, p. 5. London, 1871.

cliffs.   Others, such as the snowy owl or Egyptian vulture, are
at the best of times very rare visitors, and only driven to us by
stress of weather.   The eagles, buzzards, and almost all the
larger birds of prey are rapidly seeking the furthest corners of
the land.   The chough is extinct, save in a few favoured
localities of the West.   Game-preserving and modern agricul-
ture do not harmonise with their presence.   The readiest way
of finding any of the *raptores* in the country is to seek the
nearest wood, and there snugly sheltered at the end of a dewy
"ride," across which pheasants strut and rabbits skip, and
where chequered gleams of sunshine rest upon the herbage,
stands the keeper's thatched cottage.   On a gibbet over a row
of weasels and village cats which have taken to poaching
courses, dangles another series of criminals—owls, hawks, magpies, buzzards, &c., murdered by strychnine, or shot during the
keeper's rounds, and hung up for an example to their marauding brethren, and in order that their slayer may claim blood-
money of his employer.   Many a lesson in ornithology may
be taken at such spots, as the icthyologist eagerly scans the
mackerel seines for the treasures drawn up in them from the
Devon seas after the hundreds of opaline mackerel have been
taken out, and the worthless trash, as the fishermen deem it,
flung aside.

It is incredible how high farming will change the avifauna of
a district.   A few years may indeed see a barren moorland
smiling with corn crops, but they will also banish or exter-
minate many species of birds.   Thirty years ago a district in
Lincolnshire midway between the wolds and the sea-marshes
abounded with all the commoner birds.   Jackdaws haunted the
church towers, owls hovered over the stacks, hawks sailed over
the hedgerows and startled magpies chattering underneath
them over some unhappy, soft-billed bird which had fallen into
their clutches.   Suddenly steam-threshing machines, followed
in due time by steam-ploughs, came into vogue, new-fangled

M

ideas about cutting down timber and plashing hedges to regula-
tion height took possession of the rustic minds, and the face of
the country having thus been transformed into the neatest
series of "clean" fields that can be found even in that agricultural county, the birds departed along with summer greenery
and May hawthorn blossoms.   Owing to the destruction of the
thistles, ragwort, &c., on whose seeds the goldfinch loves to
feed, this bird is now very rarely seen in the district.   As much
corn was planted, it naturally had to be "tented," so the
nearest urchin who was too lazy to go to school and too small
to drive a plough was placed amongst it armed with a rusty
fowling-piece, and strict injunctions were given him to shoot at
every feather he could see.   Consequently all the larger birds
were massacred and the smaller ones frightened out of the
district.   As their nesting coverts in the high hedges had been
cut away, there was no temptation for the latter to return.
Beyond a few flights of larks and peewits, and the saucy sparrows of the stackyards, a bird-lover may here wander through
silent fields without being gladdened by the presence of his
feathered friends.   Even sparrows are slain by hundreds in
some benighted parishes under the auspices of the local sparrow
club, or the magnates of the vestry meeting.   Doubtless such
short-sighted wisdom will bring its own punishment.   Increased
insect ravages may compel the next generation to atone their
fathers' misdeeds by importing the very birds which the latter
so ruthlessly destroyed.   In these favoured regions, however,
lie the farmers' Elysian fields—"Everything so quiet ! none o'
them noisy *buds !* small fences for 'unting, and no trees to
shade the wuts !"

Another cause which, if it has not diminished the numbers
of the commoner birds, has decimated all the rarer kinds,
springs from what in some points has conferred a great impulse
on modern ornithology.   Numerous publications on natural
history carefully register all the more uncommon birds that are

taken or observed. This practice, however, stimulates many collectors to win a doubtful immortality by shooting every strange bird they see, in the hopes that they may appear in print as the fortunate captors. Several leading ornithologists are now making a determined stand against recording the glorious fame of those who in this manner procure rare specimens, a decision which is much to be applauded. During the winter of 1874-5, for instance, vulgar avidity or misdirected zeal killed many bitterns in England, a pair of the smaller bustard, snow buntings, grey shrikes, Bohemian waxwings, rollers, and many rare kinds of ducks. How much better to have suffered the more uncommon amongst these birds daily to have drawn near to man more confidingly, and exhibited unharmed their beauty and peculiar instincts! If such birds must be shot for the sake of science, the modern plan of preserving them as skins with arsenical soap should be adopted; these skins can be kept in a drawer and examined when required without doing them the least injury, which is far preferable to having them mounted in glass cases. Apart from scientific ends, to slay a rare bird, like the rose-coloured pastor, or even an unusual one, such as the innocent kestrel, whose fare consists of mice, for the sake of keeping its grotesque mummy in a glass case, where it may minister to the vanity of its possessor, is a crime against society at large. It requires a very observant naturalist and admirable taxidermist to set up a bird with careful reference to its form and habits when alive. Every bird-stuffer does not possess the genius of Mr. Hancock, whose case of falcons must be remembered by every visitor to the Exhibition of 1851. There is not a more depressing sight to a lover of bird-life than the boxes of so-called stuffed birds which are suspended in many suburban lodgings and country inns. Shooting birds in order that they may be converted into such miserable caricatures of their original selves ought to be an offence punishable by fine and imprisonment. Few people are aware how profitably birds

may be studied by means of a binocular, and how many innocent and beautiful lives might thus be annually saved to
brighten the face of the country. No true ornithologist will
use the gun save in extreme cases.

One of the most tantalising accidents which can happen to an
ornithologist is when a rare bird is eaten by its captor through
ignorance of its value. Oftentimes this must occur in out-of-
the-way districts where all wild-fowl shot during winter are
indiscriminately called ducks, and at once consigned to the
cook. We lately heard of a case in point. The governor of
one of England's smaller dependencies invited his secretary,
an ardent ornithologist, to dinner. After the game had
been discussed, the latter casually asked a few questions
on the birds he had just eaten, and was told by the
governor that he did not know what they were, but some
of their feathers had been preserved. The poor secretary
was broken-hearted on inspecting these. He had actually
helped to eat three of Pallas's sand grouse, for which he would
willingly have given half his substance in order to add them to
his collection. The fate of rare birds is at times even more
sad than this. Dwellers in the midland counties must often
have listened with pleasure during the short nights of June to
the monotonous croaking of the landrail from the uncut hay
beyond the garden. This bird is very local, and is shot as a
dainty morsel whenever it is seen. Luckily, like Wordsworth's
cuckoo, it has the nature more of " a wandering voice " than a
bird, and for the most part easily escapes its pursuers when it
is heard in an unusual locality. The only nightingale which
we have ever known to appear in Devon was not so fortunate.
It was seen during summer 1860 in the neighbourhood of Ex-
mouth, but was pelted to death by the idle boys of the vicinity,
much as the Bacchantes of old tore Orpheus to pieces. To
know the common birds of a district and to become familiar
with their migrations, changes of plumage, the reasons of their

abundance or scarcity in particular seasons, and the like, is a more rational and satisfactory method of studying ornithology than simply to hunt after rare specimens. It does not fall to every one's lot to secure so rare a bird as once happened to a friend who was shooting along the north-west coast of Caithness. The day was bitterly cold and the snow falling fast when he winged a wild duck and suddenly beheld what seemed an animated mass of snow-flakes swoop down upon and carry it off before his eyes. The second barrel was fired and brought down a fine specimen of the snowy owl (*Surnia nyctea*) still clinging to the duck. The two were stuffed and set up together, forming an interesting *memento* of a curious episode in an ordinary day's shooting. Nor is it every ornithologist who can boast the *nonchalance* of a writer to the Signet who dwelt hard by the North Inch at Perth. His legal slumbers were disturbed one wintry night by the rush of innumerable wings overhead. Opening his window and seizing his gun he at once discharged it into the darkness above him and placidly returned to his couch. Next morning the results of his midnight sporting were seen on drawing up the blind in a wild goose, which lay dead in the little garden. One more nocturnal reminiscence must end this part of our subject. Who that has dwelt near the East Anglian seaboard can ever forget the charm of the wailing plovers as they pass to their feeding-grounds during the darkness of winter nights? This melancholy sound harmonises well with the hour and the solitude of the country. The imaginative scholar calls to mind as he hears their weird notes the thin ghosts which Homer so admirably describes wailing, as they flitted through Hades, like so many bats,—

ὡς δ' ὅτι νυκτερίδες μυχῷ ἄντρου θεσπεσίοιο
τρίζουσαι ποτέονται, ἐπεί κέ τις ἀποπέσῃσιν
ὁρμαθοῦ ἐκ πέτρης, ἀνά τ' ἀλλήλησιν ἔχονται,
ὡς αἱ τετριγυῖαι ἅμ' ἤϊσαν;

or the disembodied spirits of the Celtic immigrants of Brittany,

who were compelled, according to Procopius, to cross the straits
for interment in Cornwall, and who wailed dismally as they
made their last voyage.

All who love birds have much reason to be thankful to the
legislature for the passing of the three Bird Bills. The wanton
and continued massacres of sea-birds, especially on the Yorkshire coast, and the complaints of mariners that they thereby
lost the invaluable assistance of the seamews' screams in warning them off rocks during foggy weather, created so strong a
feeling throughout the country that the Act which establishes
a close season for seabirds during their breeding time (April 1
—Aug. 1) was passed in 1869. How well this Act has worked
in increasing both the numbers and the confidence of that
beautiful class of birds which frequent the waves must be apparent to any one who spends a summer at the seaside. The
persistent efforts of enlightened agriculturists and lovers of the
country succeeded in 1872 in obtaining a similar Bill for the
protection of the land-birds. Some seventy-nine of the birds
most commonly seen round our habitations are thus guarded
during their breeding season (March 1—Aug. 1), and although
opinions may differ upon some of the birds included and others
which are left unprotected, the Act is unquestionably of the
utmost gain to every admirer of birds and to the cause of ornithology at large. Wild fowl are now preserved during certain
fence months by a third Act. The necessity of taking out a
gun licence protects the denizens of our fields and lanes at
other seasons from many a pot-hunting gunner, and if the fair
sex would only be true to their tender instincts and refrain from
wearing skins or feathers of wild birds in their hats or on their
dress generally, as has lately been so well pointed out by the
Baroness Burdett-Coutts in her pathetic plea for the humming-
birds, the last obstacle would be removed from the free and
full enjoyment of their lives on the part of our native birds,
and a very large element of pleasure would be added to the

existence of all who inhabit the country. British ornithology is often regarded as a stationary science which occasionally rejoices over the shooting of a rare bird. To show its progressive character, one or two curious problems may be mentioned, which, it was hoped, would be solved by the last Arctic Expedition. The great auk (*Alca impennis*), though possessing in past years a fair right to be included among British birds, has been long extinct in our islands. Its existence elsewhere may even be questioned. If still inhabiting our planet it is rigorously confined to regions high up in the Arctic Circle. There is no certain English specimen of the bird now existing, although some seventy examples of it may be found in English collections, and of two or three of these there is little doubt that they were blown ashore on our coasts. It may be interesting to gather up the most recent notices of this very rare bird in our islands. Probably the last that has been seen in English waters was picked up dead near Lundy Island in 1829. Thompson* states that one was obtained on the long strand of Castle Freke (in the west of the County of Cork) in February, 1844, having been watersoaked in a storm. It is not stated whether this bird was dead. Again, the same author states he had "little doubt that two great auks were seen in Belfast Bay on September 23, 1845, by H. Bell, a wild-fowl shooter. He saw two large birds the size of great northern divers, but with much smaller wings. He imagined they might be young birds of that species until he remarked that their heads and bills were 'much more clumsy' than those of the *Colymbus glacialis*. They kept almost constantly diving, and went to an extraordinary distance each time with great rapidity." All this exactly answers to what is known of the great auk with its curious rudimentary wings. Probably one of the last eggs taken is in the collection of Canon Tristram. It was found in 1834 at Gier-fugleshier, on the south coast of Iceland. The last notice

* *Nat. Hist. of Ireland*, III. p. 239.

of it which has reached civilisation from the Arctic regions is that Mr. Hayes was told by the governor of the Danish settlement of Godhavn in Greenland that "one had recently been seen on one of the Whale-fish Islands. Two years before one had been actually captured by a native, who being very hungry and wholly ignorant of the value of the prize he had secured, proceeded at once to eat it, much to the disgust of Mr. Hansey" (the governor), "who did not learn of it until too late to come to the rescue."* This happened in 1869. The great auk seems but too surely following the wingless dodo and moa. The type is as unfitted for the present age as would be the plesiosaurus in the valley of the Thames.

From these distant speculations it is pleasant to return to the ornithologist's study, where, surrounded by the ensigns of his craft, sits our theorist,—

> " In regions mild, of calm and serene air,
> Above the smoke and stir of this dim spot
> Which men call earth."

His bookcases groan under the volumes of Yarrell, McGillivray, Gould, and a multitude more written by men like Gray or Saxby, who have devoted their lives to illustrate the bird-life of some particular British province. Binocular, microscope, and materials for taxidermy litter the table by the sunny window-seat. One pair of Royston crows, converted into feather screens, such as Egyptian mutes might wave in one of Mr. Alma Tadema's pictures, hang over the fireplace. This bird is so destructive to game, bearing in every point a character as black as its own head, that it is ruthlessly excepted from the general amnesty a true bird lover proclaims to every other bird that visits our shores. A few—very few—choice birds, excellently stuffed, occupy some glass-cases ; the bulk of the ornithologist's collection is in the form of skins, each neatly dated and labelled with mystic signs, which are as Abracadabra to the uninitiated.

* J. J. Hayes, *Land of Desolation*, p. 291.

Taking these from the drawers in which they repose, in an atmosphere fatal to moths and insect ravagers of all kinds, owl and hawk peacefully resting next the soft-billed birds on which during life they preyed, the enthusiast lovingly smooths each feathered ghost, and lays it softly down in the limbo of winged creatures which once trilled and screamed and called and swooped and dived and hovered over many a mountain and many a well-watered woodland.   In such wise might Aristotle have sat musing over the specimens his royal pupil sent him from India, or Pliny balanced the evidence for and against the credibility of Apicius's dogma that the daintiest morsel of a flamingo is its tongue.   Draw near and desire speech with the owner of this charming room.   He either speculates on the higher problems of his science whereof we have spoken, or he is at work upon some curious fact in the economy of his favourites.   Why, for instance, in nine cases out of ten, is a piece of serpent's skin* placed loosely at the bottom of the rufous warbler's nest in Algeria, a species of which two specimens have recently been obtained in Great Britain? or what impulse in certain years brings certain species of birds to well-defined portions of Great Britain, as, for example, why in the autumns of 1866 and 1869 were there extraordinary arrivals of grey phalaropes along the south-east and southern coasts?   On such questions he will enlarge with avidity, perhaps at too great length for perfect sympathy, if his companion be not bitten with the ornithological mania.   But this is only the amiable failing of all enthusiasts, and the victim can always remember betimes the warning of the Sabellian sibyl,—

> " Hunc neque dira venena nec hosticus auferet ensis
> Nec laterum dolor aut tussis nec tarda podagra ;
> Garrulus hunc quando consumet cunque ; loquaces,
> Si sapiat, vitet."

* See the singular reason brought forward in Professor Newton's *Yarrell*, I. p. 358.

After all, the study which is most to the mind of the practical ornithologist is that bounded by blue sky and purple hills. It is when face to face with birds in their own cherished localities that their lover finds truest solace and refreshment. And it is the perennial character of these charms that forms the chief recommendation of ornithology to so many lovers of the country. By day or night, at every season, in every place, its influences appeal to their votary. Does he fling down his book, tempted by the grateful evening, and saunter through his garden to the lane beyond? The chiff-chaff, the green linnet, and the redbreast twitter at his approach; blackbird and thrush-songs are pealing from the elms that skirt the pleasaunce; the meek hedge-sparrow and bustling wren thread their way through the fences at his approach; missel-thrushes are screaming themselves hoarse at a cuckoo, which has settled on a bush too near their nest in the great thorn-bush as he enters the park; wood-pigeons murmur their ancient loves across its glades; jackdaws caw round the lightning-blasted ash-tree, and from afar,—

> " E pastu decedens agmine magno
> Corvorum increpuit densis exercitus alis."

It is a typical picture of English home life, telling of im-memorial peace and haunts securely appropriated by many a generation of birds, where never prowling urchin climbs to harry nests, and keepers seldom trouble themselves to shoot, a very Avalon of bird happiness. As our student of all these blissful creatures returns home in the mellow spring twilight, he is serenaded by the nightingale and good-naturedly hooted by the brown owl for intruding on her " ancient solitary reign," in the clump of Scotch firs. How infinitely more interesting has been his walk, because he has learned to recognise and love these birds!

Or, suppose him wandering over the russet fells of Cumber-land, where the busy world, dimly descried from a rock-ledge, slumbers far below the eastern horizon, shrouded in smoke

which is traversed here and there by a flitting sunbeam—he has
no sense of solitude when alone here with his feathered friends.
The common pipit flutters in front of him, that most characteristic bird of mountain and moorland; the dottrel and the
golden plover in his summer plumage wing their way high above
their nests ; the dunlin or "plover's page," as it is sometimes
called, also in its nuptial black-belted attire, rises before him,
while the wheat-ear flirts his tail on every boulder that lies in
his path. As he gains the crest of the granite fells, a raven
slowly flaps up with gorged maw and hoarse croaks of alarm
from the carcase of a sheep below him on the broken rocks,
the buzzard floats in mid air adown the precipices, or its bolder
kinsman the little merlin dashes off the cairn which holds its
nest. When he dips down the low-lying valleys white-collared
ousels rise from the mountain side, and the curlew screams as
it hurries over the boggy reach where cotton grass waves and
many a white and yellow saxifrage blooms to charm the
botanist. In these districts the ornithologist sees another side
of bird life, the freedom and careless audacity of the mountain
birds when bringing up their young. Delighted at being thus
admitted to the domestic life of so many species generally met
in very different localities, and oblivious of hunger and fatigue,
the ornithologist, if any one, can fully enter into the varied
beauties of such a walk. The ordinarily wild birds, now com-
paratively tamed by solitude and nesting cares, harmonize with
the stag moss and other Alpine plants flowering like a crown
for the majestic mountains. Their notes of alarm do but serve
to intensify the mystic strangeness of the scene, through which
the bird lover roams delighted, as a favoured mortal might
ramble in fairy land.

Let him now descend to the valleys, to the low ground below the last tarn, where the thin sod trembles under his foot,
and tall sedges and hillocks of marsh plants diversify a wide
expanse of shallow water. Here, if it be late autumn, Virgil's

words (himself evidently no mean ornithologist) will exactly describe the scene, as Homer, the "myriad-minded man," had taught him :—

> Jam varias pelagi volucres, et quæ Asia circum
> Dulcibus in stagnis rimantur prata Caystri,
> Certatim largos humeris infundere rores ;
> Nunc caput objectare fretis, nunc currere in undas
> Et studio incassum videas gestire lavandi.—(GEORG. I. 383.)

Mr. Knox, in his delightful book on the Spey, describes a water-piece from a Scotch loch which might well form a companion picture. If the busy crowd of fen-loving birds is to be adequately depicted in English poetry, the ornithologist must go back to an authority who lived in the palmy times of the fens, to Michael Drayton. The ducks and teal he dwells upon with all the zest of an epicure :—

> "The goosander with them my goodly fens do show,
> His head an ebon black, the rest as white as snow.
> With whom the widgeon goes, the golden-eye, the smeath,
> And in old scattered pits, the flags and reeds beneath,
> The coot, bald else clean black ; that whiteness it doth bear
> Upon the forehead starred, the water-hen doth wear
> Upon her little tail, in one small feather set.
> The water-ousel next, all over black as jet,
> With various colours, black, green, blue, red, russet, white,
> Do yield the gazing eye as variable delight
> As do those sundry fowls, whose several plumes they be." *

The plough has long since made serious inroads into the heart of the Fens. These birds and their congeners now appear by twos and threes in hard winters where their progenitors mustered in flocks of thousands,—

> "Their numbers being so great, the waters covering quite,
> That rais'd, the spacious air is darkened with their flight."

Most delightful of all rambles, however, to the bird lover, from the varied beauties of running water, curving banks and

* *Polyolbion*, 25th song.

contrasts of vegetation, is a walk down the little stream which
issues from some such fen, as we have fancied—like Dart
from the wastes of Cranmere or Tweed from its parent moss—
and merrily hastens onwards past cultivated fields till it attains
the dignity of a river, and laves the abodes of men. By its
eddies Virgil must once more limn the birds with that delicate
touch which is so characteristic of him, must tell how

> " Tepidum ad solem pennas in littore pandunt
>   Dilectæ Thetidi alcyones ; "

and again, with their note of joy from the adjacent oaks :—

> " Liquidas corvi presso ter gutture voces
>   Aut quater ingeminant ; "

and depict the falcon which pursues its quarry over the reed
beds as graphically as it would have been represented by
Landseer in the sister art. The flash of their wings in the sunlight can be seen,—

> " Qua se fert Nisus ad auras,
>   Illa levem fugiens raptim secat æthera pennis."

Onward the ornithologist fares, noticing every bird as he passes,
and still unable to shake off the poet's spell when Tereus and
hapless Itys and Procne skim before his path,—

> " Nec gemere aeria cessabit turtur ab ulmo."

Classical recollections must not, however, fascinate us too
long. The curious instincts of the birds to be met on the
river's banks are sufficiently charming in themselves. Who
can forget the thrill of pleasure with which

> " Nigh upon the hour
> When the lone hern forgets her melancholy,
> Sets down his other leg, and stretching, dreams
> Of goodly supper in the distant pool," *

he has startled the bird from its reverie, and watched its heavy
flight as it dragged its legs over the placid stream till it could

---

* Tennyson, *Gareth and Lynette.*

catch the air with its wings? The common sandpiper whistles in front, the grey wagtail struts under the overhanging bank, the water-hen and coot paddle across to the opposite tangle of sedges. Auceps will here meet Piscator—Oh! that we could overhear their colloquy as each extols his craft.

Already the roar of the ocean begins to sound in our ears, and the screams of its fowl overhead wheeling round before the coming storm warn us to conclude our walk. In pursuing this fascinating study of our native birds, it should always be remembered that kindness and protection form the surest road to their hearts. It is wonderful what secrets of bird-life may be extracted by these pass-keys to their confidence. These humane virtues have given rise to a beautiful belief in the Val St. Véronique, which is not altogether unknown in Oriental and North American superstitions, that certain wise and elderly persons can enter into and understand the language of the birds. " But there is one peculiarity in the Val St. Véronique,"* says Mr. Hamerton. "He who knows the bird-language is forbidden by the popular superstition to communicate it to any one until he lies upon his death-bed, when he may teach it to one member of his family, who, of course, is bound by the same law. Now, as it generally happens that a man lying upon his death-bed has other things to think of than the transmission of bird-lore," it is not wonderful that the secret gradually becomes known to fewer men in these degenerate days. We have attempted to indicate some methods by which lovers of nature may possibly recover the lost knowledge. With birds, as with everything else, love always begets love.

* In the *Portfolio* for 1874, p. 160.

From the Heart of the Wolds.

IN spite of old Burton's remark, "Who sees not a great difference between the Wolds of Lincolnshire and the Fens?" it may be feared that much popular ignorance exists on the point. An impression prevails that there is no scenery in Lincolnshire, and that its air is unhealthy. A glance at its farmers by the covert side, when waiting for the fox to break, or its plough-boys driving their horses afield, would dispel the latter illusion. Could a townsman follow these plough-lads home, and watch their consumption of bacon and dumplings, he would simply be amazed. As for the former belief, not three miles from where we write, rises a hill which commands a wide view over a fair champaign country, in which at least twenty church-towers can be counted. Beyond it, blue sky and a warm grey sea melt into far-distant haze, while a suspicion of Yorkshire and even the fine tower of Patrington, in Holderness, meets the eye in that white bank, like a long line of cloud stretching along to the left. Ruskin and De Wint have purged our eyes, and taught us to see beauties in the flat fenland, did we care to point them out at present. Sir C. Anderson rises to eloquence at the view from the Cathedral towers, while Turner's brush, or Seymour Haden's etching needle, might have dwelt lovingly on "that very remarkable, and, in our opinion, unique view from the bank at Burton Stather, broken by tussocks of rough grass, and interspersed with old elders and picturesque thorns and whins, among which the rabbits play and springs trickle, lurking below the damp moss and tangled fern. There have we often stood and watched the steamers, the varied sails of

billy-boys and keels, on the broad streams of the Trent and
Ouse, which at this point join the broader Humber; some
wending their way to the markets of the West Riding; some
dropping down, laden with potatoes from the warping grounds,
bound for the great vorago of London; others lying helplessly
on the mud banks, waiting the coming tide. Curlews and seagulls, and, in the winter time, grey-backed crows hover over the
water. Between the two rivers is a rich alluvial delta, with the
old church of Luddington, near which is Waterton, and not far
off Amcotts, the nurseries of those ancient names. On the
Ouse, Saltmarsh, the residence of that race for many a long
year, the modern spire of Goole, the lofty tower of Howden,
the Abbey of Selby, and beyond, rising in solemn majesty, the
minster of York."* The long outlook over the wooded valley
between Benniworth and Lincoln Cathedral, on one side of the
Wolds, and the grassy, so-called "marshes," near Great Cotes
and Stallingborough, on the eastern side, with the varied play
of sun and shadow sweeping over them on a gusty day—are
two other most characteristic landscapes, which once seen are
never forgotten.

Such, then, being the æsthetical value of the Wolds, we shall
not dwell upon their agricultural capabilities, the large fields of
corn waving in the keen air of the uplands, the huge flocks of
Leicester sheep dotted over their swelling pastures—these
pictures being at present somewhat tantalising to Lincolnshire
farmers. It will be safer to turn to their physical character.
A long ridge of chalk runs down the county parallel to the
Lincoln heights, something like the "duplex spina" extending
along the back of Virgil's well-bred horse. This ridge enters
the county after dipping beneath the Humber, near Barton,
and runs in a south-eastern direction till it dies away into the
Fens near Spilsby. On the eastern side, lower terraces break
down towards the sea, also trending to the east; while, every

* Sir C. Anderson's *Lincoln Pocket Guide* (Stanford, 1880), p. 8.

here and there, minor valleys are cut through them, with
outlets leading towards the German Ocean. Some of these
vales are deep and winding, ridged with mounds—like huge
railway embankments—of almost artificial regularity ; others
possess a more level descent, with softly-rounded lips and sides,
denuded by centuries of frost and sunshine, while occasionally,
fronting the west, a jagged bank of chalk is exposed, over
which a network of ivy trails, while dwarf elders and straggling
ashes overshadow it. Large quarries have been opened, every
here and there, on the Wolds ; and few features are more
pleasing to an artistic eye than the cup-like hollow of such an
abandoned pit in autumn, with its fringe of bents waving above,
and its tufted poppies blazing against the setting sun, which
brings out the white walls in strong contrast among the surrounding greenery, while in the moonlight these pale walls and
silvered heaps of *débris* stand like ghostly fabrics, telling of
other days and other men who worked within them. The
chief want in these verdant vales is water. When the sea tore
its way through the hills in the valleys we have been describing,
and drained off towards the east, it seems to have borne with
it the fresh water as well. No rivers, it will be seen by a
glance at the map, pour through these chalk valleys ; few or no
streamlets exist ; and a fortnight's dry weather attenuates the
few which are found into silvery threads, or in such a dry
season as 1868, leaves, here and there, a few glittering pools,
like pearls which have slipped off their string. A limestone
district is always a porous country ; but, on the other hand, as
being easily pierced by the carbonic acid gas which the rain-
water it imbibes holds in solution, it forms an excellent medium
for the formation of springs. The celebrated "blow-wells" in
the district round Grimsby are familiar illustrations of this
tendency, while every here and there on the Wolds intermittent
springs, resembling the "gypsies" of Yorkshire and "lavants"
of Hants, burst out of the hill-sides. These, as being largely

N

dependent upon previous wet weather, increase or lessen the capricious flow of the streamlets. On the Wolds above Grimsby is one of these, known as Welbeck, which Denzil Holles had intended to divert to the moats of a great house projected by him in the neighbourhood. He died, however, in 1590, before he could carry out his schemes, the regularly-planted oak trees round the house's site and the still-bubbling well-head only remaining to tell the story. It was of such an intermittent spring that a farmer roundly accused his parson, who had lately come with some new ecclesiastical ideas into the parish, of being the cause that the water had not burst for many months: "'Twasn't likely it should run when thou comedst with thy Puseyism!" We have known people on their deathbeds long, after the touching fashion of David with the well of Bethlehem, for a draught from the sparkling spring of Welbeck; and no better water-cresses can be found in the country-side than those which grow in the wide basin under the spring when it does condescend to run.

The Wold, then, being the hilly as opposed to the Fen country, and having gained the name from its wild, wooded nature, we purpose to take our readers through some of its scenery. With its northern portion is associated a book so curious in itself that it deserves mention, though we shall not dare to emulate its euphuistic English. It is almost incredible that little more than fifty years ago such a magnificently-pompous style could have found favour with book-buyers. The book, which is now scarce, is by a Miss Hatfield, who seems to have been a governess, and its pages represent the fashionable superfine diction which in those benighted days of education was taught to children.* "Dear Frederick" is never suffered to hear the commonest object named in other

* "*The Terra Incognita of Lincolnshire*; with Observations, Moral, Descriptive, and Historical, in Original Letters written purposely for the Improvement of Youth, 1816."

than the finest language, and the authoress evidently thought that when she reached such unfamiliar places as Burton Stather and Alkborough, but a very little distance further lay Ultima Thule. Miss Hatfield saw white poppies in many gardens near Coleby, and was surprised "that the simple, healthy peasants' of Lincolnshire should seek the deleterious enjoyment" of their narcotic qualities, though her amazement would be increased could she have known that, at present, multitudes of men and women in the Fens purchase weekly, on market-day, sufficient opium and laudanum for the next week's consumption. She describes, in a feeble manner, some of the northern Wold villages which she had seen, as Lady A. had told her, "I know you do not wish to remain in a quiescent state." A sunset, at page 193, is positively too gorgeous to be so much as reflected in our pages ; but the description of morning must be quoted as a sample of the boarding-school diction of the period. " This morn, Aurora, with a lively step, drew aside night's sable curtains, and began to dress the chambers of the east with crimson drapery. The god of day, quickly mounting, with rapid course rolled his chariot wheels o'er ethereal space, throwing reproachful glances upon the couch of the drowsy slumberer. Awakened by his salutation as he passed my window, round which the jessamine and woodbine twining soften his too ardent rays, I started from my pillow, upon which balmy sleep had rested upon his downy pinions," &c., &c. (p. 73). These buds of fancy, had the authoress attempted to write in verse, would naturally have blossomed into such poetry as Laura Matilda's in the *Rejected Addresses.*

Although it is said to be a peculiarity of chalk hills that they never form watersheds, we shall place the reader on the best imitation of one, on a declivity towards the centre of the Wolds, near Ludford. The Bain river, which, however, is for many miles but a rivulet, runs hence, on one side of the hill, towards Horncastle and the south. A "beck," to give its Scandi-

navian name to another rivulet, breaks from the other side of
the hill about a mile away, and flows in a north-west direction
till it ultimately falls into the sea opposite Spurn Head.   Both
rivulets flow by celebrated scenes in mediæval history; both
are equally renowned for trout.   If we follow the course of the
latter, however, a sufficiently typical view of the Wold and its
villages will be obtained.   On one side of a rough fallow field
is a sudden semi-circular break in the bank.   Three slender
rivulets gush out of as many orifices in this chalky bank, almost
immediately uniting to form a limpid streamlet, and this at
once commences babbling and prattling, in child-like fashion,
over a few handfuls of gravel, and in a dozen yards or so is
again silent, feeling the impropriety, in this busy county, of
sparkling or lapsing into playfulness, and at once settling down
to the business of life.   The natives know this cradle of the
beck as Adam's Head.   For a field or two the still youthful
stream flows at its own wayward will; a few sad wildflowers
only bloom beside it, the genius of farming here not tolerating
such gauds, else it might be the beginning of one of the happier
rivulets of the western shires.   Ere long the sterner work of
life begins.   Just as the boy of nine years, on the hill-side
above, is paid a few pence a day to shout to the marauding
rooks, so at Buttermilk Springs (where a few more streamlets
from the hill-side swell the slender thread of the main stream),
the poor little beck is caught, forced to flow through an iron
pipe, and actually compelled to work a hydraulic ram.   Civilisation has seized upon its victim.   The cast-iron pipe, the
monotonous brick-work, the plunging ram in its subterranean
cave are painfully prosaic and bare.   The east wind starves all
æstheticism out of the heart of nature in these exposed valleys.
No tender undergrowth of many-coloured mosses lovingly
softens the ugliness of these staring utilities; no ladyfern droops
her nodding fronds around the little springs; no *blechnum*
nestles beneath the obtrusive pipe, or *adiantum* depends from the

brick-work.   The artist and the searcher for beauty must look
in more favoured shires for nature's wildings.   Here all is
commonplace and wind-swept; more suggestive of the newest
colony than of old Mother England.   We sigh, and the very
name of the hamlet, Kirmond-le-Mire,* accords well with our
saddened thoughts, with earth's carking cares, and the character of the locality.   Bully Hill, too, above us, sounds aggressive, minacious, repulsive.   But even here sentiment is not
wholly strangled.   Along the High Street, above Adam's
Head, runs a long detached mound, called the Giant's Grave.
After lying for generations in neglect, a neighbouring farmer
ploughed and sowed wheat upon it; but nothing came up.   Not
to be beaten, he next year planted potatoes on it; not one ever
grew.   In despair it is now abandoned to the grass and moss
with which it has for centuries been clothed by boon nature.

Passing by an old peat bog (from which a little searching
disinters the leg bone of a red deer), the beck, which is now
a respectable stream with fish in it, runs through a magnificent
stretch of meadows from the rampart like banks near Thorpe.
Abruptly turning near Stainton-le-hole, it passes by a covert and
then a rookery, with every here and there on the hills above its
course a deserted quarry filled with stunted larches and an
undergrowth of ivy; and so, having now attained, as it were,
its majority, it reaches the meadows on which stood the religious
house known as Irford.   The trout, which, together with the
retired situation, must have first tempted the founder to build
here, dart under the bank as we draw near to the heaps and
mounds over which lambs and their mothers are now peacefully
grazing, and which show where the priory stood close by the
stream.   The chapel, with the basis of pillar forming side aisles
may be traced under the turf which covers their slight elevation.
So little is known about this secluded abode of faith that it is
even disputed whether it was a Benedictine or a Præmon-

* Prob. O. N. *myrr*, our "moor."

stratensian house.   Tanner calls it the latter, and states that it
was founded by Philip de Albini in Henry II.'s reign.   It was
dedicated to the Virgin Mary, and held six or eight religious
about the time of the dissolution, when its revenues were
reckoned in gross at £14 18s. 4d.   The prioress was one
Joanna Thompson.   On July 3, 1539, she and her sister nuns
formally surrendered the house to the commissioners, and at-
tached their common seal to the document (the Virgin crowned
and bearing a sceptre, with the Holy Child upon her lap).
The legend is imperfect, and only the following letters remain :—

   . . . ORIS·ET·CONVENTVS·DE·IRF . . .*

Lingering near these forgotten mounds it is easy to see that
some parts of the neighbouring farmhouse are built of stones
belonging to the ruins, and an old woman tells us she remembers some seventy years ago that walls belonging to the
Priory were yet in existence.   Musing among the lambs, with
rooks flying overhead in the sunshine, we recall that sultry 3rd
of July, some three hundred and forty years ago, when Joanna
Thompson and her trembling nuns, while the very foundations
of their life seemed torn np, resigned revenues and lands to the
king, who so soon would grant the latter to Robert Tyrwhitt.
They looked upon the same pastoral slopes as we do ; the

* See Dugdale's *Monasticon* (1830, Caley, &c.), vol. vi. pt. 2, p. 936,
and Tanner's *Notitia Monastica* (Nasmith, 1787), No 43 (Lincolnshire).
In a footnote Tanner observes that Dugdale places Irford among Benedictine monasteries.   He himself considers that it is more likely it was a
Præmonstratensian house, because it seems to have had some dependence
upon Newhouse, which was undoubtedly Præmonstratensian, and the
seal of the Abbot of Newhouse was affixed in behalf of these nuns to a con-
vention which they made with the Dean and Chapter of Lincoln.   The
Præmonstratensian order was a reformation of St. Augustine's rule, therefore this house might easily be called "ordinis S. Augustini " in Rymer's
vol. xiv., p. 667.

ancestors of these rooks cawed overhead; the beck ran then
as it runs now, but an impassable gulf separates the grave, self-
contained religion of the last prioress (which in these seclusions
mainly spent itself on the love of God), from the impulsive,
philanthropic character of religion at present. Missions, associations, and societies innumerable now dissipate the energies
of the serious-minded. Personality everywhere rebels against
the ecclesiastical organisation which would hold all men in
captivity round a central infallibility. Material civilisation in
too many hearts tramples down the religious sentiment itself.
Even while we linger by these verdant mounds the railway
whistle from afar penetrates the quiet valley, and at once helps
us to measure the interval between the nineteenth century and
the so-called ages of faith. Joanna Thompson in her sorrow
probably indulged in previsions of the future.* Her wildest
dream could hardly compass the free, active, inquiring England
of to-day.

A mile and a-half more brings us to one of the best-wooded
villages of the Wolds. Swinhope, (the wild swine's retreat, or,
it may be, Sweyn's abode), lies in a hollow; hall, parsonage,
and church well nigh smothered in fine old ashes and oaks.
Very few beeches are seen in this district, yet the beech probably grew here before the Conquest in vast woods similar to
those which are now seen across the German Ocean in Den-
mark. St. Helen, the mother of Constantine (who himself was
born at York), and the discoverer of the true Cross, is the
patron saint of this very small church, as of several others in
the neighbourhood. This fact seems to give an approximation
to the date at which many of the original churches of these
little villages were built, before Saxon, Dane, and devouring
Northman left their destructive traces behind, in the reddened
stones still to be seen in the church walls of the district (not-
ably at Clee), which have manifestly passed through the flames.*

* She had a pension of £6 granted her after the dissolution of the Priory.

The predecessor of the present manor house at Swinhope was burnt in the civil wars of Charles I.   A double row of gnarled hawthorns in the park strikes the passer-by and reminds him that the hawthorn, though unjustly neglected by landscape gardeners, is one of the most picturesque of our native trees, especially when bent with age, and is withal one of the most beautiful of trees twice in the year; in May, when clothed in clouds of perfumed snow, and in autumn, when its intensely red haws, touched by the faint sunlight, kindle a late glory in the woodlands.   These decrepit but striking specimens of hawthorn at once call up a panorama of human life.   How many hopeful boys have birdnested in them, and rambled underneath their shade in youth's enchanted spring time, with soft arms clad in the quaint gowns and ruffles dear to our grandmothers resting on theirs.   A few years more, and then eld slowly passes by them; the old man receiving, let us hope, the happiness that came of love which blossomed into marriage, and not unable to reckon up some good works suggested and helped on by the companionship of a good wife.

> "And once, alas! nor in a distant hour,
>   Another voice shall come from yonder tower;
>   When by his children borne, and from his door,
>   Slowly departing to return no more,
>   He rests in holy earth with them that went before."
>
>   (Rogers, *Human Life.*)

A single hawthorn tree in the North which never seems to grow larger is always an enchanted tree.*

Here the beck has become an excellent trout-stream, one of the few to be found in this district of East Anglia.   It turns round to Thorganby, a hamlet rather than a village.   More weatherbeaten ashes surround the somewhat melancholy hall with its low rooms and ancient casements.   It formerly belonged to the Caldwell family, of whom an aged man and his

---

* Thorpe's *Northern Mythology*, ii. p. 275.

wife, being Royalists, were attacked by the Parliamentarians in
1643, dragged out of their house, barbarously illtreated in
Lincoln Castle, and their servant murdered.*   The flower-
garden is formal, fragrant with memories rather than blossom.
Here the Northmen's traces are again very apparent; together
with Thoresway and Thoresby, in the immediate neighbourhood, the parish bears the name of their great deity, Thor.
Still the beck flows on, to a point where the Thoresway branch
augments it after itself has passed through Croxby Pond, a
large reedy swamp-like sheet of water, tenanted by coots and
widgeon.   Here it finds itself cutting athwart a series of chalk
valleys, the even rounded tops running along as regularly as if
carved by man's spade, while the chalk protrudes and only
leaves scant room for fringes of bents and hawkweeds to cover
its nakedness.   Lower down these scarped cliffs rise into an
amphitheatre clothed with larch and spruce.   At its base the
beck runs with some rapidity, the badgers have found a congenial haunt in the retired nooks above.   The larger willow-
herb grows along the waterside in tall thickets which provide,
in late summer, the exact tint of red necessary to blend har-
moniously with the pale scheme of colour around, but are
intensely distasteful to the keen trout-fisher, as he cannot
throw his flies by them with any comfort.   Here these willow-
herbs abound, but not to any great extent elsewhere on the
beck.   They form a sample of the little differences which a
loving eye can discern at every field of its course.   Mr.
Jefferies saves us from attempting to describe willow-herbs by
his keen appreciation of their beauty.   "They are the strongest
and most prominent of all the brook plants.   At the end of
March or beginning of April the stalks appear a few inches
high, and they gradually increase in size until in July they
meet above the waist and form a thicket by the shore.   Not
till July does the flower open, so that, though they make so

* Sir C. Anderson, *ut sup.*, p. 87.

much foliage, it is months before any colour brightens it. The red flower comes at the end of a pod, and has a tiny white cross within it. It is welcome because by August so many of the earlier flowers are fading."* At the end of this amphitheatre, where stands an old windmill, the beck finds the grey weatherbeaten church but modern village of Hatcliffe, anciently Haute Cliffe, from the above-mentioned chalky ridges. Here a student of words will remark, as well in the prefix *le* of the next village, that, like English history and the language itself, the place names of England form a palimpsest, as it were ; Keltic being succeeded by Scandinavian and Teutonic words, and they in their turn replaced by Norman-French vocables. Still the wear and tear of language everywhere continues, as Cocher Plat, a hamlet not five miles hence, testifies, which is a mere corruption in the last forty years of Cottager's Plat. A few grave-stones which have been collected within the church bear the name of Lyon de Hatcliffe, the earliest family connected with the parish which can be traced. Their manorhouse stood in the adjoining field. Some grassy mounds yet mark its site, but not a stone remains upon another.

Thence the beck flows throw wide meadows to a picturesque water-mill, with abundance of angles and gables for the sketcher, till it crosses the Roman way known as the Barton Street, from its running to that little town on the Humber. It is carried hence along the first slope of the Wolds, and commands grand views over the low country and the German Ocean, while Yorkshire like a faint blue cloud is seen across the ruddy estuary named after the drowned Hun. Memory flies back on passing over the street to its first construction, when Roman legionaries compelled the wretched peasants at the spear's point to lay down chalk and the boulders still sown broadcast over this district, in conformity with the directions of Vitruvius, which have resulted in what is still a

* *Round about a Great Estate*, p. 34.

splendid road, with broad margins of short grass on each side Fifty years ago a considerable traffic passed along it ; now this is diverted to the railway in the champaign below, and has left the street so lonely that at night the belated pedestrian, in lack of fellow-mortals, may well fancy that it was here

> Saint Withold footed thrice the wold ;
> He met the night-mare, and her name told,
> Bid her alight and her troth plight,
> And aroynt thee, witch, aroynt thee ! (*King Lear*, 3, 7.)

Two villages, one on each side of the mill at the crossing of the beck over this street, merit a word.   On the left, over the chalk ridges is Beelsby, with the deplorable shell of an ancient church, and a grand view over the Humber from its yard, whence in old days the ships of the Vikings may have been beheld by a crowd of panic-stricken hinds advancing to devastations of the country.   In an adjoining field lingers one of the few legends of this prosaic district.   A treasure is supposed to be hidden in it, and at times two little men wearing red caps, something like the Irish *leprechauns*, may be seen intently digging for it.   Do not disturb them, or on nearer approach you may find but two red-headed goldfinches swinging on a thistle.   Within a secluded vale to the right, where huge ragged ashes, the characteristic trees of this district, and still more sprawling elders cling to the bare chalk cliff as they have done from time immemorial, a couple of miles from the beck, is a green knoll with what resembles the ruins of a roofless barn.   These are the sole remains of the alien Priory of Ravendale: four walls built of rough chalk and sandstone, and one jamb of the east window and the same belonging to the south door.   A large ash shelters them, and cattle graze carelessly by them ; yet round these bare walls in lieu of ivy clings the whole history of the neighbourhood.   In their very name, Ravendale, lies, like a fly in amber, a reminiscence of the Northmen who, under their celebrated raven standard, first

harried and then colonised the district.   From this glimpse of
it lit up with flames and red with blood darkness closes round
Ravendale until its name emerges in Domesday Book as forming part of the enormous possessions of Count Alan of Brittany.
In King John's reign, 1202, one of his descendants, also an
Alan, together with his wife Petronilla, became Founders of a
Præmonstratensian Abbey at Beau Port in Brittany, itself now
a similar, only more majestic ruin than   its   Lincolnshire
daughter.   To this abbey Alan gave "in pure and perpetual
alms-gift for the salvation of my soul and the souls of my
father, and mother, and wife Petronilla, all my churches in the
Soke of Waltham, together with all my vill of West Ravendale
for the clothing of its canons."   His churches in the Soke of
Waltham (a village three miles from Ravendale) were those
belonging to some seven or eight villages of this district, in-
cluding Beelsby, Hatcliffe, and Barnoldby.   The alien Priory
of Ravendale was founded by the Abbot of Beau Port in order
to look after the English property of his abbey.   The next that
is heard of it gives us a curious glimpse into the manners of
the period.   In 1333 William, the Prior of Ravendale, is found
coursing a hare in the warren of one Edmund Bacon at Beseby
(four miles away), which, however, escaped from his greyhounds.
He was summoned for the trespass and fined £10, showing that
there was a healthy spirit of litigation abroad in those days.*
With few vicissitudes this arrangement continued until 1439,
when Henry VI. granted Ravendale, with all its appurtenances,
and the advowsons of its churches to the Chapter of the
Collegiate Church of Southwell.   The Ecclesiastical Commissioners, forty years ago, unhappily dissolved that corporation,
and vesting the revenues of Southwell Church in themselves

* Compare Chaucer's Monk (*Canterbury Tales, Prologue*) :—
> " Greihoundes he hadde as swift as foul of flight,
> Of pricking and of hunting for the hare
> Was all his lust ; for no cost wolde he spare."

distributed the patronage of these Lincolnshire churches between the recently created sees of Manchester and Ripon.
One little fact, though that a characteristic one, alone connects
at present these parishes on the beck with this long train of
history. Their rectors yet pay the same annual pensions of
six and eightpence and the like to the Ecclesiastical Commissioners, which so long ago as 1380 they are recorded in the
Exchequer Rolls to have paid every year to the revenues of
Beau Port.*

A ghost story here lightens the graver matters of history.
The belated traveller may see in the winter nights a headless
man leave the ruin of the little Church of Ravendale, and walk
down into the valley. After a little he returns happy, with his
head under his arm, sits upon the ruined walls, and utters loud
cries of joy. On one occasion a labourer hard by held the gate
open for him to pass through, and—nothing happened. The
moral of which is, always be civil, even to ghosts.

In an old stained glass window of the Church of Barnoldby-
le-Beck, the next village, is some good leafage of oak-leaves and
acorns, recalling long-past years when the county was celebrated
for its oak trees.† Anthony Harwood, the parson of this parish,
was a zealous royalist in the civil wars, and was expelled from
his cure by the Earl of Manchester for absence in the King's
army to assert His Majesty's cause, for dissuading his parishioners from rebellion, and for observing the ceremonies of the
Church.‡ Fifty years ago the "Feast" of this little village was
kept up with customs which at present seems relics of prehistoric

* See Dugdale, *Monasticon* and a paper by the Precentor of Lincoln in
Ass. Architectural Reports, vol. xiv., p. 166.
† See the ballad of *Earl Douglas and the Fair Oliphant :*
  "He carried the match in his pocket
    That kindled to her the fire,
  Well set about with oaken spails
    That leaned o'er Lincolnshire."
‡ Walker's *Sufferings of the Clergy.*

barbarism, though Barnoldby on the Beck was probably no
worse herein than its neighbours. "Lasses" ran races down
the road for "gownpieces," and every "Pharson's Tuesday"
(Shrove Tuesday) cock-fighting went on in the pinfold from
morning to night, all the population sitting round it with their
feet inside, the "bairns" doing their best to get an occasional
peep. "I mind," said an old inhabitant, "a farmer's wife in
particular who used, early every Pharson's Tuesday, to put on
her red cloak and take her seat upon the wall to watch the
mains. She would cry out—I seem to hear her now—'A
guinea on the black 'un! a guinea on the black 'un!'"

The beck now enriches deep meadows and wide arable fields
with its even streams in the steady beneficent flow of manhood,
having long put away childish graces, infantile prattle, and the
music dear alike to poet or dreamer. It has cut its way through
the chalk of the wolds into the post-tertiary deposits at their
feet, which are almost level with the sea line, and are plentifully
sprinkled with the boulders of the glacial drift. Brigsley, the
first of these low-lying villages, is chiefly remarkable for the
phonetic attrition of its old Saxon name, Brigeslai, in Domesday and the Norman-French name, Brichelai, into the Northumbrian Brigsley, the bridge on the lea.* Waithe, the next parish,
contains a very curious early Norman or, it may well be, Saxon
church tower, one of a group found in this neighbourhood.
This tower is placed between the nave and chancel. There the
beck straggles onwards in great loops, each with its pool where
the fish collect and the lovely pink spikes of the amphibious
persicaria float to gladden the wandering angler's eye. It would
almost lose itself in wide meadows, running away to the horizon,
were it not for two landmarks, the well-proportioned church
tower of Tetney and afar within a forest of masts the tall water-
tower from which the hydraulic cranes of the docks at Great

* In Ashby Church close at hand is the cross-legged effigy of a Templar,
its supposed founder.

Grimsby are set in motion. Dreary and monotonous as this district would be thought by dwellers in more hilly counties, it possesses a beauty of its own which is worth searching for, and is generally beloved when found. Perhaps the quest is better rewarded when its Egeria is discovered, in proportion as the other nymphs of this wide, wind-swept expanse are coy and retiring. The young corn, the far-reaching acres of grass, the larks drowned in the blue overhead yet still warbling, the sense of freedom and vastness which these solitudes engender, endear them to their lover in Spring. Who could quarrel with Summer and her wealth of flowers in these meadows, her fringe of aquatic plants edging our beck, the water crowfoot, brooklimes, meadow-sweet, and especially the great blue water forget-me-nots, blue as the eyes of Freya or Wordsworth's Lucy, and for the same reason, because they are retired as noontide dew or violets by the mossy stone? In autumn again, the transition is pleasant, from the uplands tufted with yellow corn to these dark green fields where the birds of winter are thus early showing themselves, the curlew with scimitar-like bill and wild cries intensifying the district's melancholy, the white-tailed sandpiper, flitting in terror up and down the beck, the grey Norway crows, true successors of the Northmen, on the look-out for cruel feastings on everything young and unprotected, the black-backed gull beating up against the stiff breeze, and only too glad to join these marauders in their forays. High overhead—and these vast skies are a peculiar attraction of East Lincolnshire—a deep azure vault in summer spreads to a limitless horizon, while the grey clouds of winter are tossed and contorted over it in graceful wreaths which would delight Mr. Black or Professor Ruskin. He who is blessed with a sound pair of lungs and a catholic sense of beauty in these wide flats need not be pitied even in the teeth of such an east wind as only here in England can be felt during March and April.

Traditions of their own linger round the lonely farmhouses,

which all down the coast of Lincolnshire dot these post-tertiary flats. An Indiaman went to pieces on the sands of this one, a lady and her child only being rescued. On a stormy winter, the sea broke in upon the lands of that one, and spread far inland like a lake, killing every earthworm in the parish, and by their loss greatly injuring the fertility of the corn land. During that winter of apprehension, 1805, when a gun fired at sea by night, or two or three shots heard in the distance by day, set every dweller in the district on the alert through dread of a French invasion, all the waggons of the different farms were numbered and every hand told off, some to fill the carts with household gear, others to drive off sheep and cattle to the uplands at a moment's notice. The present generation cannot enter into the feverish state of alarm in which its ancestors along these solitary coasts then passed their time, but old men yet tell of it by the ingle nook, and a novelist might find much valuable matter amongst their anecdotes.

Many more wonders might be mentioned in this district by the sea, the blow-wells, the so-called hut circles, the method of finding plover's eggs, and the like; but the beck here creeps in premature old age with a somewhat sullen current into a little creek, known as Tetney Lock, where a shabby barge or two lingers idle, not unlike Charon's bark and the *tristi palus inamabilis unda* of the Styx, and some Hull fishermen are trying to catch eels and dace. It is not a dignified ending to the beck's life. Outside, a few old besoms are stuck up at intervals to mark the channel along a ditch leading through half a league of greasy mud. Beyond it, red waves are flashing into white, ships beating up towards Hull, a tug with its trail of smoke, a gull or two flapping over the mud. Unsavoury and commonplace as it all looks, here closes our beck's pilgrimage. At least, it is true to nature. Each stream has its own individuality; all are not romantic like the Laureate's "Brook," which runs near Somersby in this county. It is not every beck, nor every man, who makes a good end of it.   Fitly, as some may think, is a little hamlet near at hand called "World's End."

Thus finishes our ramble from the heart of the Wolds. Choosing a stream merely for the sake of a thread on which to hang our few bright beads, a walk of some twenty-five miles at most has led us from its birth to where it sluggishly creeps into the German Ocean.   It is itself a very young stream compared with others in the kingdom which have cloven through many yards of solid rock.   This *parvenu* of ours, belonging to the last great geologic formation, chalk, has merely had to eat out a shallow track through soft banks.   Not that it could not have performed more marvellous feats in this way had the structure of the country only given it an opportunity.   The river Wily, in Wilts, managed to cut its way down, upwards of eighty feet, and developed a new course for itself, while the River Driftmen and late Pleistocene animals were living in its district.*   The remarks we have made during our ramble by the footsteps of the beck may be taken as samples of the simple joys dear to a lover of country life.   A so-called dull district has purposely been chosen to show that even it is capable of furnishing him with wealth who will take the trouble necessary to dig out ore. But little has been said of the flowers of the stream ; yet the most unobservant eye must notice that a different vegetation attends each different step of even so humble a stream as this. Again, all the bird and animal life of a district is best seen by such a stream.   Weasels and stoats regularly hunt along its banks; moles, rats, and mice come day by day to drink of it, just as all the large game of South Africa may be best seen and shot at the water holes.   A few years' investigation of any of these divisions of nature by the side of such a stream will reveal much that is unexpected and interesting.   Ghosts, bogies, and the supernatural generally have utterly vanished from this commonplace district before schools and newspapers.   Even

* Dawkins, *Early Man in Britain* (Macmillan, 1880), p. 232.

O

an old lady more than ninety years old said to us, " Fairies and
shag-boys ! * lasses are often skeart at them, but I never saw
none, though I have passed many a time after dark a most
terrible spot for them on the road at Thorpe." And certainly
a whole essay would be too short to tell of the quaint colloquial-
isms of this country side ; survivals of days before " book English " became fashionable, flotsam from the Viking ships, or
merely the irregular coinage of Want and Wont. Who but a
Lincolnshire man could fetch a " stee " (ladder) ; " lig i' the
crew" (lie down in the fold yard) ; " remble " his house ; or
" skell " (turn topsy-turvy) a heavy box ? Here, too, the
" spreeding " ploughboy fed on abundance ot milk and bacon,
though he will tell you he "is only among the middlins and
not i' very good fettle inside," will take his " docky " (luncheon)
by the hedge at ten, and afterwards work two yokes till dinner.
How expressive again is the term " heart slain," of a horse that
dies under too much work, while the general roughness of North
country perceptions comes out in a favourite proverb, " a beal-
ing cow" (*i.e.*, a lowing cow) "soon forgets her calf !" Such
matters as these, which might easily be added to, lend an interest to the dullest district. Happy the man who is not above
noticing them.

> " Wisdom there, and truth,
> Not shy, as in the world, and to be won
> By slow solicitation, seize at once
> The roving thought, and fix it on themselves."†

* *I.e.* hogboys, a corruption of the Norse word *haug-bui*, the tenant of
the *haug*, how, or tomb ; a ghost or goblin. See Anderson's Introduction
to the *Orkneyinga Saga*, p. ci.
† The " Winter Walk at Noon.'

Amongst the Sea-Birds.

GREAT was the exultation on board the *Firefly* as she lay under the tall water-tower that rises with the grace of a Venetian campanile above the masts in the docks of Great Grimsby, when the master had sent word,—

> " Mak ready, mak ready, my merry men all ;
> Our guide ship sails the morn ! "

Captain Try laid aside his pipe and woke up the crew's activity; Peter, the cook and steward (who was a chattel of the master's, be ing, as it were, *navi ascriptitius*, having been rescued by him on the Atlantic, so ran the story, from a derelict laden with timber), put on the blue checked shirt which, worn outside his other clothes, formed his full dress while waiting at meals ; the other hands holystoned the deck, scraped the masts, yellow-washed the funnel, and out-vied one another in rendering the yacht presentable.   So it came to pass when we went on board the *Firefly* at luncheon time (would that we were nautical enough to translate this into the proper number of bells !) on the last day of July, she looked as well-formed and trim as a navy tender.   Her beautiful lines, broken by the crimson curtains of the saloon windows in the deck-house, could not fail to delight all lovers of naval architecture ; steam was up, and the Union Jack flying at her stern looked as impatient as the men.   The moment we stepped on board the burgee of the Vice-Commodore of the —— Yacht Club fluttered up to the main truck, and our voyage had begun.

A sailing yacht has many advantages in the way of romance,

cleanliness, and beauty to which a steam yacht can never lay
claim. In a golden age when such sublunar cares as letters,
telegrams, and business could not exist, without question a
sailing yacht would be infinitely preferable to steam ; but in
the present changeful scene, when time must be seriously taken
into consideration, and when it is absolutely necessary to be at
the office or the House on a certain day, commend us to a steam
yacht, and let it be of one hundred and thirty-four tons, with
ample saloon, state rooms, forecastle and the like, and a
glorious hurricane deck high above the smell of oil and vibration of the engines, commanding a large prospect on all
sides, and catching every wind that blows. For all these desirable points, and many more perfections which the discerning
reader will take for granted, meet in the yacht of our heart, the
Firefly. Over to Spurn is some seven miles, but we left the

> " Humber loud that keeps the Scythian's name,"

and stretched out past light-ships and buoys (for the mouth of
the Humber is a network of shoals) to the open sea. Cleethorpes, the watering-place of Mid-England and Sheffield, is
passed, and the beacon of Donna Nook is seen on the right.
The shallow seas and long expanse of sand here are fatal to
many ships in winter. Numerous gate-posts and "briggs" in the
adjoining marsh-farms are mementoes of wrecks, and curious
legends of splendid port wine rescued from sunk vessels, and
coverlids of embroidery a couple of centuries old kept in the
farm-houses, float from mouth to mouth in this district. Just
beyond lies classic ground to the imaginative, Somercotes, the
scene of the Laureate's " Locksley Hall," with its barren sands
and waste, where rabbits and rooks live in amiable contiguity
in the same burrows. Trees are not to be expected on this
bleak cost. Every one will remember

> "The sandy tracts
> And the hollow ocean-ridges roaring into cataracts,"

precisely the scenery of winter on these shallow seas. And as we are in pursuit of birds it may not be amiss to remind the reader that by slightly altering the punctuation of a line (placing the comma after moorland), in the recent editions of the poem, Mr. Tennyson has succeeded in giving a most vivid description of the curlew's flight, seen against the lowering clouds of a wintry sky,—

> "As of old, the curlews call,
> Dreary gleams about the moorland, flying over Locksley Hall."

Once outside the mouth of the Humber, the vessel suddenly becomes very lively, where tide and currents meet, and plunges and rolls for a quarter of an hour in a manner to try a lands-man's equanimity ; but the *Firefly* soon overpasses the broken water, and stretches out into the German Ocean. All this time, beyond an occasional herring gull and a distant glimpse of a great black-backed gull, the only birds we have seen are several of the graceful terns, which breed on the gravel spits round the Spurn lighthouses. The lesser and the arctic tern could be distinguished (*sterna minuta* and *arctica*) ; beautiful members of a beautiful family, whereof we have a dozen species. Their flight and mode of fishing, as they wheel round in graceful circles and then plunge down upon their prey, has earned them the name of sea-swallows, but they do not possess a tithe of the swiftness and agile grace of the swallows proper. Their delicate build and lovely plumage, however, quite compensate for this inferiority. They are occasionally seen inland, but not often, preferring the open sea and any wide extent of marshland to cultivation. After a storm we have, however, noticed them flitting up and down a brook in the centre of Notts. He must be very sea-sick, or very insensible to beauty, who does not love to watch their flight from a vessel's deck, now rising, now skimming the surface of the waves, wheeling, passing and re-passing one another in airy circles, and describing a graceful

maze like the Dædalean dance on the shield of Achilles, where
the youths and maidens—

> " At once rise, at once descend,
> With well-taught feet ; now shape in oblique ways,
> Confusedly regular, the moving maze :
> Now forth at once, too swift for sight, they spring,
> And undistinguish'd blend the flying ring." [*]

As we look on delighted, down flashes a bird on the waves
with its harsh scream and breaks up the aerial dance, while it
secures the little fish on which it feeds.   The noddy, so familiar
to us from many narratives of voyage and shipwreck, is a member of this pleasing family.   Like the beautiful Kittiwake gulls,
the terns form the light troops of nature's army of larger gulls,
cormorants, and the like, wherewith she does battle against the
impurities and super-abundant life of the ocean.

When well out of the Humber, with the Dimlington high
land on our left, the first " land-fall " usually made by vessels
bound for Hull or Grimsby, the *Firefly* bears down upon a
smack sailing out to the Dogger Bank.   A boat is dropped and
two sailors board her, returning with a pailful of whelks.   When
land and clouds are almost commingled behind us, the engines
are stopped, the *Firefly* suffered to drift, and all hands betake
themselves to fishing for cod with the whelks.   Two large
hooks, depending from a cross arm of iron heavily weighted
with lead, are let down to the bottom with a line of small rope,
and before long a very respectable cod-fish is hauled up by one
of the crew.   Let no delicate fly-fisher of the Test or Itchen
attempt this kind of sport.   Play there is none, and the fish is
dragged up as quickly as possible hand over hand.   Yet there
must be some skill required in detecting the bites of the cod
and hooking them, for the weight of the apparatus effectually
prevented any but the crew from catching these fish, and several
of them had gained experience from having served in Grimsby

---

[*] Pope's Translation, Il., xviii. 682.

fishing smacks on the Dogger Bank before they joined the *Firefly*. Nine or ten big flapping cod were thus unceremoniously dragged up, and then the roll of our craft as she drifted proving decidedly unpleasant to weak stomachs, much to the relief of some who did not yet betray themselves, the *Firefly's* steam was once more turned on, and her head directed landwards. Rain came on in violent squalls, the sky and waves assumed angry darkened lines, wind blew in strong gusts, and no one was sorry when Peter pulled his forelock and announced "tea." Alas! the faint-hearted, on descending to the cabin, found a trying state of things. The swing-table, with the teathings, was rolling suggestively backwards and forwards, the lamps around joined in the dance, dizziness speedily ensued, incapability of eating or drinking, and a rush to the upper airs. There we will leave these weak members of the crew telling their sea-sorrows to old ocean, while we, with the snug tea-table and its rolls, typing unmistakeably the ups and downs of life, take that philosophical view of existence which is so natural to those who feel themselves superior to sea-sickness, the plague of lower mortals.

On adjourning in coats and comforters to the hurricane deck for our evening stroll, the sea and sky seemed a painting *in sepia*, ragged clouds were driven before the wind, the shore was gloomy and flat, very few birds showed themselves, and a huge collier under steam ploughed her sooty way past us. Farther out a few fishing-vessels scudded along with reefed sails, and there was every prospect of a dirty night. But we were cheerful enough, and Dr. Johnson's view of a ship being a gaol with the chance of being drowned superadded, never presented itself to our mind. It is seldom realised that apart from the buccaneering spirit of the Elizabethan era, the present sentimental love of the sea, which people suppose always distinguished Englishmen, only dates from the general peace at the beginning of the century. Amongst its best

results are the numerous yacht clubs of the country. We had
left Kilnsea far behind, and were now approaching Withernsea,
which serves as a convenient watering place for Hull, much as
Cleethorpes does for Grimsby. All this coast, it is well known,
is now and has for ages been subject to continual erosion by
the sea. Shakespeare's Ravensprug has long disappeared with
many other villages. Some forty-six years ago, Kilnsea church
was washed away, and the waste is very noticeable even in a life-
time. At Bridlington we noticed that several houses, which we
remembered twenty-six or twenty-seven years ago, had disappeared from the edge of the cliff. North of Withernsea darkness fell and we steamed on till we gained Bridlington, as the
captain maintained. The lead was flung, but the soundings
hardly answered the depth of water in its bay. However,
Captain Try stoutly insisted that he knew the lights well, which
we saw glancing over the waters. It was true the harbour
lights were not lit, nor would they be for another two hours
when there was water enough for vessels to enter. So a riding
light was run up the rigging, the engines stopped, anchor let
down and an anchor watch set, while we adjourned like old
salts to the cabin; and the Vice-Commodore, to celebrate the
first night at sea, served out to all hands fine old Jamaica pine-
apple rum. After a last stroll on deck, finding the weather
improving, we sought our state-rooms, and rocked like "the
wet sea-boy, in an hour so rude," soon fell asleep.

Next morning the roll had ceased, and holy-stoning overhead having effectually routed sleep, we all found ourselves
in very airy costumes—there being no ladies aboard—on the
quarter-deck. And great was the merriment : we had fancied
ourselves at Bridlington, all, save the vice, who had his suspicions from the soundings, and lo! there was Hornsea, flat,
dark, and dull, in front of us. The sun was doing its best,
however, to struggle through the mists, and every now and
then a beam shot over the dark waves, and seemed to promise

a still further improvement. Soon we appeared at breakfast, and did ample justice to the cod-fish—cooked by Peter as appetisingly as if Carême, or his pupil, Francatelli, had been the *chef*—while the anchor was being hauled in, and the good ship once more put under steam. The clouds rolled up, a thundershower burst overhead, and the heavy plunging sea assumed indigo colours as the waves were ruffled into foam by the blast. The shore did not look cheerful, nor even picturesque, and we wondered what manner of people could spend their summer holidays at Withernsea or Hornsea. Doubtless they have their compensations undreamt of by scoffing yachtsmen. At Bridlington the grand cliff-scenery of Yorkshire commences, though the lias runs north and south here in beds much lower than those above Filly. The place itself resembles a Dutch seaport town, so quaintly is it built (of course we are alluding to the old part, with the new terraces and big hotels we have no sympathy), old, red brick houses jostling each other, and seeming, from the bay, to face every way, a bustling throng in the streets, ships with dark sails flapping idly in the harbour, irregular windows, and stone staircases outside the houses, with the sea lapping underneath them—all this swept by a few sunbeams under the dark cloud-canopy—formed a pleasant sight to artistic eyes. As for the new town, with its prim lodging-houses and long lines of regularly built mansions, we will only say that it brings out in stronger relief the charming irregularity of the quay and its environs. The natives appear to bathe largely here, if one may judge from the enormous number of machines drawn up, like regiments on parade, along the shore. Captain Try, leaning abaft the funnel, looks on them with silent contempt, and suggests that, if the weather hold up, we shall be likely "to catch some whitening" (whiting). He is a thorough old malaprop, and being once sent to a naturalist with some parasites from a sea-bird, informed him, "master's compliments, and he has sent you some Pharisees, sir." Sea-

birds now begin to fly across the *Firefly's* bows in little parties
of three or four, skimming the waves, and soon as we draw
near the magnificent cliffs of Flamborough they grow tamer,
and ride on the waves as we approach.   It is the 1st of August,
and to-day their slaughter, according to the sea-fowl Bill, may
legitimately begin.   Two of those on board want a few for
their own and their friends' collections, and are now crouching
down, gun in hand, one at the bows, the other by the stern,
watching their opportunity.   Most abundant are the guillemots
(*Uria Troile*), swimming very low in the water, and dipping up
and down iu the swells, with their brownish dark plumage rendered more conspicuous as they rise by the pure white of their
breasts.   Generally speaking, not having been disturbed of late,
they do not take the trouble to fly, but fix their sparkling
timorous eyes on us until, a sudden access of terror coming
over them, down go their sharp black bills, and they dive, to
reappear fifty yards further from the yacht.   Constantly we see
them floating thus on each side of us in little family parties of
seven or eight.   Enormous numbers haunt the sea off the
headland here, and roost or breed on the ledges of its chalk.
Their solitary egg is laid on the rock-shelf without any attempt
at making a nest, and the bird incubates in an erect position,
like the attitude in which the great auk is depicted.   So little
is its dread of man at that time, or, indeed, at any time, that
it has earned the sobriquet of "Foolish Guillemot" thereby.
Besides two rarer species, another is common in Scotland with
black plumage and patches of white, and red legs, whereas our
bird has dusky legs like his neck and back.   Little parties of
gulls and kittiwakes, containing perhaps fifty birds, scream
and wheel around our track and in front : herring gulls, the
common gulls, lesser black-backed, and others apparently of
different kinds, but more probably the same in different stages
of plumage (for no family of birds changes its plumage in so
marked a manner as do the gulls, and no one but a professed

ornithologist can, in consequence, detect the birds' ages or sexes), fly on either side, and amongst them wheel, in a very shy manner, some black birds with swift-clipping wing, pronounced to be Manx shearwaters (*Puffinus Anglorum*) by the sportsmen. Together with his larger relative, the greater shearwater (*P. major*), this is considered a desirable bird from its rarity, and the *Firefly* is turned towards first one and then another of the friendly parties of gulls in which they are discerned. These rise as we get within a hundred yards of them, in a noisy desultory manner, but the shearwaters, with characteristic caution, dash off sea-wards at once, their long clipping wings opening and closing like a pair of scissors, speedily putting them out of our reach. On nearing the Head, little households of puffins (*Fratercula Artica*) meet us swimming round the *Firefly*. They do not seem to go far from home, and look as comical while swimming with their black collar and coloured bill, as when sitting in their absurd fashion so gravely on the rock-ledges. But as we laugh down they too go, for they are splendid divers, but fly in an awkward manner, getting under weigh by splashing along the top of the water for several yards with a hasty fluttering which reminds the looker-on of a family of rats scuttling away when disturbed by a terrier. These birds only remain the summer with us. Amongst the crowds of different birds which scream and dive and swim and fly round the yacht, every now and then a gannet may be seen, having probably wandered thus far down from the Bass Rock. Its size renders it very conspicuous, to say nothing of its milk-white plumage and long bill. Then a little band of petrels skims by, or a flock of jackdaws flies up and down by the cliffs, cawing with rage at our venturing so near their domains. It is curious to see how completely these clerical birds secularise themselves when they quit the church towers. Here they are as noisy as gulls, and fly about with a great loss of dignity. We look upon their antics with wonder, and this unaccustomed laying aside of their

gravity is as amazing as it would be to see the Upper House of
Convocation playing in a cricket match while wearing their
episcopal aprons. Especially numerous around us, as they
rock on the waves, are the razor-bills (*Alca torda*). Their mode
of swimming and diving much resembles that of the guillemot,
and in shape and plumage they are much like the bird, but
even the most careless of observers would at once distinguish
them by their curious black bill, with its three or four transverse
flutings, of which the middle one is white.

All these birds in vast numbers, as we approached the headland, screamed and clanged and flew under the windy walls, or
swam and dived and fluttered over, around, and beside us, with
a bewildering frequency and uproar. The sun came out, and
the waves sparkled and dashed in white curls of foam on the
little beach strewn with huge fragments of chalk, and a more
enlivening scene could hardly be found. We might have been
Pisthetærus seeking his fortune in the kingdom of birds.
Certainly the citizens of King Epops were responding to his
call,—

        " Hoop ! hoop !
        Come in a troop,
        Come at a call,
        One and all,
        Birds of a feather
        All together ;
        Birds of a humble gentle bill,
        Smooth and shrill,
        Dieted on seeds and grain,
        Rioting on the furrowed plain,
        Pecking, hopping,
        Picking, hopping ! "*

All this time but a couple of guillemots have fallen to the
sportsmen's guns, so it is determined to lower a boat and let
one of them be rowed towards the cliffs, while the *Firefly* is

* Right Hon. J. H. Frere's Translation of Aristophane's *Aves*. Pickering, 1840

allowed to drift with the tide. The birds still retreat before the gig and seek the cliffs evidently, as of old, remembering the chorus,—

> " Since time began,
> The race of men
> Has ever been deceitful, faithless ever. *

Meanwhile we rig out lines for whiting, and take a good look at the fine headland of chalk as we are borne past it on the tide. It was a fine sight on an autumnal morning, two or three years before, to stand at its verge, and, looking out upon the impervious mist, all at once see the seething volumes part and disclose a ghost-like procession of thirty colliers and traders silently streaming onwards almost under our feet, so closely did they hug the Head. And then the mist curtain came together once more, and even blotted out the sea below, though ever and anon we could hear

> " The blind old ocean maundering,
> Raking the shingle to and fro,
> Aimlessly clutching and letting go
> The kelp-haired sedges,
> Slipping down with a sleeping forgetting."†

As is generally the case, however, the view of the great bluff's wrinkled and storm-beaten face from the sea is immeasurably grander. The chalk is streaked with these darker furrows, which seem to soften its stern expression ; and, as a stray sun-beam flits across it, the contrast between its whiteness and the heaving dark swells below appears to light it up with something of a sentient smile, though in all conscience on a November night during an on-shore gale it is a grim step-mother to ships ! Then we have seen the gleaming, smoking crests of the waver-ing masses of water hurl themselves far up the rock-walls, till their tops were torn off by the wind and sent flying in foam

---

* Right Hon. J. H. Frere's Translation of Aristophane's *Aves*. Pickering, 1840.
† Lowell's Poems—ed 1873, p. 393.

over the fields behind, while the vast weight of water fell back with a din like thunder, and was struck by the next incoming surge, when both leapt up and roared and broke once more into maddened sheets of spray. That is a sight never to be forgotten. But now we float placidly along in deep water only a few hundred yards from the Head, and note the ruins of the old fire-beacon (for the place has for centuries earned its name of Flameborough), and then the lighthouse with its neat white cottages below. It is 80 feet high, and stands 250 feet above the sea. Its revolving lights had cheered us last evening off Hornsea, and are nightly blessed by many a ship, for immediately off it lies the Smithwick sand which at low tide is only just covered with water. We see the buoy tossing on our left, and large ships, which do not take the inner channel as we are doing, are careful to give it a wide berth, standing well out when they have rounded the Head.

And now we drift past the end of the Dane's Dyke, and here are two fantastic columns of chalk, called the King and Queen, standing out from the cliffs and showing how, together with the large caves which are also visible below, the sea gradually saps this natural fortress, as it is doing, only at a quicker rate, all along the Yorkshire coast. And here is Thornwick, a natural opening or *wick*, in the chalk-walls which forms a capital shelter for the fishing boats of the village of Flamborough. Itself lies some way at the back of the cliffs. We have lost sight now of the great cliffs to the north, near Whitby, and of Scarborough Castle, standing out so boldly against the sky, the Headland intervening, while a few shots and clouds of frightened birds, rock-pigeons, daws, gulls, and the like tell that our friend is finding the game he desires. Presently he comes off, with nothing much, however, to show; a kittiwake in immature plumage with a brown head, instead of the pure white it would have attained when a year had passed, a puffin, and some razor-bills form his bag. He reports that no rare birds are to be seen to-day, but any number of those we have already been sailing amongst. They sit overhead in long lines, apparently absorbed in thought, scarcely caring to fly even when fired at, as the old Roman senators were found sitting in native dignity when the Gauls broke into the Senate House and literally bearded their august department and silent majesty. The birds are soon slung by Captain Try on a spar at the stern of the *Firefly*, and as they hang head downwards in all the freshness of their unsullied plumage, we could not help wishing for Hook to portray their slender forms and pure tints in a sea-piece worthy of their beauty. How wooden and un-natural will they look when set up, even by the most cun-ning of taxidermists, compared with the flexibility and grace of their deathful charms at present. Before the Sea-Bird Protection Bill was passed, scenes of sickening butchery were of daily occurrence here in summer; especially at the breeding season, when the birds are tamer than at other times. Artisans and tavern keepers from the inland large towns used to hire boats and go out, often in a drunken state, shooting at everything that flew near them, frequently to the dread and peril of the boatmen themselves. Multi-tudes of the poor victims were never picked up, and their death too often meant the destruction by starvation of their broods on the cliffs.

Besides their innocence and beauty, and their use as sea-scavengers, the birds of Flamborough are of positive advantage to sailors during a fog. They hear their windy screaming and wrangling on the cliffs, and keep well off the rocks. This aspect of the bird's usefulness was finely described by the Rev. Richard Wilton in his poem on the "Flamborough Pilots" at the time of the agitation for the Bill. We had been eager pro-moters of the Bill, and were certainly amply repaid by the sight we saw to-day, the increased number of birds sporting, feeding, and clanging, like the wish-hounds of Dartmoor in full cry, around us: Needless to say, not one more was shot than was necessary for the collections.

No whiting were caught, but the grey gurnard bit briskly, and we took ninety-seven while the boat was absent. This fish is amongst the few British fish which can emit a groan or sigh on being pulled out of the water, hence it is known in Scotland as the " crooner," and its brother the red gurnard is aptly named by science *trigla cuculus*. The skilful manner in which the seamen in a trice exenterated, skinned, and beheaded these fish was very striking. They were supposed to be dead before this process was commenced ; but as the ninety-seven were by captain Try's order laid out in the sunshine, like so many sticks of celery, muscular motion, *horrendum dictu*, still existed amongst the trunks in a manner which opened up many avenues of serious thoughts, leading from this borderland of sensation up to the very Fountain of Life. Our speculations, like those of many much more renowned naturalists, needless to say, soon lost themselves in the outer darkness which surrounds this mystery. And then we adjourned to tea and eat the unfortunate gurnards with much satisfaction on which we had been philosophising.

The shooting party having returned, and a brisk breeze springing up, fishing tackle was hauled in, and the word passed to steam homewards under all sail. Then, indeed, the sailors were proud of their craft; and we had an opportunity of seeing how each hand knew his own work, and was forward in doing it. It was like the heroes of old setting sail, such activity prevailed.

> Nauticus exoritur vario certamine clamor.

The casings were taken off the trim spars, the sails hauled up from the forecastle and run aloft in a twinkling, and then the good ship *Firefly* staggered along through a stiff tideway under steam and sail, raising at her clear-cut bows what yachtsmen know as " a very pretty feather." Everyone had

found his appetite, and when Peter announced dinner, great
was the consumption of roast beef and puddings, albeit the
latter was an inch and a-half thick, and yellow enough to have
terrified a robust landsman who had never known dyspepsia.
At sea, with the old Greek "ox-hunger" upon one, such trifles
are never considered, and all viands taste equally excellent.
On the horizon we now saw a good example of sea mirage, the
distant vessels seeming much larger and looming distorted in
the haze.   The phenomenon is not unknown in the fens, where
the vast flats lend themselves to such optical illusions as readily
as the wide sea horizon.   Next we pass several dandy-rigged
Yarmouth cutters going up to the herring fishery off the Tyne.
These are wonderfully stiff sea-boats, and sailed as steadily as
a rock, while their inmates leaned against the side enjoying the
spell of idleness, or smoking innumerable pipes, near the booms
rigged out astern, partly to clear the decks, and partly to steady
the vessel.   All these fishing vessels have a wonderful similarity,
and their sailors in oilskins and sou'westers might all belong to
one family.   Most inland readers must have noticed pictures
of them in full sail on the side of the Yarmouth herring paste
tins ; they are characteristic features on the north-eastern coast.
The heavily-laden iron screw-colliers labouring away in the
offing, the weather-bound Grimsby smacks, the trading vessels
and tugs, greatly diversified the sea ; while on the coast, as we
successively ran past the different watering-places, their visitors
could be seen walking and riding on the sands.   Every now
and then, too, we shot past fishing parties from Withernsea or
Hornsea, some returning home, and many of them looking
sufficiently cadaverous to claim our pity ; others yet anchored,
and fishing with all the zeal peculiar to the lover of this sport,
whether he seek to capture a Tweed salmon or Thames
gudgeon.   Anon a busy tug meets us, disgorging volumes of
smoke, so that Captain Try, terrified for his spruce masts,
gladly goes to windward of her.   She is towing a huge raft of

P

teak to the Tyne. A small spar is rigged on this to carry lights at night, for it would be an unpleasant rencontre to run foul of these heavy balks of timber.

But the look-out man here gives notice to the sportsmen to take their pieces ; five hundred yards ahead is a noisy parliament of gulls, kittiwakes, and shearwaters, some floating in a dipping white line, others wheeling over them with eager screams, and every now and then splashing into the waves. There is probably a " school of fish " underneath them, and they are waiting to seize what fortune may throw in their way as the fish rise near the surface, whither they are driven by the repeated attacks of clouds of dark skirmishers round the main body of gulls, guillemots, razor-bills, puffins, and the like, which dive underneath, and pursue the hapless fish in deep water. Captain Try turns the steamer's head towards the gulls ; we cower behind the bulwarks and anxiously await the result. Long before we get within shot the cautious shearwaters flap up and fly seaward ; then the lesser black-backed gulls follow their example. Up with a whirr of numberless wings gets the whole body now, most of them seeking the cliffs, while some cross the *Firefly's* bows and give a chance of a shot. Two barrels of a breechloader are emptied at them in vain ; then they wheel and pass overhead, so that the Vice-Commodore at the stern leaps up and also gives his two barrels. Vain—vain are the sportsman's efforts, not a feather is damaged, and the gulls soon disappear, leaving behind only a detachment of terns. These light troops wheel and dash into the sea with loud clanging and screams at the side of the *Firefly*, but prudently remain just out of shot. Indeed, no cunning old carrion crow in a ploughed field in the country seems to possess a better idea of distance than do the terns. Somewhat annoyed at their ill luck (for one of the sportsmen won a Queen's badge at Wimbledon, and reasonably thought himself able to shoot a sea-gull), while comparing notes the look-out once more descries a similar collection of birds, all as before engaged in fishing or riding in long white lines on the dark sea. Forthwith the *Firefly* bears down upon them, and all in eager silence again watch the gunners. The same tactics as before are repeated by the different kinds of birds, the Vice-Commodore being much chagrined at the wildness of the Manx shearwaters; again some incautious birds cross the yacht's bows and wheel overhead, and once more with a similar result to the last attempt, four barrels are simultaneously poured into them. These sea-birds seemed to bear a charmed life; and the last we saw of the flock was its whirling and falling like huge snow-flakes before a dark cloud on our port bow. But only those who have tried know how difficult it is to hit a bird in one kind of rapid motion, from the deck of a vessel, itself in uncertain motion, with an undercurrent of throbs and spasms from the ceaseless plunging of the piston-rods. When memory turns to the incredible slaughter which used to take place amongst these very sea-fowl before the Bird Bill was passed for their protection in 1869, it is perhaps matter of satisfaction that even now, when the fence months have expired, it is not quite so easy to hit a sea-gull from a boat as it is to knock down a fieldgare from its perch on a hedgerow. And should the main- tenance of the Sea Fowl Preservation Act seem to anyone, while contemplating the enormous number of birds on these shores at present, a useless restriction on sportsmen, it will be as well for him to bear in mind that, just before the passing of that Bill, on a strip of coast eighteen miles long near Flam- borough Head, 107,250 sea-birds were destroyed by pleasure parties in four months; 12,000 by men who shot them for their feathers wherewith to adorn women's hats, and 79,500 young birds, which died of starvation in the nests thus bereft of pro- tectors. Commander Knocker, who was stationed at Flam- borough, and reported these facts, saw two boats loaded above the gunwales with dead birds, and one party of eight guns killed 1,100 birds in a week. Practical ornithology, besides the

"Sea Birds' Bill," can now boast of two more triumphs in the way of protection. The "Wild Birds Preservation Act" of 1872, amended in 1876 and 1880, protects the ordinary birds of coppice and woodland during their breeding months, and the "Wild Fowl Act" of 1876 imposes penalties for taking wild fowl between 15th February and 10th July. Not merely naturalists, but also all lovers of the country, ought to be sincerely grateful for this kindly legislation.

At Withernsea two large posts are erected to enable ships to try their rate of speed at a measured mile. The *Firefly*, under steam and sail, but against the tide, made her mile in seven minutes and thirty-five seconds. This quick travelling soon brought us once more to the shoals, sand-banks, lighthouses, and light-ships on and about the Spurn. Running the gauntlet of these, and avoiding a wreck buoy over a hapless vessel which here went down with all her crew, in the destructive gale of Good Friday, 1876, when the Lincolnshire coast was strewn with wrecks, we left the buoys on our right which mark the channel for Hull, and struck across the Humber for Grimsby. It was such an evening and such a scene as Turner would have loved to paint. A brilliant sunset flooded the Humber with crimson, and brought out in all their vivid colours the green-painted "billy-boys," and smacks with dark-red sails, and red-night-capped fishermen aboard, now falling upon a passing tug, now a stately barque anchored in mid-channel till she could go up the river. As the strong light shone through the crowded masts and busy life of the fish-dock, and danced over the ripples brightening beside the ships at anchor, and then dying away left them dusky ghosts of their former selves, the long line of Lincolnshire coast, with its trees and farmsteads, faded into blue mist, while overhead the moon, almost at her full, glided out of a long cloud, and from the point where we dropped anchor for the night, seemed like a vast riding light suspended near the summit of the tall water-tower. Then it was easy to understand the witchery which sea life has for an artistic eye, and the incomparable effects of colour not unfrequently to be observed on the waves. Amid these solemn greys and softened purples and blues of evening the Spurn lights were lit, and immediately the view on all sides was confused by the number of lights run up into riggings, or extending in long-drawn lines when the lamps along the shore were lighted. The many noises of a busy dockyard gradually composed themselves, and the wash of the waves round our bows made itself more distinctly heard. Our cruise had almost ended. The grog-locker was opened for the last time, and then we turned in. During the dim grey of morning we were faintly conscious that Captain Try and his men were getting us into the yacht's snug berth in the dock. But at seven, when the steam began to blow off, sleep was effectually murdered, and we awoke to dress to its roaring accompaniment. And then came the last breakfast in the comfortable little saloon, not unmixed with a tinge of sadness at the breaking up of a merry party, and the return to the anxieties and duties of life, the last shaking of hands and cheery farewell to Captain Try and his crew. The dead birds were duly carried on shore, and save that the most cherished memories need no sensible object to evoke them, will long in the mute isolation of their glass cases, remind their owners of the delightful trip of the *Firefly* among the thousands of their screaming, diving, swimming kinsfolk off the wave-eaten cliffs of Flamborough.

All our care not to commence shooting till the earliest legal date had been futile. It seems that the Flamborough authorities had passed a bye-law to postpone all shooting of sea-birds till 15th August, so that our doings on board the *Firefly*, though committed in sheer ignorance, were doubtless viewed with much reprobation from the cliffs.

POEMS,

BY

MAY PROBYN.

Square 16mo, cloth, gilt.   Price 3s. 6d.   (Post free.)

PRESS NOTICES.

"Miss Probyn's small and modest volume displays much brightness of fancy and sweetness of feeling, united with excellent metrical science. . . Perhaps we shall give the best idea of Miss Probyn's manner by quoting one of her bright and picturesque pages, taken from the quaint poem called 'Soapsuds' :—

> "'Her arms were white as milky curds ;
> Her speech was like the song of birds ;
> Her eyes were grey as mountain lakes
> Where dream of shadow stirs and breaks.

We would willingly linger longer over this charming little book, which we leave with reluctance, and with the hope of meeting its author's name once more before very long."—*Saturday Review.*

"Very sweet, very simple, and very skilful."—*Vanity Fair.*

"May Probyn has written the prettiest and daintest volume of verse we have met with for a long time. . . She has a fresh, sweet voice, very delightful to listen to. It is positively fascinating to read these bright, pure verses. . . . Hers are exquisite fancies, tender thoughts, and a joyous delight in the beauties of colour and sound and summer ; hers, too, is a sweet melancholy, the fair sorrow of love which lingers in the lines of our old English ballads. There are many of May Probyn's poems we should like to quote had we space, especially 'Soapsuds,' which is a delicious piece of work. She has written a volume of verse that is worth reading, some bits of which linger like perfume in the memory."—*Westminster Review.*

"There is pathos in these little poems, and once or twice a sign of the rarer gift of humour."—*Pall Mall Gazette.*

"She has a genuine vein of fancy and sense of rhythm, coupled with much felicity of expression."—*Daily News.*

"She has a free touch, and imparts to her songs a movement and swing which are charming, the more so as these do not constitute the sole attraction. We look forward with pleasure to Miss Probyn's next volume."—*Lloyd's Newspaper.*

"Her volume is noteworthy for its simplicity, its sincerity, and for an underlying tenderness and pathos which are rarely met with in modern verse in the same degree. Each poem carries its impression direct to the heart, and we are greatly mistaken if several of them do not become household words in English homes before long."—*Belgian News.*

"If lightness and elegance are qualities to recommend a charming book, exquisitely got up, May Probyn's little volume should be popular. A bright, clever volume, in which we find much good rhyme and still more genuine and pleasing poetry."—*Newcastle Courant.*

THIRD EDITION.

MY LIFE AS AN ANGLER.

By WILLIAM HENDERSON,

AUTHOR OF THE "FOLK-LORE OF THE NORTHERN COUNTIES."

Crown 8vo. With Autotype portrait and twelve full-page Illustrations, engraved by EDMUND EVANS. Cloth, top edge gilt. Price 7s. 6d. (Post free.)

PRESS NOTICES.

"The pleasure, the friendships, and the experience gained by fifty years of angling for salmon and trout are told with spirit and abundance of interesting detail in this book. . . . Clear in style and free from

PRESS NOTICES—*Continued.*

the vulgarity, slang and trite quotations which disfigure so many modern angling books, these reminiscences will be read with pleasure by all who enjoy country life and admire the old-fashioned virtues of diligence and contentment ; nor does it require an angler to relish the many anecdotes of Northern life and natural history which the writer intersperses among the fishing experiences. . . . Nothing that is beautiful and of good report appears to escape him when he wanders, rod in hand, by the river side, and it is this pleasant natural mode of interesting his readers which will endear the book to a wide circle of readers. . . . The contents, and, above all, the tone of this book, by far the most important contribution of late years to angling literature, deserves much commendation. The publishers are entitled to credit for the excellent printing, the stout paper, and the dainty woodcuts which adorn the volume. . . . There is no modern book about angling which could be put in the hands of either novice or veteran with greater chances of charming both alike. It holds a copious store of information and anecdote, and reflects in every page its author's kind heart, ripe experience, and soundness of judgment. Like Auceps, in a book which Mr. Henderson, in common with all anglers, must reverence, we close this delightful volume with the words, ' I assure you, Mr. Piscator, I now part with you full of good thoughts, not only of yourself, but your recreation.'"—*Athenæum.*

"If our readers are not fishermen, they will nevertheless find ample reward in the general matter, lively and thoughtful, with which the author has diversified his story of river-side life."—*Spectator.*

"Mr. Henderson writes on an ever popular subject in a charming style. . . . It is, in fact, a choice book on a choice subject, choicely produced, and we congratulate both author and publishers."—*Publishers' Circular.*

"A lively and picturesque collection of scattered experiences."— *Saturday Review.*

"The illustrations display a high degree of artistic merit."—*Pall Mall Gazette.*

"Gives many capital accounts of sport. . . . An indispensable edition to the collector's library."—*Field.*

"A volume in which luxurious typography and the amenities of artistic illustration are by no means unworthily expended."—*Daily Telegraph.*

"A work rich in humour."—*Leeds Mercury.*

"One of the most genial, chatty, and entertaining narratives ever penned by a Piscator."—*Yorkshire Post.*

"It proves that a genuine, ardent sportman can not only be genial and gay, and write a book more entertaining than a novel, but that he can also have ever present to his mind the truest and purest religious sentiments."— *Durham Chronicle.*

Foolscap 4to, cloth, gilt.   Price 6s.   (Post free.)

THE ANGLER'S NOTE-BOOK AND NATURALIST'S RECORD.

A Repertory of fact, inquiry, and discussion on Field-Sports and subjects of Natural History.   With six illustrations on plate paper.   The *Green* Series Complete.

CONTENTS :—"The Oldest English Treatise on Fishing," and "Anglo-Saxon Fish-Names," by the Rev. Professor Skeat; "An Unknown Angling Poet;" "One of the Mysteries of Angling Literature;" Conrad Heresbach: "Concerning Fishing" (a translation of his *De piscatione*; &c., by Thomas Westwood, author of the *Bibliotheca Piscatorta*; "Fishing Cats,," &c., by William Henderson; "Invitation to Coquet," by Joseph Crawhall, editor of "Newcastle Fishers' Garlands;" "Fishing a Scotch Loch," by the Rev. M. G. Watkins; "Notes from the Journals of Jonathan Couch," and several hundred papers and short notes—in prose and verse—by many other well-known writers and naturalists.

"Wading through its pages is like wading up a Devonshire trout-stream at every turn there is something interesting to note and store away in the angler's memory."—*Fishing Gazette.*

"Brimful of eminently readable matter."—*Nottingham Sunbeam.*

"We strongly recommend it to all anglers and lovers of nature generally."—*Bath Journal.*

"A very charming volume."—PROFESSOR G. BROWN GOODE, U.S."—*Fisheries' Commissioner.*

Crown 8vo. Price, paper cover, 1s. ; cloth, 2s. (Post free.)

THE ART OF GARDENING :

A PLEA FOR ENGLISH GARDENS OF THE FUTURE, WITH PRACTICAL HINTS FOR PLANTING THEM.

By MRS. J. FRANCIS FOSTER.

PRESS NOTICES.

"In this pleasant and original little book the authoress not only enters a vigorous protest against the bedding-out system and the so-called 'natural' style of gardening, but gives very good practical advice for gardens of a different sort."—*Gardener's Chronicle.*

"This little book proceeds from a true lover of flowers, and will be welcome to all who take an interest in their care and culture."—*Civilian.*

"A pleasant and unpretending little volume."—*Saturday Review.*

"The charm consists in its author's evident love of her subject. Like a true lover, she has gone far and wide in her search for old plants and old plant lore. We agree with Mrs. Foster that the most perfect herbaceous border is one that has an old wall behind it. Blue larkspurs and white lilies, roses, phloxes, and evening primroses never look so well as when they are seen against a background of wall, mellowed with age and clothed with its beautiful garment of wall-growing seedlings. . . . Mrs. Foster's book, too, is most useful in its lists of flowers that bloomed in the days of Chaucer and Shakespeare. She also devotes one chapter entirely to quotations from old poets on gardens, and all the delights that spring from them. If it helps her readers to know for themselves those authors, who found among the flowers of the garden apt similes of all that is truest in human nature, she will have added a very substantial addition to the pleasure already enjoyed by those who love gardens, but yet are unfamiliar with the pages of the poets who knew well how to speak their praises."—*Spectator.*

"A pleasant book."—*Athenæum.*

"A charming little tractate. . . . a collection of pleasant thoughts and poetical fancies, not incapable, however, of very practical realisation, about gardens and flowers, and the enjoyment that may be extracted from them. Mrs. Foster speaks lovingly of the old-fashioned gardens, and the old hardy flowers, ever changing with the season and ever presenting some new charm, from the first snowdrop peering slyly out of the snow, herald and harbinger of spring, to the last blossoms of the hardy pompones and chrysanthemums, lingering in the rectory garden as if striving to endure till they could lend their aid to the Christmas decorations of the village church. . . . Mrs. Foster devotes one very pleasant chapter to the old herbalists. . . . It is impossible to leave Mrs. Foster's little book without noting her earnest pleading for that purest pleasure of a garden which arises from the capacity for bringing sweet and innocent delights into lives that sadly want some brightness and sweetness brought into them from without."—*Guardian.*